A Taste of Death

by

Suzanne Rossi

The Snoop Group, Book 3

This is a work of fiction. Names, characters, places, and incidents are either the product of the author's imagination or are used fictitiously, and any resemblance to actual persons living or dead, business establishments, events, or locales, is entirely coincidental.

A Taste of Death

Cover Art by *Kim Mendoza*

The Wild Rose Press, Inc.
PO Box 708
Adams Basin, NY 14410-0708
Visit us at www.thewildrosepress.com

Publishing History
First Crimson Rose Edition, 2018
Print ISBN 978-1-5092-2219-3
Digital ISBN 978-1-5092-2220-9

The Snoop Group, Book 3
Published in the United States of America

Gil chuckled. "Opposites attract. Look at us."

"Yeah, just look at us," she drawled. "You thought I'd killed Isadora Powell."

"And I can admit when I'm wrong."

Anne finished the last glass, wiped her hands on a towel, and faced him again.

"Thank goodness for that!"

He pulled her close and kissed her. A moment later a cough had them breaking apart.

"Sorry to interrupt, but I just came down for a bottle of water," Lisa said with an amused expression. She retrieved the bottle from the fridge and looked at them. "Carry on."

Gil and Anne both laughed as her daughter exited the room. Before they could take her advice, Gil's phone rang.

He pulled it from his pocket. "Collins here… That's not surprising." He paused for a long while as he listened. The look on his face turned grim. "That is. What would be the purpose… I have no idea. I'll have to ask the husband. I take this to mean it's official now… Yeah, I never really figured it any other way. I'll get on it first thing in the morning."

He hung up with a frown. "That was Gilson at the lab. The reports came in. The only peanuts found were on Ms. Harrison's food. All the other plates and the breading from the kitchen are clean. And here's an interesting twist. Mixed in with the ground peanuts was a healthy dose of ground lobster shells. She was definitely murdered."

Dedication

One thing I've learned throughout my life is that people come and go. A few remain close friends forever. Others enter, leave an impression—some good, some bad—and then move on.

I've been lucky enough to connect with several very special people over the years, especially writers, and while I may not see them often, I still rely on their postings on social media to keep up with their lives—and they mine.

Twenty years in South Florida gave me the opportunity to meet many authors, so when I moved to Memphis eighteen months ago, I cried knowing I would likely never see most of them again.

But I've also discovered there is always a ray of sunshine wherever we go. I have met quite a few authors here who welcomed me into the fold of River City Romance Writers like an old friend.

So to all those wonderful members, thank you for making me feel at home.

Chapter One

Anne Jamieson paused outside the meeting room doors and swallowed, hoping the action would ease her slightly upset stomach. She wiped her palms down the side of her skirt, licked her lips, and glanced at her watch. Ten-forty-five. She was late. Procrastination? Perhaps. Today marked the first time she'd step through those doors as President of the Southeast Florida chapter of the Writers Association of America. It was mid-October and she'd only held office for a month. Her election had been hard fought and the margin of victory larger than anticipated.

And am I really ready for this? It's another huge change in my life.

Her divorce, the murder of bestselling author Isadora Powell last summer, followed by the murder of two agents at the chapter's conference this past spring had been worse than difficult. The only good thing to have come out of it was Detective Gil Collins. Their relationship was going strong.

"Gonna take root out here?" a familiar voice said from behind her.

She turned to face her critique partner and the new chapter Secretary, Rose Bennett.

"I may. Can't decide. I never thought much about actually running a meeting. Guess I'm a little intimidated. Kathy told me we've got over eighty attendees this month," she explained, naming the recently re-elected Vice-President.

"Well, don't be worried. Ignore those who didn't vote for you and just be yourself."

They stepped aside as two members walked up in full Halloween costumes—one as a witch, and other as a clown.

"Hi Anne, Rose. Not in costume for your first meeting?" the clown asked.

"Uh, no. To tell you the truth, I totally forgot this was our Halloween meeting. Maybe I'll be a Pilgrim for Thanksgiving."

The ladies laughed and entered the room. From inside came the babble of voices. Down the hallway, waiters and waitresses moved carts filled with covered plates against the wall.

Anne checked her watch again. "Looks like lunch is here. I guess we should go in."

"Good idea, and don't pay any attention to whatever Fran says or whatever gossip you may hear," Rose told her.

Fran Harrison had been the previous chapter president and her opponent in last month's election. The woman was not taking her loss with grace.

"Gossip?"

Rose sighed. "I heard from Terry Whiting that Fran accused Barb Hamilton of miscounting the votes so you'd win. Needless to say, Barb was not only upset, but furious. It might be a good idea to keep them as far apart as possible."

"Barb's as honest as a nun. Fran needs to accept things and move on."

Another member dressed as a ghost glided past

them and into the room. The costume startled Anne. A sheet with a hole cut out comprised the main part of the getup, and a pillowcase with eye, nose, and mouth openings covered the head. In her opinion the costume resembled a Klan outfit.

"Who was that?" Rose asked.

"I have no idea, and I didn't forget this was the Halloween meeting. I never liked dressing up or trick or treating as a kid."

"I'm with you there, but with five kids I have no choice except to go with the flow. I think as board members we should show a little decorum."

More food carts rattled down the hall.

"Come on, let's go in."

Anne opened the door and entered the room. It was packed. Tables stretched from one end of the room to the other. Conversation dropped, and then picked up again as she made her way to one at the front. Nancy Carlyle, another critique group member was already seated. She waved them over.

"I was beginning to think you'd bailed," she said as they took their seats.

"Came close," Anne replied.

"I talked her out of it," Rose said with a laugh.

Anne glanced at the table next to her and made eye contact with Fran Harrison. The woman glared back with a decidedly unfriendly look.

Looking away, Anne sucked in a deep breath.

"Ignore her," Nancy said. "She's a sore loser."

Another glance showed their re-elected treasurer, Jane Whittaker seated next to Fran. Also at the table was the board member-at-large, Ellie Campion. She dealt with the hotel meeting reservations. Not rocket science. Relatively new to the chapter, she wasn't as yet involved in personalities or politics.

Jane, however, bothered Anne. She hadn't seen the detailed financials from the past year and wasn't sure the woman was qualified to be treasurer. The monthly treasurer's report distributed at the meetings showed a substantial amount of money allocated to Miscellaneous Expenses, which suggested the checkbook didn't balance all the time. Still, Jane was likeable enough to squeak out a win over another lady for the position.

Also at the table with Fran was Susan Lynch, a former critique partner. Susan had been asked to leave the group last spring. She wasn't a good fit, and her galloping paranoia drove them all crazy. She did not respond well, and took every opportunity to tell whomever would listen how mistreated she'd been.

Vice-President, Kathy Samuels entered the room along with their guest speaker for the day, Cindy Romero, a bestselling author of historical romance. Anne rose and hustled over to greet them.

"Cindy! Hello, I'm Anne Jamieson, chapter president. Welcome. I'm looking forward to your presentation."

Cindy shook hands with her. "Thank you so much for having me. I've heard a lot of good things about you here in South Florida."

"I've reserved a seat for you at our table," Kathy said.

They took their seats and more introductions were rendered.

"Looks like a good turnout this month," Kathy commented. It was her job to find speakers. She seemed to have no axe to grind with anybody.

Anne gazed around the room. About two-thirds of the members were in costumes. "So is this where I make some kind of announcement?"

Kathy laughed. "I guess so. Just say hello and enjoy lunch."

Taking a deep breath, Anne laid her napkin on her plate and made her way to the podium. The microphone stuck up like a weed in a garden. Stepping behind the intimidating pedestal, she tapped the microphone. A hollow thump resounded in the room.

"Well, I guess it's turned on," Anne said with a nervous laugh. "As your new President, I want to thank you all for coming today, especially those of you who took the time to celebrate Halloween with costumes. Everybody looks terrific and I understand there will be certificates awarded for best costume, most imaginative, and so on. Lunch is about to be served, so enjoy and I'll speak to you again later."

As she left the podium, she heard Susan say to Fran, "Not very welcoming, if you ask me."

"Stiff and not friendly at all," Fran replied.

Anne ignored them even though several at their table nodded in agreement. One of the exceptions was Ellie Campion, who stared at her plate. She shifted in her chair as if uncomfortable.

Instead of returning to the table, Anne circulated chatting with people and trying to act presidential, whatever that was. The longer she did so, the more she relaxed. This wasn't all that different from her normal procedure at any other meeting.

Noting a newcomer, she paused at a table near the back of the room and introduced herself.

"Hi, I'm Anne Jamieson."

The blonde lady smiled and extended her hand. "I'm Dr. Mary Smith. I write medical romances."

"How thrilling. Are you in private practice?"

"Yes, up in Highcrest about thirty minutes north of here. I work with several other doctors in a family practice."

"Well, I'm glad you joined us today."

Toward the end of her meet-and-greet session, someone tapped her on the shoulder. She turned to find Ellie with a nervous smile on her face.

"Anne, I want to apologize for Fran and Susan's words. I know you had to hear them."

"Don't worry. Neither woman is a fan of mine. We've had our differences."

"Well, I'm in a critique group with Susan and three others, and have to admit, I'm not happy."

"How so?" Waiters and waitresses entered the room bearing trays with plates of salad.

"Susan's very bossy, opinionated, and sometimes says things during critique that are just plain wrong. Yet if you call her on it, she gets huffy and says she knows what works and since the rest of us are new to the writing game, we should listen to what she says. She also takes every opportunity to bad-mouth you and several other members. I'm thinking of dropping out. Should I?"

Anne didn't know what to say that wouldn't sound bitchy, but tried anyway. "Susan isn't all that experienced either. She's only been writing about two years, so go with your gut feeling. If you don't think the group is working for you, see if you can find others who'd like to critique. As a matter of fact, would you be willing to head up a critique group committee partnering people together?"

"Me? Gosh, I never thought about that, but I guess I can do it."

"Good, I'll make an announcement later."

Ellie glanced toward Susan. "Maybe I should inform Susan I won't be in the group anymore before you do. Not really looking forward to that. She takes everything so personally."

Doesn't sound as if Susan's changed much.

Anne made her way back to the table and covertly watched as Ellie resumed her seat next to Susan who immediately leaned in to talk. Ellie answered with an apologetic expression. The conversation didn't look particularly nice. Susan jabbed at Ellie's shoulder with her finger. Ellie swatted her hand away. Susan sat back in her chair and glared at the woman before transferring her gaze to Fran who took a deep breath and also glared.

Oh boy, this situation needs to be defused fast.

Rising, she approached Fran.

"Fran, I'd like a word with you privately, if I may."

"What for?"

"Yeah, what for?" Susan echoed.

Anne ignored her. "Privately, please, and now."

She turned on her heel, not waiting to see if Fran followed, and exited the room. Fran appeared a moment later.

"Well, what do you want?" the former president snapped.

"For starters, did you bring the rest of the papers and other materials I requested last month? Rose and I need the correspondence and the details from prior meetings."

"I said I'd get them to you as soon as I could."

"Good. Suppose I come by your place Monday morning?"

"Fine!"

"Also lay off Barb Hamilton. Your accusations are absurd and hurtful."

Fran curled her lip. "And you will never convince me the election wasn't rigged. I think *you* are a cheat and a liar!"

Anne clenched her teeth and resisted the urge to smack Fran right in the mouth.

"Fran, the election was fair and square. Get over it. And quit making snide remarks to others about me. It just isn't professional."

Three costumed members—a Raggedy Ann, the Klan/ghost, and someone in a bunny suit—came around the corner from the restroom area. The Klan/ghost stopped by the food cart to lift a lid from one of the meals. Time to terminate this conversation. She didn't want anyone to see the past and present chapter presidents having an argument.

"Now, may I suggest we go back inside? Lunch is being served."

Fran, her face turning an interesting shade of red, whirled and reentered. Anne followed. She paused near Ellie and leaned in to whisper. "Could I speak with you in the hallway?"

Ellie nodded and the two women exited.

"So, did you say something to Susan about the critique group?"

"She told me not to spend too much time with you because you were a bad influence on new writers. I told her I found you very helpful and pleasant. She then

8

stated that I was a lousy judge of character. I got mad and told her that must be true since I was a member of her critique group. I then said I'd no longer be critiquing with her."

"I think I saw that."

"Called me a traitor and said I'd never find another group."

"You aren't, and you will. I'll make an announcement that you'll be heading up the critique committee right now if you're game."

"Let's do it, but first I'd better change tables. I don't think the atmosphere at this one will be conducive to eating."

"What was that all about?" Nancy asked in a low voice as Anne stood behind her seat.

"Just clearing the air." She waited until Ellie had found a new seating arrangement, and then made her way to the podium. "If I could have your attention for a moment I'd like to make an announcement. I know many of you are searching for a critique group, but aren't sure how to go about it. I'm happy to announce that Ellie Campion, our board member at-large, has graciously agreed to head a committee to match authors to each other for this purpose. I'll post all the pertinent information on the loop later this week. And thank you, Ellie, for taking on this responsibility."

Many of those present applauded as Anne made her way back to her seat. She cast a quick glance over at Susan who glared at Ellie with what could only be described as an outraged expression.

"Well, that's chopping her off at the knees," Nancy said in a low tone.

"I'll figure out the details tomorrow and get with

Ellie. She may be a gem of a board member."

Out of the corner of her eye she saw Rose approach Fran. Fran angrily jerked her head and waved a hand in dismissal. Rose straightened, bit her lip, and said something, then nodded to Susan who sniffed, stuck her nose in the air and turned to a woman sitting next to her.

Rose pulled out her chair and rolled her eyes. "Well, that was unpleasant."

"What happened?" Nancy asked.

"I asked when I would get the minutes from the last two meetings and was told 'the new president has it covered.' The tone was downright hostile."

Nancy glanced at Fran. "Why does she have the minutes?"

"When Mary Beth Wilkins left in late June, she turned all the correspondence over to Fran until a new secretary could either be appointed or elected," she replied mentioning the former Secretary.

"And Fran, in all her wisdom, didn't see any reason to appoint someone for a two month interim, so she did it herself. Plus, I think she thought her candidate for secretary would win," Anne added.

A salad plate was placed in front of her. She selected the balsamic vinaigrette dressing boat, dribbled some on her greens, then picked up her fork and took a bite. The dressing and the crunchy veggies were better than usual.

Anne looked around the room.

Wonder who that ghost person is. Funny, most of the costumed people I can identify, but not her. Oh well, sooner or later she'd have to take the pillowcase off in order to eat.

Anne let her attention wander as the rest of the table discussed books turned into movies and Hollywood in general. She was concerned about expenses. The sit down lunch was way too expensive for a chapter meeting. Perhaps a buffet or a time change to earlier in the morning for breakfast would work.

Thank goodness they were no longer in the conference business. The vote was close, but jettisoning the conference prevailed.

Anne had also pushed for changing the writing contest, In Other Words, to an electronic format. Her view had won by a large margin.

Little things. Baby steps. But what else can we do to generate income?

"You're awfully quiet," Nancy said in a low voice.

"Just thinking of ways to cut costs and increase revenue for the chapter."

From her other side, Rose leaned in. "Good for you. Keep it simple."

Nancy nodded. "I heard that in spite of some creative bookkeeping by Jane we lost over four grand on the conference last spring. Not to mention two dead agents."

"If you ask me, I think Jane's bookkeeping is always creative. I have an idea for the treasurer's position, but I'm not sure how it will go over," she replied in a hushed tone.

"What's that?"

"We hire an accountant to keep the actual books, file the taxes, and stuff like that. The treasurer does the day-to-day operations like writing checks, balancing the checkbook, and whatever. I have no idea how much it might cost, but think it would be money well-spent."

"Isn't Mavis Holloway's husband or son a CPA?" Rose asked, mentioning a fellow member. "Maybe he'd cut us a deal on cost."

As a non-profit organization, the paperwork and Federal regulations could be daunting to a well-meaning amateur.

Anne shifted her gaze to the treasurer sitting next to Fran. "I'll bring the subject up at our next board meeting and demand Jane present a budget by the January meeting."

"Good luck with that," Nancy said. "I don't think she really understands the word in this context."

Someone brushed past Anne's chair. She looked up to see Barb Hamilton with a determined look on her face striding toward Fran's table.

"Oh crap," Anne said in a low tone. "This could be trouble."

"You could be right," Rose said.

Barb poked Fran in the shoulder, then spoke in a loud voice. "We need to talk, lady, and now!"

Fran glared. "I have nothing to say to you, so go away."

"Well, I have plenty to say to you, and if you don't want everyone in the room to hear it, you'll get your ass out of that chair and into the hallway."

"Who do you think you are?" Susan demanded with a scowl. "Fran doesn't have to talk to you if she doesn't want to."

"You stay out of this," Barb said with a curled lip. "It has nothing to do with you."

"I can defend myself, Susan," Fran interjected.

Susan swallowed and sat back.

Fran half turned in her seat. "I'm tired of having

my lunch interrupted every few seconds to talk to idiots. Get away from me."

"And I'm tired of being accused of fraudulent vote counting!"

"Well, I think you did cheat," Susan said emphatically.

Barb glared at her. "I don't give a rat's ass what you think, Susan. From what I hear you're a paranoid, critique group Nazi, so don't you dare try to tell me I'm a cheat!"

Susan gasped and half-rose from her chair. "Who said that! You take it back!"

"Anne, do something," Kathy said in a frantic tone.

Anne glanced at their guest speaker Cindy who took it all in with wide eyes. In fact, other than for Barb, Fran, and Susan, everyone stared at the scene unfolding in front of them. Kathy was right. Decisive action was needed.

Get your head out of your butt, and put a stop to this now!

Anne rose and strode to the other table where she placed her arms around Barb's shoulders and steered her away from Fran's side.

"Barb, Fran, Susan, out in the hallway. Now!"

"You're not my boss!" Fran said with a snarl.

She leaned down and hissed in the woman's ear. "Yes, I am! I'm the President and you're coming with me." She looked over at Susan. "You, too."

She guided Barb toward the doors as the former president and Susan followed.

Outside, they sidestepped a couple of waitresses with more trays of salad.

"Down here, out of the way." She pushed the group

farther along before stopping near the door of an unused meeting room. "What the hell is the matter with you people? This is embarrassing! We have a bestselling author inside, for crying out loud. How do you think this looks to her?"

"Not my fault," Fran said. "I didn't start it."

"Yes, you did! You started it by making an absurd accusation against Barb with no facts to back it up. Susan, I don't know where you suddenly grew a spine over the past six months, but butt out. Get rid of your Uriah Heep complex."

Susan looked both angry and puzzled. "My what?"

"Uriah Heep," Barb answered with a sneer. "A sniveling, kowtowing, favor-garnering character in Charles Dickens' *David Copperfield.* I'm assuming you've heard of Charles Dickens."

Anne jumped in before Susan could reply. "Barb, I understand how angry you are, but this is neither the time nor the place to air dirty laundry."

Barb bit her lip. "You're right, Anne. I apologize. And I'll apologize to the whole room."

"Thank you. That would be a class act."

"Well, I'm not apologizing to anybody," Fran said.

"Me neither," Susan echoed.

"I didn't expect *that* from either of you. Now, may I suggest we put the drama aside for the rest of the day, have lunch, and enjoy Cindy's presentation?"

Anne turned and walked back into the room, which was once again buzzing with conversation, and resumed her seat. Barb followed and made her way to the podium. Fran and Susan did not reappear immediately.

"Ladies and gentlemen, may I have your attention?" The room quieted. "A few minutes ago, I let my temper get the best of me. The result was not pleasant for anybody in the room. I would like to offer my sincerest apologies to you all, and especially to our special guest speaker, for putting everyone in an embarrassing position. It won't happen again."

As she moved away from the microphone a few people clapped.

Susan reentered the room and took her seat.

Anne checked her watch. The luncheon service was taking forever. The hotel had only provided three servers to cover over eighty people. *Just another reason to make a pitch for a buffet.*

Finally, the wait staff entered with trays containing the entrees—chicken in a basil cream sauce, cheese tortellini, or salmon with a bread crumb and herb-crusted topping. Rice pilaf and green beans rounded out the plates. Not the most exciting fare in the world, but adequate.

Anne's table was served first. The server matched the entrée with a color-coded card in front of each diner. Anne's choice was salmon. She popped a morsel into her mouth. Only moderately dry, which was better than usual. She sampled the rice and was pleasantly surprised—moist and flavorful. The green beans needed more cooking, but overall, the meal was edible.

Fran finally reentered the room and sat. She looked across the table at Susan and shrugged.

Anne sighed. "What a way to start a presidency."

"You did the right thing," Kathy said. "I swear I don't know what's come over Fran in the last few months. She seems to be bitter about damned near everything."

"I heard her latest love affair hit the skids," a

woman seated next to Rose said.

"I thought she was married," Rose countered.

The woman, Sally Crenshaw, grinned and leaned over to say softly, "She is. So was the man she was seeing. And it's not the first time she's treaded on some other woman's territory. I heard she had a fling with Rebecca Lawrence's husband last year."

Rebecca Lawrence was a member of the chapter who wrote erotic romance.

"Sally, maybe we should dispense with the gossip for now." Nancy cast a glance at Cindy.

Sally nodded. "Of course. Later."

Anne leaned toward Rose and lowered her voice. "Is it true? She had an affair with Becky's hubby?"

Rose nodded. "I critique with Becky and a few other erotic romance writers, too. Happened about a year ago. They supposedly broke it off, but when I talked to Becky a couple of weeks ago, she thought it had heated up again. No proof. Just suspicions."

Fran really is a piece of work.

"How's the chicken?" she asked Nancy a few minutes later.

"Not too bad for a change."

She was about to make a comment to Rose when suddenly someone screamed.

Anne jerked her head to see Susan with her mouth wide open and her finger pointing across the table. Fran's hand grasped at her throat. Her eyes bugged out and her other hand clutched at the edge of the table. Her face had a bluish tinge to it.

"Help! Help!" Susan shrieked. "She's choking!"

Fran toppled to the floor gasping, her face turning bluer. She now waved her hands as though trying to say something.

Anne jumped to her feet and paused next to Fran who writhed on the floor. She had no clue what to do.

From the back of the room, the visiting doctor rushed forward.

"Everybody back away. Give me some room."

Anne shooed people away. The doctor hauled Fran into a sitting position and applied the Heimlich maneuver several times. Nothing happened. Fran's face was now a deep blue. She no longer gasped, but made horrible, gurgling sounds. Suddenly she went limp.

"She's not breathing. Damn, my bag is in my car. No time to go get it. Someone call 9-1-1."

Nancy was already on her cell making the call.

The woman laid Fran back on the floor and began CPR.

Anne's heart raced as she stared and regretted the harsh words of earlier.

Nancy joined Anne. "Paramedics are on the way."

Several minutes passed as Dr. Smith performed the procedure. Finally, she put her ear to Fran's chest, listened for a few seconds before raising her head.

"I'm not getting heartbeat."

"No, what did she choke on?" Rose gasped.

The doctor continued CPR. "I have no idea. Hopefully, the paramedics will be here soon and can do a tracheotomy. I don't have the tools."

"Someone should inform the hotel," Nancy said.

"I'll do it." Rose headed for the house phone. A minute later she returned. "They're trying to find a security guard with medical training. I told them we called 9-1-1."

After what seemed forever, the paramedics raced in

and took over. They quickly examined Fran and resumed CPR while getting information from the doctor who now stood off to the side.

"She's not choking," one of the medicos said. "She's in anaphylactic shock. Her throat is swollen shut. I'm not getting a heartbeat either."

He retrieved an instrument from his bag and tried to insert it into her throat. It refused to go. Without hesitation, he opened a sterile pack, whipped out a scalpel, and carefully cut a slit in Fran's throat just above her breastbone. A tube was inserted. An airbag was attached and one of the men squeezed it at regular intervals.

"She's still not breathing." He started more CPR as his partner listened through a stethoscope.

Silence reigned from everyone except Susan who sobbed hysterically. Her cries had a piercing sharpness that irritated the crap out of Anne.

Nancy walked over to the distraught woman. "Susan, knock it off!" When the noise continued, she pulled her around and slapped her on the cheek. "Get a hold of yourself."

Susan hiccupped and glared, but the caterwauling ceased.

"What did the paramedic mean by shock?" Anne asked the doctor.

"Anaphylactic shock—usually from some kind of food allergy. Sometimes insect related. Often deadly. Geez, I hope we got to her in time."

Anne was almost in shock herself. This meeting was turning into a disaster of monstrous proportions.

Finally, the paramedic ceased CPR to check vital signs. He looked at his partner and shook his head.

"Doctor, would you like to take over?"

The woman nodded, checked for a heartbeat again.

"There's nothing. No heartbeat, no blood pressure, not breathing. I'm sorry, ladies, but she didn't make it."

"Didn't make it?" Kathy said.

"I mean she's dead."

Chapter Two

Anne's hand flew to her throat as a collective gasp rose from the others in the room.

"D...dead?" Rose asked in a high-pitched voice.

"It's all your fault!" Susan pointed a finger at Anne. "You upset her so much she choked to death."

"Shut up, Susan," Nancy said. "The doctor said it was anaphylactic shock."

"Brought on by Anne's constant badgering," Susan insisted.

The hotel security man finally rushed into the room and spoke with one of the paramedics. The doctor eyed those standing nearby, including Susan.

"Anaphylactic shock is a strong, often deadly, reaction to an allergen."

"Allergen? As in ragweed pollen or something?" one of the women asked.

"No, this was most likely brought on by something highly toxic to her system. Usually insect or food related," she replied.

"Food?" Susan's finger once again pointed toward Anne. "You! You put something in her food."

Nancy stepped forward and glared at the woman. "Susan, if you say one more word, I swear I'll hurt you. Quit making accusations and go find a seat."

Jane led a sniffling Susan toward the back of the room.

"I've called for an ambulance," one of the medicos told Anne. "And the police."

"The police? Whatever for?" a member asked.

"I imagine it's just routine," Anne replied.

The servers entered bearing more trays of entrees, and then stopped to stare at the body on the floor.

"I don't think we'll be finishing lunch," Anne told them. "As you can see, there's been an unfortunate accident. The police and an ambulance are on the way. I think it best if you wait outside."

The servers turned and exited.

She made her way to the podium. "Ladies and gentlemen, may I have your attention? A terrible tragedy has just taken place. I suggest you all return to your tables. The police are on the way and may want to speak with some of you. Needless to say, there will be no program today."

"Was she bitten by an insect?" someone inquired. "Maybe one of those brown recluse spiders bit her or something."

"A bee," another member added. "I had an uncle who was allergic to bees. Almost died one time. Maybe a bee stung her. Was she allergic to bees?"

"Maybe it was something she ate," a third lady said. "I've heard people can have allergic reactions to fish."

Rose heaved heavy sigh. "Oh, for Pete's sake. If she was allergic to fish, do you think she'd have ordered the salmon?"

"Maybe it was served to her by mistake," the woman continued.

Rose glanced at the table where Fran had been seated. "Nope, the card by her place setting is blue.

21

That means she got fish. Besides, I'm sure she could tell the difference between a hunk of salmon and chicken."

Anne held up her hand and spoke loudly into the microphone. "Please, speculation is useless. Let's all try to remain calm. I'd also like all board members to come up here for a few moments."

Rose, Jane, Kathy, and Ellie joined Anne at the front of the room away from the podium.

"Oh, my God, I don't believe this," Kathy moaned.

"I…I don't know what happened. She came back to the table and a few minutes later…" Jane didn't finish her sentence.

Anne took a deep breath. "I know what happened is horrible, but we need to keep calm and put a cork in useless speculation. Jane, you and Susan seem to be on good terms. I suggest you try to keep her active imagination silent. Throwing out silly accusations is not only dangerous, but slanderous as well."

"I'll try, but she's pretty upset."

"Kathy, I'm sure Cindy has had about all she can stand of the Southeast Florida chapter. Maybe it would be best if you got her out of the room. Buy her lunch or a drink in the bar and see she gets to the airport."

"Good idea. She looks pretty bewildered."

"Ellie, Rose, and I will go from table to table saying soothing things to members. The police should be here soon."

They had no sooner broken ranks when the ambulance crew arrived complete with a gurney. Out of respect, Anne asked those sitting at nearby tables to move farther back and partially pulled one of the sliding panels dividing the rooms into place, blocking the view from attendees.

Fran's body was placed in a body bag and loaded onto the cart.

"Umm, gentlemen, where are you taking her?" she asked.

"To the morgue. ME will perform an autopsy as soon as possible. Uh, doctor, would you meet us at the hospital to sign off on all this?"

"Yes, of course." The woman retrieved her purse from where she'd been sitting and left.

Anne watched as the ambulance crew wheeled the macabre cargo out of the room, then reopened the divider before heading to one of the tables.

She had barely begun to speak when two police officers walked into the room. A moment later they were followed by Detective Gil Collins, Anne's boyfriend. She hurried over to the group.

"Gil, what are you doing here?"

"I heard the call come in, knew you were here today, and then called the hotel. When I learned a death had occurred at your meeting, I came to see if I could help. There's nothing suspicious about this, is there?"

"I doubt it. One of our new members is a doctor and she said it may have been an allergic reaction to something like an insect bite or food. She left with the paramedics to meet them at the hospital."

"In that case, I'll let the officers do their job."

One of the men stepped forward. "Ma'am, could you tell me the victim's name?"

"Frances Harrison. I don't know her address or anything like that offhand."

"And she was part of this group?"

"Yes, we're all authors."

The policeman wrote in his notebook, and then looked up. "Is this some kind of Halloween party?"

"This was our regular monthly meeting, but since it's so close to the holiday some members like to dress up." She paused. "I guess someone should notify Fran's husband."

Susan chose that moment to come forward.

"Ah, Ms. Lynch, we meet again under tragic circumstances," Gil said.

Susan glared at him before turning her attention to the other two officers.

"My best friend, and our beloved *former* President, was poisoned," she said, her voice dripping with drama.

Anne drew in a deep breath. "Oh, for God's sake, Susan…"

"Poisoned?" Gil interrupted. "By whom and why?"

"By the new president, Anne Jamieson. She and Fran had been arguing all meeting long. Fran was so upset she had to leave the room. I was with her. When we returned, Fran started eating. Within a couple of minutes, she was gasping for air and turning blue. I think that while we were gone, Anne dumped poison in her food."

"And exactly how was I supposed to do that with at least five other people sitting at the table? And if I'm not mistaken, I was with the two of you in the hallway," Anne said in a furious tone.

"I have no idea, but you did it."

Gil sighed and pinched the bridge of his nose between his fingers.

"Ms. Lynch, do you have any proof Ms. Harrison was poisoned?"

"Uh…Ah…Of course she was," Susan snapped as

she shifted from foot to foot.

"Just as I thought. Might I suggest you stop making accusations? It could get you sued."

Susan sniffed and curled her lip. "Oh sure, you'd some to her defense. You're sleeping with her."

The tips of Gil's ears reddened, while Anne's face burned, a sure sign she was also flushed.

"Perhaps it would be a good idea to talk to the others at the table," the second cop, silent until now, said. "I notice the food is still on the table. Where was the victim sitting?"

Susan pointed with a flourish to Fran's chair. "Right there."

"I see. Would you happen to know the deceased's address and if she had a landline or not?"

Susan nodded and gave the desired information.

The first officer looked at Gil. "Detective, would you like to take over?"

He shook his head. "No, you men continue. There's no reason for homicide to get involved—yet."

The policeman nodded and turned to Susan. "In that case, ma'am, why don't you ask the ladies sitting at the table to meet me at the back of the room. Bill, why don't you bag any food left on Ms. Harrison's plate? See if the staff can provide containers for the iced tea and water, too. As soon as we're finished here, we'll go break the news to the husband."

"It also might be a good idea to talk to the wait staff. See if they noticed anything unusual," the second officer said. "By the way, Ms. Jamieson, what was the doctor's name who assisted the paramedics?"

"Ah, Mary Smith. I believe she said she was in practice up in Highcrest. I don't have her address or phone number, but I'm sure Kathy Samuels, our Vice-President can get it for you. She's off right now dealing with our guest speaker."

"Thank you."

"Anne and I will go with Ms. Lynch." Gil removed a small notebook from his pocket.

Susan turned away and strode to the back of the room.

"Gil, I swear to God, I didn't poison Fran."

"Of course you didn't, but now that the accusation as been tossed out, we have to see if it has legs."

Anne weaved through the tables. Her heart pounded and her face still burned. Only good breeding had kept her from punching her former critique partner in the mouth. Anger was a useless emotion—one she tried to stifle—but in this case, she felt justified. She was tired of being accused of murder every time a body popped up.

She and Gil found the group that had sat at Fran's table standing near the back wall. Susan and Ellie glared at each other. Jane wrung her hands and bit her lip. The other four ladies looked both afraid and apprehensive, their gazes darting from person to person as if trying to ascertain if one of them was a killer. No doubt Susan had already let them know how she felt.

A moment later the first officer joined them.

"Good afternoon, ladies. I am Officer Winters. If you don't mind, I have a few questions to ask." He gave a soothing smile, his pen and notebook in hand, then nodded toward Jane. "Let's begin with you, ma'am. What is your name and can you tell me what happened at your table during lunch?"

Both the officer and Gil had pens poised to write.

Anne decided Gil was being proactive in case this wasn't an accident.

Jane wet her lips and gave her name. "I...I don't think anything out of the ordinary occurred—other than Fran dying, of course."

"Anne here began harassing both Fran and me from the moment she stepped into the room," Susan interrupted. "And Barb Hamilton had some very nasty words with Fran, too."

"Barb Hamilton? Which one is she?"

One of the other ladies pointed to a nearby table. "She's the woman wearing the yellow blouse."

"And what was the argument about?" Gil sent the policeman an apologetic look.

"Barb was in charge of our recent elections. Fran suspected the votes weren't counted correctly," another of the women explained.

Officer Winters eyebrows rose. "And were they?"

"Of course they were." Ellie continued to glare at Susan. "My name is Ellie Campion, and for the record, Fran and Susan were the ones making derogatory remarks about Anne."

"What was your reaction, Ms. Jamieson?"

Anne took a deep breath and told them about the conversation in the hallway and its aftermath.

"Ms. Whittaker, will you please ask Ms. Hamilton to join us?"

Jane nodded and scurried off to whisper in Barb's ear. The woman immediately rose and walked up to the group.

"I'm Barb Hamilton, officer. What can I do for you?"

"I understand you had an argument with the

deceased. Could you tell me about it?"

Barb cast her gaze at the rest of the group, and then frowned. "Why? What has that got to do with anything?"

"The lady died under strange circumstances. We just want to get a picture of what happened. Routine, that's all."

Barb shrugged and described her confrontation with Fran.

"Did you talk to her again?" Gil asked.

"Certainly not. Why should I? I returned to my table and ate my salad."

"Thank you, ma'am."

"Did anybody else approach Ms. Harrison or the table in general during this period?" the officer inquired.

Another lady wrinkled her brow before replying. "There were a lot of people milling around, especially before the food was served."

"I mean during the actual lunch."

"Several."

Gil gave her a sharp look. "Any in costume?"

"Yes, but I didn't pay much attention. I was talking to others or eating my salad."

Gil tapped his finger against his lips. "Anne, when you and the three women were in the hall, did you all return at the same time?"

"No. Susan and Fran remained behind for a few minutes."

His attention turned to Susan. "Why, Ms. Lynch?"

Susan shifted her weight from foot to foot. "Fran was very upset at the hateful things Barb and Anne had said. She knew they'd colluded to rig the election."

Gil waved his hand. "Yes, but what else was said?"

"I don't know. Fran said she'd get even with both of them, along with Nancy, Rose, and Jen. They all campaigned against her."

"And what did you say?"

"She was my best friend. I told her I'd do anything I could to help."

"And then?" Officer Winters asked as he and Gil wrote in their notebooks.

"I came back inside just as Barb walked away from the podium, sat down, and ate. Fran came in a few minutes later."

"And how long after that did Ms. Harrison get sick?"

"Ten minutes, maybe a little longer. She finished her salad and started on her salmon."

"Do you need us for anything else?" one of the other ladies asked with a sick expression. "My appetite is totally gone. I want to go home."

Officer Winters glanced at Gil who nodded.

"In a minute, but I will need a list of who attended today's meeting for the record."

"Jane is our treasurer and has the list. I'm sure she can make a copy and give it to you," Anne told him.

Jane nodded. "Yes, of course. I'll take a photo of it and send it to you immediately."

Jane got the e-mail address from Officer Winters, who then made the announcement that people could leave. Most of those assembled did so rapidly. Others lingered a few moments longer and whispered among themselves. Ellie stayed.

The police officers spoke briefly with Gil, and then also left.

Ellie shuddered. "Anne, if there's anything I can do to help, please let me know. I've never seen anyone turn blue before. I mean it was awful. She was almost purple."

She patted Ellie on the arm. "I know. And we had at least five new people attending. Not a very good way to pump up the chapter."

"I see you, Ms. Bennett, and Ms. Carlyle here, but where's Ms. Swanson?" Gil asked.

"Jen's up in Atlanta for a few weeks. Her mother had some minor surgery and she's keeping house for a while." Anne shook her head. "She's not going to believe this one when I tell her."

Rose and Nancy joined them. "How do I write up the minutes for this meeting? 'New President welcomed guests. Former President dropped dead. Meeting was adjourned. Respectfully submitted by Rose Bennett.'"

"I wouldn't even bother," Ellie said. "The meeting was never officially called to order."

"Ellie's right," Nancy concurred. "I'm thinking the chapter is about to take a mammoth financial hit this month."

"How so?" Anne asked.

"We have to pay the hotel for the food, but will also have to refund everyone's money because most lunches hadn't been served."

"Oh God, I never thought of that," she groaned.

"And I need those minutes from the last couple of months, too, so I can bring myself up to date on what went on. I missed the July and August meetings. Fran also did the minutes for September. She had them all," Rose reminded her.

"If you'd like, I can drop by her house on Monday

and pick them up. I'm sure her husband or someone will be there," Ellie offered.

"Thanks, Ellie, but I don't think that's a priority now. We can deal with them later. She also had some papers from board meetings and such that I needed," Anne said. "She kept them on her computer, but told me she had the hard copy backups in a couple of large boxes in her office."

Gil eyed Ellie and smiled. "I know Anne, Ms. Bennett, and Ms. Carlyle, but I've not had the pleasure of meeting you. I'm Gil Collins."

"Ellie Campion. I'm the board member-at-large—elected last year."

"Gil, I think that by now you can call me, Rose."

"And I'm Nancy. Ms. Carlyle sounds so formal, and we've been through a lot together in the past year."

"That we have. I just hope we aren't going through it again."

Anne cast a sharp glance at him. "You think there's something…strange about this?"

He raised his eyebrows and shrugged. "It just seems odd, that's all. The food looks pretty average to me. And Ms. Harrison wouldn't be likely to order something she's allergic to, but a bee sting is even stranger. Normally, people react to a sting."

"That's right," Rose said with a thoughtful expression. "They jump, wince, yell 'ouch' or something."

"Plus, a bee buzzing around here would have been noticed by someone else," Nancy added. "Could it have been a spider or some other insect?"

Anne sighed. "I have no idea. Somebody suggested a brown recluse, but I don't know if they cause allergic reactions. They are toxic, however. I wonder about fire ants. They pack a pretty powerful bite."

"I've also heard some medications can cause serious allergic reactions," Rose added. "My cousin is allergic to penicillin."

"If she was allergic to a medication, then her doctor wouldn't have prescribed it," Gil said.

"Then that leaves the food," Nancy stated.

"Good grief." Ellie frowned. "You don't suppose Susan was right and someone poisoned her, do you?"

They all looked at each other.

Allergies—food. Why does that sound familiar?

The thought hovered on the edges of Anne's mind like a moth advancing and retreating from a teasing flame. She drew a deep breath and concentrated. Finally, she remembered.

"Peanuts!"

"What?" Gil asked.

"Peanuts! Fran was allergic to peanuts. I don't recall the exact circumstances, but I remember her saying that once."

"I do, too," Gil said. "It was at the conference. We were eating breakfast. Ms. Harrison stopped by the table and you offered her a bagel."

"With peanut butter on it! That's when she said she was highly allergic to peanuts."

Nancy nodded. "I also remember someone offering her peanuts in the bar. She backed away fast."

Gil pulled out his cell phone and walked several steps away.

Rose's forehead wrinkled. "I wonder if she was allergic to just peanuts or to any kind of nut?"

"Peanut allergies are well-documented," Ellie

commented. "I was once on a flight where the attendants didn't serve the usual peanut packages because someone had an extreme allergy to them. I guess even the smell can bring on a reaction."

"So, I doubt a hotel would take a chance and use any kind of nut on a topping or crust without declaring it on the menu," Nancy told them. "Ellie, you were at her table. Did someone stop by to chat?"

Gil returned to the group.

"I left that table when Susan and I had a spat about the critique group. The food hadn't been served yet."

"That means we'll have to talk to those seated at the table again," Gil said with a deep sigh.

Anne noticed Susan, Jane, and another lady from earlier still in the room. Gil moved toward them. She and the others followed.

"Ladies, if you don't mind, I have a couple of questions." He withdrew the notebook from his pocket. "Can you recall who stopped by the table to chat with Ms. Harrison?"

"You mean other than Anne?" Susan said in a snotty tone.

"Yes."

"Well, there was Barb, of course," Jane added. She then rattled off several names. "And someone in a ghost costume. She just kind of paused near us."

"Any idea who it was?"

She shook her head. "She never spoke to us and I didn't pay any attention."

"I remember the ghost," Ellie said. "She came and sat at my table for a while."

"What do you mean 'for a while?'" Gil inquired.

"I remember being served my salad and by the time

I'd put the dressing on, she was gone."

"Did you recognize her?"

"No, the costume totally covered her. Even the eye slits were tiny."

"It could have been a man," Anne added. "We have several men who are members."

"Good point," Nancy concurred.

"You know, now that I think about it, I saw the ghost lift the lid on one of the dishes in the hallway. Didn't seem like any big deal at the time," Anne said.

Gil continued writing. "What about after the entrée was served? Anyone stop by to chat?"

Susan shrugged. "I don't think anybody came by, but I wasn't paying much attention. I was mad at Anne."

Jane shook her head. "I don't recall either. The waiter served us and that was that. I do recall that Fran and I were the last ones served at our table."

"We had a waitress," Susan said. "The short, fat one."

"No, it was a guy," Jane insisted. "I remember his hands when he put the plate in front of me. Fran came back into the room a few minutes later and began to eat. Then all hell broke loose."

Gil finished writing and looked up at Anne. "And you're sure you saw the ghost lift a lid to one of the dishes?"

"Yes. I thought he or she was just curious."

"Seems to me that if a ghost had served Fran, or anybody else for that matter, someone would remember," Nancy said.

Anne cast a glance at her former critique partner. "You and Fran didn't come back into the room together. Where were you?"

"None of your business," Susan shot back.

"Make it my business." Gil gave her a hard stare.

Susan looked away and shifted her weight from side to side again. "Fran was very upset. I tried to comfort and calm her down. She wanted to deck both Barb and Anne."

"Yes, but Fran came back a good ten minutes after you," Anne reminded her.

"She said she didn't need my help and was going to take a walk to cool down—and before you ask, I have no idea where. I went to the ladies' room."

"Thank you for your help, ladies." Gil smiled and nodded.

Jane got the hint that they should leave. Susan didn't. She still glared at Anne, but moved away as the treasurer grabbed her elbow and steered her toward the door while whispering in her ear. Susan's comments as she exited were clearly heard.

"I don't care what you say; he needs to arrest our new President. She's always hated both me and Fran. Why, she wasn't in the least bit nice when she won the election. Didn't phone Fran or…" Gratefully, her voice faded as they women moved down the hall.

"Whew, what a morning," Rose said. "I don't know about the rest of you, but I'm confused."

"Me, too," Ellie echoed.

Kathy Samuels reentered the room shaking her head.

"Oh my God, what a day! Poor Cindy was so upset—too upset to eat, so I bought her a glass of wine, then shoved her into a taxi for the airport. I don't think she'll ever come back."

"I'm Detective Gil Collins. Could I ask your name?"

"I'm Kathy Samuels, the Vice-President of the chapter." She glanced at the others. "Did anything happen while I was gone?"

"Looks like Fran may have had a serious reaction to something in her food," Nancy told her.

"Ms. Samuels, did you notice anything or anybody unusual this morning?"

"Not really. Some people were in costume, but I didn't bother to look too closely. I was more concerned with Cindy's welfare."

"Did you by any chance notice a person disguised as a ghost?"

Kathy frowned. "Yeah, I did, but had no idea who. I was going to call out whoever it was for looking like a Klansman. Bad taste, if you ask me. Do you need me for anything else? I just want to get home and try to forget any of this happened."

Gil snapped his notebook closed and smiled. "No, I don't need you. I may be in touch later, however, and naturally if you think of something, no matter how insignificant you consider it, please let me know."

"Oh, Kathy, the officers would like the address and phone number of Mary Smith, the doctor who helped out. She said she was a new member."

Kathy frowned. "She was? I don't recall her offhand. Let me check when I get home."

Gil handed Kathy and Ellie his business card. The women nodded, gathered up personal items, and left. Rose, Nancy, and Anne remained.

Anne looked at Gil. "What next?"

"Next, we talk to the wait staff."

Chapter Three

Gil moved to the door and stepped into the hallway.

"This is looking more and more like no accident," Nancy commented.

Anne took a deep breath. "I know, and once again I'm involved with a dead body."

"As Jen would say, the Snoop Group to the rescue," Rose said.

Their absent critique partner, Jennifer Swanson, had dubbed them this during the conference last spring when they'd assisted Gil in solving two murders.

Anne mentally crossed her fingers. "Let's hope that this time, it's an accidental death. Maybe the hotel is at fault."

"Well, if they are, they can expect one massive lawsuit coming their way," Nancy added. She pulled out a chair and sat. "I'm tired of standing, but don't want to go home just yet. This investigation stuff is getting to be fun."

Anne and Rose also took seats.

"I wonder at what point in time Susan is going to go completely around the bend," Rose said. "Her accusations are totally insane."

"Well, no one can possibly believe I had anything to do with Fran's death. How much longer will Susan's present critique partners put up with her?" Anne wondered.

Gil reentered the room with three waitresses. All wore black slacks, black shirts, and black shoes. Very nondescript. Anne immediately noticed that none of them matched the description Susan had given of her server.

So much for short and fat. Leave it to Susan. Doesn't pay attention to details, but has an opinion anyway.

For once she didn't feel guilty at being judgmental.

One of the women glanced at the table where Fran had been seated and shuddered.

"I appreciate you coming. Could I have your names, please?" The women complied as he wrote in his notebook. "Ladies, I'll make this as quick as possible. Which of you served this table?"

The tall dark-haired woman who shuddered raised her hand. "I did."

"Could you please give me some details?"

"Details? I filled water and iced tea glasses. I brought in the salads, and then took away the empty plates. It took a while because I had to deal with four tables. The others only had three."

"And why was that?"

"Jeff was a no-show. We had to rearrange the stations. Since I'm the most experienced server here today, I was told to pick up the slack."

Anne was itching to ask more about Jeff, but knew better than to interrupt Gil. Nancy and Rose also knew the drill by now. They, too, kept silent.

"What can you tell me about the table where the lady died?"

"Not much. It was fairly straightforward."

"Tell me about the food," Gil asked.

"The salad was mixed greens with tomatoes and cucumbers. The dressings were in boats on the table—balsamic vinaigrette and ranch. There were also two baskets of bread and some butter."

"I see. What about the entrees?"

"There was a choice of three, one chicken, one fish, and one vegetarian."

"Can you describe how they were cooked?"

Anne leaned forward in her chair. She saw where this was going.

"The chicken was in a sauce of some kind. The fish had a coating of bread crumbs, and the meatless dish was cheese tortellini in tomato sauce."

"Can you describe the breading in more detail?"

The woman shook her head. "Not really. I don't cook it, I just serve it."

"Excuse me for a moment," Gil said. He walked over to the house phone, lifted the receiver, and spoke softly before returning.

"Did anybody notice anything unusual during service?" he continued.

"You mean other than half of them were in Halloween costumes?" another server asked. Her iron gray hair was cut in a severe, almost masculine style.

Gil smiled. "Must have been amusing."

"Would have been if it hadn't been for this one who lifted the lids from a few of the plates."

"Can you describe the person?"

"Yeah, a ghost."

"She was a ghost?" the last woman, a short, slender redhead said. "I thought she was a Klansman. Tacky if you ask me."

"Why do you say 'she'," Gil asked.

The waitress shrugged. "The room was mostly women. I just assumed."

"And you saw her at the cart with the food on it? Salad or entrée?"

"Definitely entrée," the redhead told them.

"No, it was the salad," the second server insisted.

Gil turned to Anne. "Do you know which it was?"

She shook her head. "Didn't see the plate, only the action, but my guess is it was the salad. I remember it was the first time I called Fran out into the hallway for a chat about getting Rose and me the necessary papers."

The redhead shook her head. "When I saw her, it was definitely the entrée. I remember because I was carrying some empty salad plates to the cart."

Gil's attention swiveled back to the waitresses. "Tell me, where do you take the empty plates?"

The gray-haired server answered. "There's usually a cart or two just around the corner near the freight elevator. When they're full one of us takes them to the kitchen. If we're real busy, we just call down for a busboy to come."

"And today?"

"Didn't need to call," the redhead replied. "The busboy came with a bunch of entrees just as I filled up the space on the last cart. He left with one of them. I assume he returned for the others."

"Did you know the busboy?"

The head waitress nodded. "Sure, it was Miguel."

"Miguel? Can you describe him?"

"Early twenties, five-six, slender."

Gil smiled once again. "Thank you for your help. Now, I'd like to know if I could get, say about a dozen ziplock baggies."

"Of course, won't take a minute."

Anne and her friends had remained silent during the interrogation. Now, however, she jumped to her feet and walked over to the group.

"Hello, my name is Anne Jamieson. I'm the new president of the chapter. I just want to tell you that this staff always does such a nice job. I'm so sorry this had to happen." As she spoke, she shook hands with each of the women. "I hope next month is less traumatic."

The women left. Anne turned to Gil.

"Jane may have been on to something. None of those women served her or Fran."

"How do you know?" Rose questioned.

"Jane said it was a man because she remembered his hands. They were definitely masculine. Two of the servers wore rings and one nail polish."

"She would have seen that," Nancy agreed.

"What about the busboy?" Rose added. "Could he have served a plate or two to help out? The waitresses may not have known, or may not have wanted to admit they let a busboy do their jobs."

"This is beginning to look strange," Gil said. "I called down for the head chef to come up. Where is he?"

The server arrived with the requested baggies.

He stuffed them into his coat pocket. "Are there any more entrees still in the hall?"

"Yes, sir. A full cart. "

Gil left the room and returned a few minutes later with three of the baggies containing samples of the salmon. He then went from table to table taking random samples of fish and salad from other plates.

"What are you doing with those?" Rose asked him.

"Comparison samples. Someone in the kitchen could have accidentally put peanuts into the mixture or on the salad."

He zipped the last bag shut as a man in a white coat and pants walked into the room.

"Mr. Collins? I'm Chef Michael Barnes. I understand there was a problem here."

Anne wanted to roll her eyes. *That's putting it mildly.*

Gil told the servers the room could be cleared, and then explained to the chef what had happened. "You didn't know about this?"

"No, I came in about eight-thirty or so to oversee prep for lunch and tonight's service. I gave the sous chefs and line cooks their orders, and then met with the head of catering. We had several large bookings for today, including a small wedding reception for this evening."

"So you didn't prepare this particular menu?"

"I made the decision on what to offer. I try to change it up from month to month. I give the sous chefs the menu when they come in and begin the process."

"What is in the breading on the salmon?"

"Toasted bread crumbs, chopped parsley, a little thyme, some..."

Gil held up his hand. "Peanuts?"

"Peanuts? No. Never. Too many people are allergic to peanuts and nuts in general. If we use any kind of nut, we always state it on the menu. There's a macadamia encrusted grouper, but that's all."

"Could a mistake have been made in the kitchen?"

"Not likely."

"Would you have any of the breading used for the salmon still available?"

Chef Michael frowned. "I don't know, but we can go check."

Gil turned back to Anne and the others. "I'm staying here for a while. Why don't you all head for home?"

Nancy nodded. "Sounds like a plan to me."

He touched Anne's arm as Nancy and Rose exited. "Dinner tonight?"

"Sure. I'd like that."

"Do we go out or do I bring in something for four? Are Lisa and Ken at home this weekend?" he asked naming Anne's thirteen-year-old daughter and sixteen-year-old son.

"They're home. However, they can order in a pizza or eat leftovers. Let's the two of us go out for a nice meal."

He grinned, leaned down and kissed her lightly on the lips.

"See you around seven."

Anne joined Nancy and Rose in the hallway.

"I know this sounds really callous, but I'm starving," Rose said. "Lunch?"

"Fine with me as long as it's not here," Nancy replied. "I've had about as much of this hotel and its food as I can stand."

"Rafferty's?" Anne suggested. They always went to Rafferty's during times of crisis.

"Rafferty's," Nancy and Rose concurred at the same time.

As they left the hotel, Anne couldn't help but wonder if she was once again up to her ass in a murder.

****

The Saturday lunch crowd at Rafferty's had thinned, so the group had no problem finding a table. After ordering white wine all around, they looked at each other.

"So, was this all just a horrible mistake or was Fran murdered?" Nancy asked in her usual blunt way.

"I can think of a lot of people who'd want to kill her," Rose said.

"Yeah, but how many knew about her peanut allergy? What a way to start my presidential term," Anne lamented again. "And just once, I'd wish someone would put a muzzle on Susan or stuff a sock in her mouth. Anything to shut her up."

Rose waved her hand. "Don't worry about her. I noticed a lot of members looking at her like she had two heads when she was accusing you. Susan Lynch will not be taken seriously by many after today."

"But it's so annoying to be on the end of her barbs. I always feel like I have to defend myself."

"I talked to a few people while Gil was there. She's going through critique partners like water over a dam," Nancy said. "Pretty soon she won't have anybody left to bully."

"Any idea who's still putting up with her nonsense?" Rose questioned as the waiter brought their wine.

Anne sipped and shook her head. "Not a clue. Ellie dropped out this morning. Susan wasn't happy about it."

Nancy took a large drink and sighed. "Oh, who cares about Susan? Her paranoia will bury her. Let's talk about Fran. Any idea who this ghost person was?"

"No. She was there before lunch was served, but gone when Fran died," Anne said.

"And Jane was convinced she was served by a man. The busboy?" Rose mused.

Anne tapped her finger on the rim of her wine glass. "Possibly. Of course, we don't know if it was the food yet. There *might* have been an insect involved."

The waiter stopped by their table. "Are you ready to order, ladies?"

Nancy opted for a burger and fries, while Rose settled on a turkey wrap with chips. Anne didn't have much of an appetite, so decided to keep it light by ordering a Caesar salad. Besides, she'd eat her fill tonight.

"I don't care what anyone says, it was no insect," Nancy stated when they were alone again. "And it could have been an accident. A line cook or sous chef deciding they could improve on the recipe and making it up as they went along."

"I hope that's the case," Anne answered. "I'd feel sorry for whoever did it, but that explanation would get the chapter out from under suspicion."

"And what are we going to do about those missing papers Fran had?" Rose asked. "I need to see those last couple of months of minutes."

"Ellie said she'd drop by and get them, but I think I'll go with her. She seems nice, but I don't know that much about her. I'm not sure I'd trust her to hand them over without reading them. I just hope Fran's husband will let us in to look," Anne said.

"I'd wait until after the funeral," Nancy suggested. "They aren't that important."

"Speaking of the funeral, I suppose we all have to

attend," Rose commented with a sigh.

"Unfortunately," Anne stated. "At least you and I do. All board members should be there."

"I'll go, if for no other reason than to support you," Nancy added. "I'm keeping my fingers crossed that this won't adversely affect the chapter."

Anne stared out the window, her mind racing as Nancy and Rose talked about the chapter.

This is the third time in a little over a year the chapter has been involved in violent death. Membership renewal starts in January. Wonder how many will drop out. And how will the Writers Association of America view all of this?

The national organization had suspended chapters in the past, but usually for lack of a full board of directors or weak membership numbers. Anne knew that as President, she was responsible for keeping the chapter on the straight and narrow. And Lord knows the past year hadn't been this chapter's shining hour.

Rose's voice brought her out of her thoughts.

"How does that sound to you, Anne?"

"What? I'm sorry, I was thinking. How does what sound?"

"You put out an announcement on the chapter e-mail loop about Fran, and we hold an emergency board meeting to see who takes her place on the board. According to the by-laws, the past president sits on the board for a year in a non-voting position as a kind of liaison. Technically, Fran should be replaced," Rose said.

"Oh crap, I forgot about that. I suppose the best thing to do would be to ask the previous president to do it."

"I'm not even sure who that is," Nancy stated. "The one before Fran, Carol Peters, moved away as did the one before her. I think Luella Cranston did the honors before that."

"I'll check when I get home. I hope I can pull off a sincere message for the loop. Praising Fran might be an impossible task for me. If I lavish too much, everyone will know I'm lying."

Rose patted her hand. "You're very diplomatic. You'll do just fine."

Their food arrived and the conversation ceased.

Anne picked at her salad and tried to form the beginning of her announcement. No matter how she mentally structured the statement, it sounded cold. Surely there was some way to word the statement that sounded both sincere and warm at the same time.

She sipped the last of her wine, and hoped Fran's death would be called accidental. But deep down, she was certain it wasn't.

****

Anne entered her house and met her daughter, Lisa, in the kitchen.

"Hi Mom, how was the meeting?"

She wasn't sure how much to tell Lisa. At thirteen, the kid knew what was what. However, did she want to burden her with the full truth?

Inhaling a deep sigh, Anne compromised. "Awful! Fran Harrison passed away right in front of everyone. Something she ate, I think."

Lisa stopped pouring her soft drink and stared. "Are you kidding? What? She like choked?"

"She was certainly blue enough. Nobody could revive her, not even a doctor or the paramedics. Really frightening."

"Wow, that must have been horrible to watch. Wasn't she the woman you ran against for president?"

"Yes." She hoped this explanation sufficed.

"It was an accident, wasn't it?"

"As far as I know."

Her daughter resumed pouring her drink into an ice-filled glass. "I just asked considering your track record with death."

Anne bit her lip. "I assume we'll know the full circumstances soon. By the way, Gil and I are going out for dinner tonight, so you and Ken are on your own."

"Which means he'll want pizza and I'll want Chinese. Brothers are a pain."

Lisa made a face and left the room.

Heaving another huge sigh, Anne trudged upstairs, closed the door of her bedroom, and pulled her cell from her purse. Plopping down on the chaise in the corner of the room, she called Jen.

"Hey Anne, how was your first day as prez?"

"Not the best." She gave Jen the news.

"Holy shit! Was it like a heart attack?"

She spent the next ten minutes telling her friend the details and her suspicions.

"A peanut allergy? I sort of remember her reaction when I offered her some one day in the bar at the conference. She backed off like I held a sword to her chest. Did anyone check her purse for an injection pen?"

"A what?"

"A lot of people who are highly allergic often carry an injection pen with them, just in case, although I think that may be more apropos for insect stings like from a

48

bee. I mean, if you go out to eat and have a severe allergy to some kind of food, then it makes sense to tell the waiter about that allergy, so maybe she didn't have one with her."

Anne almost ran out of breath listening to Jen who tended to talk in long sentences.

"To the best of my knowledge, no one did. Not even the paramedics."

"And you think it may have been deliberate?"

"I don't know, but Gil took samples of the food from both Fran's plate and others."

"Gil was there? If he was called in, then someone must suspect murder."

She explained how Gil had come to be there and how Jane swore she was served by a man, not a woman.

"Sounds like a job for the Snoop Group," Jen said. "What a shame I won't be there to help."

"I may have to take an interest in the case, since I'm the chapter president, but Susan was there and made accusations."

Her friend made a rude snorting noise over the phone. "Screw Susan Lynch! And I'm sure no one thinks you did it—if it turns out to be murder."

"I suppose, but it's still upsetting." Anne changed the subject. "How's your mother?"

Jen rattled on about her mother's surgery and recovery before they ended the call. Bottom line—Jen might be home by late next week.

Anne rested in the chaise and thought about what her critique partner had said regarding an injection pen. She assumed it contained some sort of hypodermic pre-filled with a specific amount of a drug to counteract the allergy. But if Fran possessed one, why didn't she reach for her purse when the attack began?

Because the dose was so massive, she didn't have time?

And she didn't remember seeing a purse or anything like that near Fran at the meeting. Could someone have removed it? She made a mental note to ask Gil tonight.

****

Since Anne had no idea where she and Gil were dining, she kept her wardrobe choice casual—a pair a black denim Capri pants, an aqua tank top, and bronze-colored sandals. Inspecting her reflection in a mirror, she decided she looked pretty damned good. A recent haircut had taken her shoulder length auburn hair to a sleek, asymmetrical short bob. It took some getting used to. Change was not often in her vocabulary, but the last six months had given her incentive—both professionally and personally.

Three months ago, her agent had presented her with a contract from a small press on her latest vampire story. It might be her last. Her old publisher who specialized in the subgenre had not shown any interest in more of her work. The realization she was dropped hurt like hell, but at the same time gave her the impetus to move on. Her work in progress was a total departure into the world of romantic suspense. Plus, she was seriously dating a cop, which gave her a leg up on research regarding police procedures.

She was heading downstairs when the doorbell rang. Both of her kids raced through the foyer to answer.

"Ha! Pizza!" Ken exclaimed giving his sister a wicked grin.

"My General Tso's Chicken won't be far behind."

Ken paid and tipped the delivery person with money Anne had left on the hall table and carted the box toward the kitchen. Her daughter took up a position by the sidelight to watch for her Chinese order.

"What time is Gil picking you up?"

"Around seven. What are you and Ken going to do—besides eat, I mean?"

Lisa shrugged. "I may read. I picked up some home decorating magazines when I was visiting Dad the last time."

"Sounds like a good idea."

"Gil's here." Lisa opened the door. "Hi, Gil, how's it going?"

Gil stepped into the foyer. "Hi, Lisa. Things are fine. And you?"

"It'll be great as soon as my dinner arrives."

He looked over to Anne. "And speaking of dinner, are you ready?"

"More than ready. I didn't eat much at lunch." She hitched her purse onto her shoulder. "Where are we going?"

"How about Harbor Lights?" he said naming a popular restaurant on the beach. "It might be a little crowded on a Saturday, but nothing like during season."

"Sounds fun. I haven't been there in a long time. Maybe we can take in a movie later." She turned to Lisa. "Try to get along with your brother."

"I will, and you be good," she said with a grin at both of them.

****

Anne settled into a cozy booth at Harbor Lights with a wonderful view of the ocean. The drive over had taken less than ten minutes, so the conversation had been general. Now, with Gil finally seated across from her, she could ask the questions burning a hole in her tongue.

"Any news yet about the food samples you sent in?"

He shook his head. "Not yet. I requested a fast track, but it's the weekend. May not get it until Monday."

"But you're thinking this was no accident, aren't you?"

"If it hadn't been for the one lady insisting she'd been served by a man, I'd pass it off as just that. However, it's best to play it safe."

"I called Jen this afternoon with the news. She said that people who are allergic to things often carry a hypodermic with an antigen in it. Did Fran have one in her purse?"

"I never saw a purse. Maybe the paramedics took it with them or the officers. Could be one of the other ladies picked it up." Gil frowned and slid from the booth. "I'll go check. Order me a vodka and tonic if the waiter comes. Be right back."

The waiter appeared shortly after Gil had left. She placed his drink order along with her choice of white wine. The drinks arrived at the same time Gil returned.

"Well?" she asked taking a sip from her glass.

"The officers do not have a purse belonging to Ms. Harrison. Neither do the paramedics—and they said the doctor who assisted them at the hotel never showed at the hospital to fill out the paperwork, so we'll definitely need *her* address and such." He took a long swallow of his drink. "Now, I'm tired of discussing murder and mayhem across the dinner table. I'd rather concentrate on you. By the way, you look fabulous. Those pants or whatever they're called are delightfully tight in all the right places, and that top shows just enough to make me curious."

Anne had to suppress a giggle. Gil did this to her all the time. His comments made her feel young, sexy, and desirable. A melting sensation slipped over her. Forget dinner. She wanted Gil. She bit back a sigh. Later.

When the waiter came back, they ordered—grouper for her and surf and turf with lobster for him. The conversation veered toward family and her work.

"How's the new book coming?" he asked.

"It's amazing at how fast I cranked this one out. Took only eight weeks from start to finish. It's going through critique at the moment. So far, the group likes it. Thanks for your help with the technical points of a police investigation. They helped."

"My pleasure. Mention me in the dedication." He grinned as their food arrived. "What's the title again?"

"*Conferences Can Kill You*, but that may change. I'm still not sure if to keep it under my own name and brand or to use a pseudonym."

Gil's eyebrows rose. "Conferences? As in dead agents?"

"Yep. They say to write what you know, and I certainly know about dead agents."

The meal was delicious and Anne couldn't resist the vanilla ice cream with both chocolate and caramel sauce. But as she ate, the tug of desire reappeared. He sipped his coffee and smiled.

"So are you really interested in a movie?"

"Nope." She popped a spoonful of ice cream and gooey sauce into her mouth, then slowly removed the spoon.

Gil stared. "Your kids are home, but I'm all alone."

"I've got a remedy for that."

His smile widened. "But you promised your daughter you'd be good."

She dipped the spoon into the caramel and licked it clean with slow lapping motions, all the while returning his stare.

"I plan to be good. I plan to be very, very, good."

He took a deep breath and signaled the waiter. "Check, please!"

Anne inwardly chuckled.

The trip to his house took under fifteen minutes. It took even less time for their clothing to hit the floor and for them to hit the bed.

"God, you're gorgeous. Gorgeous and sexy," he whispered, his hand caressing her shoulder.

"So are you."

"No, I'm not."

She ran her fingers through his hair. "You are to me, and that's all that counts."

Then he kissed her, letting his actions speak for him.

An hour later they were redressed and cuddling on his sofa in the living room.

"So what movie did we see—if Lisa wants to know?" he asked as his lips found her temple.

"I noticed that the Vintage Movies Theater in the mall was showing Casablanca. I can recite the dialogue."

He chuckled. "What a tangled web we weave…"

"Oh, shut up."

His phone rang. "Collins here…That was quick…I see…What about the rest of the samples…All right, that works for me. Have to wait for the autopsy results anyway. Thanks."

He hung up and stared at Anne with a serious expression. Her stomach fluttered and her heart thudded in her chest. This was not good news.

"That was Gilson at the lab. He analyzed the remains of Ms. Harrison's food. Definitely ground peanuts. Lots and lots of them."

Chapter Four

Anne banged her fist on the arm of the sofa. "I knew it! I just knew it. What about the rest of the food?"

Gil shook his head and set his phone on the end table. "Don't know yet. Gilson analyzed Ms. Harrison's food first knowing I wanted the information as soon as possible. He just checked for peanuts—nothing else."

"And if the rest of the food is peanut-free, then we can assume this is murder."

"Unless she did it herself."

Anne sat up and stared. "Suicide? Fran? No way in Hell. She was much too fond of herself to do something like that. And besides, who commits suicide by anaphylactic shock? That's bizarre."

"Most of the bodies *you* deal with come under that heading—or at least the circumstances of your finding them do, not to mention the motives."

She ignored his sarcasm. "What would be the motive here? Fran was an embittered pain in the ass. She really wanted to remain as president of the chapter. I certainly didn't do it. She'd have more of a motive for killing me than the other way around."

"No one is suggesting you had anything to do with it."

"I'm sure Susan Lynch would disagree with you."

He sighed. "That woman needs to have her lips

sewn shut. One of these days she's going to get sued for slander."

His phone rang again. "Now what?" he muttered as he answered. "Collins here…Oh really, that's interesting. Don't mess with anything and I'll be there shortly. Thanks."

"I guess that conversation means the evening's over."

"That was the hotel. Seems a cleaning woman found Ms. Harrison's purse hanging on the back on one of the stall doors in an out of the way restroom off the lobby."

"You're kidding. What was it doing there?"

Gil kissed her temple and rose. "That's what I'm about to find out. I'll run you home first."

Anne also stood. "Can't I come with you?"

"I guess it won't hurt, but let me do the talking."

"No problem. How did the hotel know to call you? You're homicide."

"I spread my business cards around this afternoon after you left."

"Which means you suspected Fran was murdered."

"It means I was being proactive."

"I hate that word."

"So do I. Are you ready to go?" he asked in an impatient tone.

"I'm ready and I won't ask any more questions."

The drive to the hotel took twenty minutes. After parking, Gil rummaged in the trunk until coming up with a large, folded, grocery sized paper bag. They walked in the entrance and approached the front desk. A band was playing in the lounge area, yet the lobby seating was empty.

Either the band is really good or the place is dead on a Saturday night.

"Hello," Gil greeted the desk clerk before flashing his badge. "Could I please speak with Mr. Goodson?"

The clerk nodded, picked up the phone, punched in a few numbers, and said, "Mr. Goodson, there's a man from the police department here to see you... Yes sir." She hung up and smiled. "Mr. Goodson will be out in a second."

"Thank you." Gil smiled back and moved to end of the long counter.

Anne fidgeted as they waited. A moment later, a short, balding man emerged from a hallway carrying a blue purse.

Retrieving fingerprints from that textured faux crocodile surface will be a hard task.

"Hello, Detective Collins? I'm Thomas Goodson, the assistant manager of the hotel. The cleaning lady discovered this about an hour or so ago. I opened it to find a wallet with an owner's ID. The minute I saw the name, I found your card and called. Carl Roberts, the manager told me what happened earlier today. Thought you'd be interested."

"Thank you. I appreciate it," Gil said as the man handed over the purse. "Is this Fran's?"

Anne shrugged. "I guess so. I didn't notice her purse at all. She was here and seated when I arrived for the meeting this morning."

He snapped on a pair of latex gloves and opened the clasp. Anne peered around his shoulder at the contents. Nestled in the bottom was a yellow box with a brand name and a picture of a syringe along with the numbers .03.

"Is that…" she almost asked.

"Looks like an injection pen to me." He carefully opened the box and shook out the hypodermic. "Doesn't appear to have been touched." He next pulled out the wallet. "This is Ms. Harrison's without a doubt. Money and credit cards are all here."

"Maybe it was taken after Fran went down. I mean, surely Fran would notice if someone took off with it. And if not Fran, then another person at the table."

"Where did you put your purse?"

She shrugged. "If it's a shoulder bag I hang it from the back of the chair. If it's a handbag, I put it on the floor next to my chair."

"And this is a handbag?" he asked.

"Yes. Chances are she had it on the floor. And Fran was in and out of the room several times. *Plus* she was also distracted by all that went on, so she may not have noticed it was missing. Maybe no one at the table saw anything that suggested somebody picked it up."

Gil replaced the items, closed the handbag, put the purse in the paper bag, and pulled off the gloves.

"When people are talking or eating, they often don't pay attention to others walking by."

"That's true." Anne turned to the manager. "And this was found on the back of a stall door?"

"Yes, ma'am. The cleaning lady said it was the far end stall."

"Where is this restroom?"

"You go down this corridor, turn left, and then right. It's down a short hallway."

"Thank you." Gil cupped her elbow and led her away.

"Certainly is out of the way," she commented as

they followed the passages.

They passed the men's room and finally stopped in front of the ladies' room door. Another door was nearby. Gil opened, and then closed it again.

"Meeting room."

A door with the word "Stairs" was just beyond the meeting room. Across from the restrooms a glass door, now locked, led to the parking lot.

"Awfully convenient," Anne murmured.

"Very," he replied as he scanned the ceiling. "There's a fisheye surveillance camera at the junction of the corridors. Looks like I'll be pulling more tape—lots of tape from all the cameras on the first floor. Let's check out this stall."

"Maybe I should go in, in case someone's inside," she suggested.

"It's eleven o'clock at night and this is an obscure area. Who'd be in there?" He pushed the door open. As predicted, the room was empty. He used a paper towel from the dispenser to open the last stall door.

Anne surveyed the restroom. It was small, only three stalls and one sink. It had no doubt been designed for use by those attending a meeting in the room next door.

"Nothing of interest here," she said. "Are you going to dust for fingerprints?"

"Maybe on the door to this stall, but that's it. The cleaning lady would have done her thing on the rest of the surfaces. And somehow, I don't think the person who took the purse would spend time washing their hands. Come on, let's go."

They stopped by the front desk again where Gil requested Goodson put up an "Out of Order" sign on the ladies' room door, asked that the tapes needed be available, and informed him a fingerprint crew would be by as soon as possible. He then called it in to the station. Goodson promised to pull the tapes tonight.

"Forensics won't be here until tomorrow," he informed the assistant manager who nodded and moved away.

"Why wait until morning?" Anne asked as they left the hotel.

"Because it's Saturday night and this is a low priority. Goodson is pulling those tapes right now, which means my Sunday will be spent looking at them, and before you ask, no, you can't see them yet."

She ignored his comment. "There were over eighty people at the meeting. You may need some assistance with talking to some of them."

"Let me guess, you and your group are volunteering for the job."

"It makes sense. I know these women—well most of them—and they might tell me more than they would you. After all, someone went to an awful lot of trouble to kill Fran. This was no spur of the moment plan." She drew in a sharp breath. "And maybe whoever took the purse knew she carried an injection pen."

"That thought crossed my mind, too. That purse could have saved her life." He heaved a sigh and gave her a stern look. "You can help as long as you keep it simple and report everything you discover to me. No sleuthing on your own."

"Deal!"

On the drive home, Anne's mind drifted back to this morning. Sally Crenshaw had made comments about Fran having affairs. And one of those affairs involved a member's husband.

Fran's love life just took center stage.

****

Anne awoke the following morning with a mental checklist, at the top of which was reading the chapter by-laws. She rummaged through the file cabinet in her bedroom looking for the document.

"Damn it, where is it, Gary?" she asked, talking to a stone gargoyle sitting on top of the metal cabinet. The silly looking thing had been a gift from her kids years ago as tribute to her paranormal books.

"Are you talking to Grotesque Gary again," a voice said from the doorway.

Anne turned to look at a grinning Lisa.

"I was hoping maybe he had a glimmer of where I'd stuffed the chapter by-laws in this thing."

"Well, I don't think old stone face is going to answer. By the way, Carrie Phillips called last night and invited Ken and me over for a barbeque this afternoon with her family. Is that all right?"

"What? Yes, I guess so," she replied absently, opening another drawer. "Just make sure you're home by nine. Is your homework done?"

"Yep. Did it all last night. How was your date with Gil?"

"Great." She flipped through a couple of useless folders. *I've really got to clean this thing out.*

"What movie did you see?"

"Casablanca." She hated lying, but no way was she ready for her thirteen-year-old daughter to know the truth.

"Old movies—blech. Have fun searching. I'm going to grab some breakfast, and then read some of an assigned book for English."

As Lisa headed downstairs, Anne finally found the by-laws.

"Gotcha! Thanks, Gary, I know you helped in some way."

She settled in at her desk in the corner of the room and flipped through the boring legalese until coming to the part she needed.

"Nuts," she said out loud a few minutes later. "I was hoping I wouldn't have to do this, but I guess I do." She laid the thick packet on the desk and took out a sheet of paper along with a pen. A to-do list was in order. "Talk to you later, Gary. I've got work to do. Have a nice day."

It looked as if a board meeting was necessary, but she'd call board members in the afternoon. *I'll set it up for Monday sometime.*

She then called Kathy Samuels to see if she had found Dr. Smith's address and phone number and to inform her of the meeting.

"I'll be there. Anne, I've looked in all the new member files for the past six months and a Doctor Mary Smith from Highcrest is not there. Maybe she was planning to join."

"Could be. I'll let Gil know. He and the police can track her down."

It's odd that she wouldn't show up to do the paperwork and fill out a death certificate.

Next she jotted down some words of condolence for the chapter loop. That should go out today. Neither of the two sentences she'd written sounded very warm or comforting. *Work on it later.*

She also made a mental note to call Fran's husband

with condolences. Having never met the man, she had no clue what to say. She didn't even know his name.

Of course, also on her list was how to begin helping Gil with what was certainly a murder case. Sally Crenshaw was near the top for interrogation, along with Jane. Maybe the treasurer could remember who sat where at the table.

But first, Anne needed to talk to Rose. Her confirmation of the gossip about Fran's love life made talking to her better sense. Sally wasn't always discreet.

Downstairs, she headed for the kitchen where she fished her cell from her purse. Lisa had finished her breakfast and was sitting on the patio with a book.

She dialed Rose and waited through four rings until her friend finally answered.

"Hey, Anne, what's up? Any more news on Fran's death?"

"Some." She gave Rose the details of the lab report and of her trip to the hotel.

"So someone took Fran's purse and hid it. You know what this means, don't you?"

"Yes, this was a meticulously planned killing. And by someone who knew Fran carried an injection pen in case of emergencies. Do you know who might have been close with her? I have to be honest; I never paid that much attention to who she hung out with—other than Susan. By the way, Gil gave us the green light to do what we usually do."

"Get in his way?"

"Don't be funny. He said we could ask questions."

"Might be a good idea to wait until we have the rest of the lab reports in," Rose suggested.

"I'll just ask a few innocent questions."

"Uh-huh. How innocent, Anne?"

"Well, Sally Crenshaw mentioned Fran having an affair with another member's husband. You seemed to know a lot about it. What gives?"

"Ah, that would be Becky Lawrence. I critique with her in the erotic romance group. She wasn't at the meeting. I can give her a call on the excuse of telling her about Fran. I'll also call Sally and pump her for more information if you'd like."

"Good idea. I need to call Fran's husband and express the chapter's condolences. What's his name?"

"George. I met him at the last Christmas party."

Anne suppressed a giggle. "George? *George* Harrison? Like the Beatle?"

"Yeah, I know. Made me want to laugh, too. You know if you're going to discreetly ask about Fran's love life, don't forget to talk to Jen. She knows everything. I guess somebody should call her."

"Already done. She's the one who brought up the injection pen theory. But I'll give her another call. As Jen would say, the Snoop Group is on the prowl."

Rose groaned. "Leave it to Jen to come up with a silly name."

"But appropriate. By the way, I'm calling a board meeting here at ten-thirty tomorrow morning. We have to replace Fran."

"Ten-thirty? I guess I can make it, but may have to bring a toddler and the baby, so this better not take too long."

"No problem." Rose's five kids often made for interesting critique group meetings, too.

"I've gotta go. I'll call Becky this afternoon and see what she has to say. Talk to you later."

Anne hung up and tapped her finger against her lips. It was too early to call the rest of the board members, but she could call Nancy with the information she'd learned last night.

"After the conversation at the hotel, I'm not surprised," Nancy said when Anne finished. "The killer had to be either the ghost or the mysterious waiter."

"You mean the busboy?"

"If it was him. I don't suppose Jane paid any attention to what the waiter wore, did she?"

"She didn't say. Why?"

"Waiters and waitresses usually have some kind of identifying uniform, like the black worn by the waitresses we talked to yesterday, but busboys generally wear T-shirts and jeans. Maybe a place like the hotel would ask them to wear black pants or something."

Anne hadn't thought of this angle. "I'll ask. I'll also talk to Jane again. And by the way, Gil said we can talk to people who were at the meeting. You know, gently question them."

Nancy sighed. "At least this time I'm not on deadline. I just turned in my last round of edits."

"I'm going to call a few people this afternoon. Perhaps we can develop a network for asking questions. Kinda like we did when investigating Dorie's murder," she said naming their late critique partner and first case.

"The meeting was packed, so that makes sense. Why don't you tackle board members and I'll talk to a few others who I know had problems with Fran, like Janine Barrett."

"Janine? What kind of problems did she have with her?"

"When Janine first joined the chapter, Fran demanded she show loyalty by volunteering to work on the conference."

"Loyalty? You're kidding. That's crazy. No newcomer wants to jump in headfirst before knowing how the chapter works."

"Janine was there yesterday. I'll give her a call and see what she has to say."

"That's okay. I'll do it." Anne sighed. "I guess I'd better get busy and write this condolence announcement for the loop. I have to have an emergency board meeting to appoint a new past-president liaison. Hope I can find one. Talk to you later."

Anne hung up, had a quick breakfast, and then sat down to compose the announcement for the members.

"Like there's anybody left who hasn't heard," she said to herself as she wrote.

An hour later, she had what she hoped would be received as warm and sincere.

Dear fellow members,

It is my sad duty to inform you of the tragic death of our former President, Fran Harrison, at yesterday's meeting. Fran was a valuable member of our writing community and will be missed. Her dedication to this chapter was strong. Her loss will be keenly felt by all of us. Our deepest condolences go out to her husband and family.

As of now, I do not have any details regarding the funeral or a memorial service, but will keep you informed as to when and where such will be held.

With great grief,

Anne Jamieson, President

She contemplated erasing the *with great grief* part,

but decided to let it stay. It might not be the most heartfelt piece she'd ever posted, but would have to do.

With that chore finished, Anne fished the roster from her files and scanned the names, making a list of who to call when a something licked her ankle.

"Hello, Bruno," she said addressing the little shih-tzu.

His fluffy tail wagged and his eyes sparkled. Technically, she was Candace Warren's dog, but Anne had taken him in when his owner had been convicted of manslaughter. Candace, also a member of the group, was doing time at a minimum security facility about two hours away from San Sebastian where they all lived.

"I'll bet it's time for your walk." At the word "walk," his tail wagged faster. Anne laughed. "All right, you win. Let's go."

In the kitchen, Lisa was stuffing a swimming suit and beach towel into a tote bag.

"What time are you leaving?" she asked as she snapped Bruno's leash on.

"Twelve-thirty. Her brother's going to pick us up."

"Speaking of brothers, where's yours?"

"Still in bed. I was about to go up and roust him out."

"Well, have a good time and be home at a decent hour."

"Will do. I don't think I'll be home for dinner, but it won't be too late. Promise."

Anne nodded, walked through the house and out the front door. As Bruno stopped to thoroughly sniff every vertical surface he came across, she thought about the questions she'd ask the people on her list.

Thirty minutes later, she reentered the house in time to wave goodbye to her kids as they left for a fun-filled afternoon of barbeque and swimming.

With a deep sigh, she settled down at the kitchen table and placed her first call to Luella Cranston, the last president still living in the area. She explained the situation and asked if Luella would accept the position. She breathed a sigh of relief when the answer was, "Sure, what the hell."

Her next call went to the treasurer.

"Hello, Jane, it's Anne. How are you doing?"

Jane sighed. "As good as can be expected, I guess. I'll be seeing Fran's blue face for a long time."

"An awful tragedy. I just wanted to let you know I'm calling an emergency board meeting for tomorrow morning. According to the by-laws we have to replace Fran on the board."

"We do? Why? Her position wasn't a voting one."

"I know, but it's in the by-laws. I had to dig back over ten years to find who was still in the area. Luckily, Luella Cranston agreed to do it."

"She was President when I first joined. I don't know her very well. She doesn't come to a lot of meetings."

"She's getting on in years and lives about an hour away from San Sebastian. She agreed to help out and that's all that matters." Anne took a deep breath. "By the way, who was sitting at your table yesterday? I know Susan and Ellie were there, but who else besides you and Fran?"

"Let's see, there was Carolanne Rogers. She was dressed as some kind of a princess—wore a tiara, I remember. Then there was Cheryl Johnson. She was in costume, too. A clown complete with a Bozo wig, a fake nose, and lots of silly make-up. Linda McIlroy sat next to Susan, if I recall. And Olivia Leonard sat next to me. Neither of them bothered to dress up. Ellie moved after she and Susan kind of got into an argument. About critiquing, I think. Susan made a couple of nasty comments about Ellie after she left the table."

"Was everyone at the table, other than Ellie, when the food was served?"

"I don't remember. I was talking to Olivia when the waiter served me. Fran had been gone for a while."

"And a waiter, not a waitress, served you? Did you notice his clothing?"

"Not really. Like I said, I was talking to Olivia and had to break off the conversation to lean back when he placed the plate in front of me. That's when I noticed his hands. Definitely male."

Anne thought for a moment about what Jane had just said. She remembered Fran as being to the left of Jane. "You leaned back? Where was Olivia sitting?"

"To my right. Fran was on my left. The waiter served me, and then left the plate in front of Fran's spot. Why?" Jane asked.

"Oh, no reason. I was just curious. The wait staff thinks a busboy may have lent a hand. I've got to go and finish my calls. How about we gather at my house tomorrow at ten-thirty? That way we can officially meet and enter Luella as the replacement into the records."

"Aren't all meetings supposed to be open to the membership?"

"I'll post something on the loop around nine-thirty. If someone wants to come, they can, but I'm not going to knock myself out over it. I'll see you tomorrow."

Anne hung up with one vital piece of information. The waiter was no waiter. A professional would have never served from the right, but from the left of the guest.

So it could have been the busboy. She made a mental note to tell Gil.

Rose already knew about the meeting. That left Kathy and Ellie to contact. Neither answered their phones, so Anne left messages in their voicemails, then followed up with e-mails to all.

Her next call was to Gil.

"Good afternoon, gorgeous," he answered in a cheery tone.

"Good afternoon yourself. You sound chipper today. Any news about Fran?"

"No, nothing new yet, and if I sound chipper, as you say, it's because I'm talking to you, not viewing old surveillance tapes."

"See anything interesting?"

"Not much, but I've only seen the lobby tapes and the hallway tapes near your meeting room so far. Lots and lots of people coming and going, some in costume. Seems your group wasn't the only bunch with a Halloween themed event, including the Italian Opera Lovers Club. I've never seen so many Enrico Carusos in my life."

"You're kidding," Anne said with a laugh, and then sobered. "That means a man could have slipped into our meeting to serve Fran."

"Their meeting was on the lobby level. Yours was on the second floor. I've still got a lot of location tapes to view yet."

"Did you see the ghost on those tapes?"

Gil sighed. "Yes, three times in the hallway. Two times to lift the lids off a couple of plates, and once walking the opposite direction and disappearing."

"So it looks as if the ghost left before eating, just like Ellie said. When?"

"Shortly after you, Ms. Harrison, Ms. Lynch, and Ms. Hamilton had your little chat. You had returned to the room as did Ms. Hamilton. Ms. Harrison and Ms. Lynch continued talking for a few minutes, then Ms. Lynch returned. The victim remained walking up and down the corridor. The ghost lifted the lid of one of the plates, replaced it, and walked right past Ms. Harrison a few minutes before she returned to the room. The tapes also showed the wait staff coming and going, but since they dress alike, it was hard to tell who was male and who was female. The resolution isn't that great. It's an old system."

"Hmmm, interesting. I talked to Jane Whittaker a while ago. She had some information." Anne relayed her suspicions that the waiter was not a pro.

"The busboy is named Miguel Suarez. He's due here for his shift at three. I'll talk to him then. I also tried getting in touch with the no-show waiter, Jeffrey Wainwright, but he doesn't pick up his phone. I'll keep trying." Gil paused. "Did I remember to thank you for a fabulous night last night?"

"Several times over. And the restaurant was good, too. Would you like to come for dinner here tonight?"

He chuckled. "I'd love it, but am pretty much committed to those tapes. Is the invite open for tomorrow?"

"Sure is. Six-thirty?"

"Six-thirty. Talk to you later."

Before hanging up, Anne relayed the information—or lack thereof—regarding Dr. Smith to Gil.

"We'll check it out."

She sighed. Here she was alone in the house for the entire afternoon and Gil was unavailable.

"Well, damn!"

Chapter Five

The rest of Sunday had been a combination of quiet and semi-chaos. Soon after the e-mail posting, her phone started ringing from members who had not attended the meeting. All demanded to know details of Fran's death. Her pat answer had become, *we don't know, perhaps a food allergy.* She had also called the Harrison home to express condolences to Fran's husband. He was unavailable, but she talked to Fran's sister.

"Yes, we were all shocked," the woman had said in a somber voice. "Poor George is devastated. He isn't able to cope at the moment."

"I totally understand. Please convey my sympathies and those of the chapter on this horrible tragedy to him and the rest of her family."

"I will and I'm sure he'll be in touch when he's able. Thank you."

And now Anne prepared to host an emergency board meeting. She set out a pitcher of iced tea and a small platter of pastries on her dining room table. The board members would arrive shortly.

The doorbell rang and she hurried to answer. The sooner they got started, the sooner it would be over.

Rose rushed in minus kids. "I hope this doesn't take long," she said. "My neighbor agreed to look after Graham and Brian for a couple of hours. Thank God,

Bethany is in first grade this year and the twins in kindergarten. I'm slowly whittling down the group at home."

As she spoke, she made a beeline for the dining room where she flopped in a chair.

"Tea? Pastry?" Anne offered.

"Tea, yes. Pastry, no. I'm on a diet."

Amused, she poured a glass of tea. Rose was always on a diet. Five kids in eight years of marriage had seen to that. It also explained why she never seemed to have time for a haircut or manicure, although Anne noticed today that Rose's hair was in place and her fingernails clear of color. Maybe having three out of five at school gave her some extra time for herself.

"Did you talk to Becky Lawrence?"

Rose nodded as she drank. "Yes. She was shocked, but not in the least upset. I'll tell you more details later."

The doorbell rang again. Within the next five minutes, the rest of the board arrived, along with Luella Cranston.

"Luella, I'm so glad you agreed to do this. Such a shock about Fran."

The woman walked past her and into the foyer. "Yeah, heard she croaked at the meeting. Oh well, I've done this before, and if you ask me, it's a total waste of time. You need to change the by-laws regarding this position at the next board meeting and present it to the membership for a vote. Don't know why it was there in the first place."

At seventy-five, Luella had long ago passed diplomatic and moved straight into crusty old broad. She spoke her mind and didn't care. Although still a member of the chapter, she had stopped writing her sweet romances years ago saying she'd achieved her goal of five publications and called it quits.

With everyone present, Anne turned to follow Luella when the doorbell rang again. It was Nancy.

"Hi, come on in."

Nancy grinned and headed for the dining room.

Jane leaned forward in her chair. "Nancy, what are you doing here?"

"I represent the non-board membership. I'm keeping you honest for an open forum." She turned to Anne. "Loved the way you popped the announcement of the meeting on the loop at ten o'clock this morning. By the time most of the membership reads it, it'll be over."

"That was the whole idea. This is merely a formality, but we had to meet in person to do it. Luella's right, we need to change the by-laws." She didn't add that if seen early enough, Susan Lynch would have been at the door, too. No way was she ready to deal with *her* again.

"I take it there's no more news about Fran," Ellie said.

"Not to my knowledge. I'm sure we'll find out the details sooner or later."

Rose sent her a glance. So did Nancy as she bit into a pastry. Anne had a lot to discuss, but not with Ellie, Jane, Luella, and Kathy around—at least not yet.

"Let's get this show on the road," Luella said. "I've got a lunch date with an old friend. Figured I might as well roll this cockamamie meeting in with a little fun."

Anne sat at the head of the table. "In that case, if Rose is ready, I hereby declare this meeting has come to order."

Rose nodded. Ten minutes later the meeting was adjourned. Luella thanked them and trotted out the door closely followed by Jane and Kathy. Ellie hesitated.

"Just thought you'd like to know I've had four people contact me about critique groups already, and what with Fran and all, I guess you haven't even had a chance to put it on the loop."

"That's great, Ellie. When you get enough people together, make sure you have a good mix of experienced and new authors in a group. You'll do well at this," Rose told her.

Anne patted Ellie's shoulder. "Thanks for coming, Ellie. I know it wasn't much of a meeting, but it was necessary."

Ellie paused again as if wanting to talk further, but Anne headed for the foyer giving the woman no choice but to follow.

She opened the door only to step back in surprise. Susan Lynch stood on the doorstep.

"What kind of stunt are you pulling?" Susan said. "All board meetings are open to the membership."

Getting her breath back, Anne swallowed a tart reply settling instead for a cool comeback.

"You obviously saw I made the announcement on the loop this morning. We needed to fill Fran's position as soon as possible."

"Fran's barely cold. You could have waited a while." She shot an evil glance at Ellie. "And you, you are nothing more than a suck-up. You don't have the experience to head a committee, especially one dedicated to critiques."

"Well, we'll just have to find out about that, won't

we," Ellie shot back. "I'll talk to you later, Anne."

Ellie sailed out of the door, brushed past Susan without a look, and strode to her car parked at the curb.

"Sorry you missed the meeting, Susan," Nancy said in a civil, but tight, tone. "Better luck next time."

"And may I ask whom you selected to replace Fran or is that a secret, too?" their former critique partner snapped.

"Luella Cranston graciously accepted," Anne replied.

"Who the hell is that? I'd have been a much better choice. You should have had nominations."

Nancy straightened to her full five-foot-nine-inch height. "The by-laws state that the position be filled by a past-president of which you aren't nor ever likely to be. Now, if you'll excuse us, we're going to lunch—and no, you're not invited."

Susan's nostrils flared, but she turned and marched away.

Anne closed the door. "Well, that was interesting. Good thing I didn't post the meeting last night. She'd have been here for sure. Do we want to go out to lunch?"

Rose shook her head. "I need to get back home. Let's talk here."

"So, what did Becky have to say?" Anne asked as they seated themselves in the living room.

"Like I said, she wasn't in the least sorry to hear Fran bit the big one. Becky was a member of Fran's critique group and it all started when Fran held a little cocktail party for them and their husbands at Christmas. That's how Becky's husband, Jim, met Fran."

"I take it that's when the affair began," Nancy said

as Rose paused.

"Not at first, but a few months later Jim began working late on what he called special projects. Becky didn't think a thing about it. *Then* she met the wife of one of Jim's co-workers at the grocery store and mentioned the late hours."

"And the woman answered, what late hours?" Anne said.

Rose nodded. "Exactamundo! So Becky staked out his work. When he drove out of the parking lot, she followed him to a cheap motel, watched him enter the lobby and come out again, then head for a room. A few minutes later, Fran pulled in, knocked on the door, and when Jim opened it, planted a big, juicy wet one on his lips. An hour later they came out, got into Jim's car and headed for a restaurant."

"So, did Becky confront him? I'd have done it right in the restaurant," Nancy stated.

"Becky did something better. She followed him for a couple of weeks and every time he and Fran met, Becky took tons of photos and videos with her cell phone. Finally, she confronted him. He promised to break it off. Then she confronted Fran with the evidence. Fran was not in the least contrite. Becky, of course, withdrew from the critique group."

Anne shook her head. "And did her husband break up with Fran?"

"So Becky claims. Said things went back to normal."

"Until..." Nancy prompted.

"Until about a month ago. Once again, Jim started working late. Becky thinks this time it was legit, but she wasn't sure."

"How did you know about the affair?" Anne inquired.

"Becky told us during critique group one day. She was pretty upset and I guess she needed to talk. She didn't go into details then, only that Jim and Fran were having a fling. At any rate, during the election, Becky said she'd vote for Ghengis Khan over Fran."

Nancy's eyebrows rose. "And Becky just spilled her guts to you with the details yesterday?"

"More or less, she was only too happy to let me know what a snake Fran was, but you know, I had the feeling her reaction to Fran's death was all rehearsed—like she knew what had happened, yet pretended not to when I called. I probably wasn't the first person to get in touch with her." Rose glanced at her watch and rose. "I've got to go. If you need me to talk to anyone else, let me know."

"Well, that was interesting. Becky wasn't at the meeting, but I suppose she could have heard about Fran from someone else," Nancy said after Rose had left.

"Maybe a former critique group member. She had the motive, but not the opportunity. And over eighty of us had the opportunity, but not necessarily the motive."

"And the means," Nancy added. "Someone had to know about her peanut allergy."

"The only reason I knew was because of an incident at the conference last spring. I wonder who her other critique partners are. They must have known. And maybe even known she carried an injection pen."

"That's highly possible." Nancy paused. "You know, Becky could have been at the meeting—dressed like a ghost."

Anne drew in a sharp breath. "And Becky is on the

tall side. With short dark hair. If she slicked it back, she could easily pass for a waiter."

"*And* she used to critique with Fran."

"Oh my, do you think Becky could have done it?"

Nancy shrugged. "On the surface, I'd say no. And she'd be taking a hell of a chance on someone recognizing her as either a ghost or a waiter."

Anne didn't know Becky all that well, but suspected a woman scorned once was one thing—a second time and she might not be so forgiving.

"The ghost and the waiter could have been anybody. Jane gave me the names of the others at their table yesterday. One of them may have noticed something unusual."

"Want me to call them?" Nancy asked.

"Would you? That way I can talk to Ellie about this ghost person in more detail, and to Kathy. She may have noticed something, too. Today wasn't a good time what with Luella around." She gave Nancy the ladies' names, and then chuckled. "I think Luella may liven up board meetings."

"If she even bothers to attend."

Anne's phone rang. Caller ID showed it was Jen.

"Hi Jen, what's up?"

"Uh, this and that. Anything new?"

Anne told her of finding the purse and injection pen at the hotel.

"I read the loop and saw your announcement about Fran and the board meeting. When did you last read the loop?"

"Last night when I posted the condolences. I didn't bother this morning. Too busy. I just posted. Why?"

"I think you'd better read it. Susan posted about an

hour ago."

"Oh God, now what?"

"The comments coming in thoroughly back you. I've gotta go. I just wanted to give you a heads up on this. Talk to you later."

Anne hung up and stared at Nancy. "That was Jen. She says Susan's been posting on the loop."

"Oh shit!" Nancy rolled her eyes.

They entered the kitchen where Anne opened her laptop and pulled up the information highway for the chapter. She found and read Susan's posting with Nancy looking over her shoulder.

Anne slammed her fists on the table. "That bitch!"

The gist of the long, rambling, slightly incoherent posting was that Fran would be alive if Anne hadn't been harassing her.

"Something's got to be done about this woman," Nancy said in an anger filled voice. "Who owns the list serve?"

"The person who set it up about twenty-five years ago. I think that might be Georgia Yancey. I'm calling her. Even if she isn't the owner, she'll know who is."

Anne pulled up the roster, found Georgia's number, and dialed. The woman answered on the fifth ring.

"Georgia, it's Anne Jamieson."

A loud sigh came over the phone. "I wondered when you'd get around to calling me. I've had over a dozen calls in the past hour complaining about Susan Lynch. I don't know her, but this post is way out of line. I've already sent her a warning. If she doesn't cease and desist, she'll be suspended from posting for however long I decide. I was also just about to post a reply saying the loop is for chapter business only and personal vendettas are strictly prohibited."

Anne breathed a sigh of relief. "Thank you, Georgia. Susan has problems. She hates me and considered herself a good friend of Fran's. Hopefully, this will be the end of it."

She hung up and turned back to Nancy who continued to read the computer screen.

"This was posted about an hour ago. Already over thirty people have replied—all of them on your side. I don't think we'll have to worry about Susan for a while. Can't believe she had the gall to post this, and then show up for a board meeting." She glanced at the time in the bottom right hand corner of the screen. "Oops, I've got a hair appointment at noon. I'd better scoot."

"Are you going to do something totally different with it this time?"

Nancy grinned. "And be unpredictable? Nope. My hair has been like this for years. No reason to change now. Although, I may have to give in to coloring it. The gray shows up well against the dark brown."

Anne waved as her friend walked to her car. Tall and lean, Nancy moved with a grace she'd always envied.

With the meeting done, she decided to follow up with Ellie and Kathy on what they may have seen or heard on Saturday. She called Kathy first.

"Hi Kathy, it's Anne. I just wanted to ask a couple of questions. I didn't want to bring up what happened with Fran in front of Luella. Have you got a minute?"

"Sure, I guess so."

"Did you see or hear anything that was unusual at the meeting on Saturday?"

"Not really. Not until Fran turned blue and hit the floor. I'm sorry if that sounds insensitive, but Fran was a real piece of work."

"How so?" She had a pretty good idea yet wanted to hear it from another source.

"As you know, I was elected to the board a year ago. I had some ideas for guest speakers that would touch on all aspects of writing. In order to save a few bucks on hotel and travel, I wanted to use two or three members as speakers. Fran shot that down immediately. Said a chapter was judged by the caliber of its speakers and that we needed name presenters."

"What did she mean 'name' presenters and judged by whom?" Anne asked.

"I made the same comment, and she suggested people like BriAnnon Ridgeway or Sarah Grant."

Anne almost choked. "BriAnnon Ridgeway? She lives in Seattle and rarely travels outside the area. Getting her would have cost a fortune, not to mention impossible. And Sarah Grant only does the national convention."

"I know. I brought that up and she said it was my job to extend the invitation. Then she followed up by stating the national organization would be impressed with her leadership skills."

"The national organization doesn't give a flying flip about the chapter programs."

Leadership skills? Probably planning on running for a board position at WAA.

"I told her a few months later that I'd tried, but was turned down. But as much as she hassled me, that was nothing compared to the grief she gave Terry Whiting about the conference."

Terry had had the misfortune to be the last conference chair.

"When and what about?"

"Before the conference. Fran didn't like the keynote speaker. She didn't like the editors or agents Wendy Travers had invited—especially Carmella Radcliff. She wasn't impressed with the food selections or the facility. Terry finally told her to cram it and run the chapter. She'd deal with the conference. The real dust up came in April, after the conference and the murders."

"How?"

"Fran worked herself up into a frenzy of rage over damned near everything. She screamed at Terry and at Wendy. Wendy was in tears and Terry almost attacked her. We had to literally get between them. Thank God the only outsider at that board meeting was Susan Lynch. And speaking of Susan, I saw her posting. I posted right back that her comments were inappropriate."

"Thanks, Kathy. Georgia Yancey is taking care of it."

"About time somebody did something with that woman—Susan, I mean. The instant you decided to run for the presidency, she and Fran started a campaign of character assassination. And just so you know, I voted for you."

"I appreciate that. And thanks for looking after Cindy. I suppose she was upset."

"Very much so. I was going to call her in a little while to offer more apologies and see if she's willing to come back."

"Good idea. I should probably do it myself, but I'm

so busy at the moment."

"No problem."

"Thanks, Kathy. I've got to make some more calls. I'll talk to you later."

Her next call was to Ellie, asking the same questions as she had Kathy.

"I've thought and thought on this and can't think of a thing. Anne, is Susan Lynch mentally ill? I mean, I don't want to pass judgment if the poor woman has a problem, but her behavior is so odd."

Anne tiptoed through the diplomatic minefield. "I'm not sure about being mentally ill, but I think she's a bit paranoid. You said the other day that the ghost sat at your table. Did he or she do anything unusual?"

"She never talked if that's what you mean. Just nodded or shook her head if anyone asked a question. I thought it was all a part of the costume and theme of Halloween. Kinda mysterious and a joke as to discovering who she was."

Anne doubted the ghost had been in a joking mood.

"You know, she did get up and move around a lot," Ellie continued. "She'd sit for a while, look around the room, then get up and leave."

"Did you see her talking to Fran?"

"Not that I recall, but I did see her pass by her table at one point. The only reason I noticed was because the waitress served my salad. I don't think Fran was there, but don't quote me on that."

"You sat on the board with Fran. How did that go?"

Ellie sighed. "Not good. Fran was always carping about something. If she had won the election again, I was going to resign. I don't need negativity."

"In that case, I'm doubly glad I won. I've got to go. I'll put up a notice that you're in charge of forming critique groups and post it on the loop as soon as possible. You do a good job with the reservations, so I have confidence you'll do just as well with this. Have a good one."

Anne hung up and composed a brief message concerning critique groups, then posted it. She was glad to notice that the replies to Susan's vitriolic comments were all supportive of her and not the sender.

A glance at the clock showed it to be almost two. Gil would be coming for dinner at six-thirty. Time to figure out a menu and go to the store.

Her heart beat faster at the thought of seeing him.

Girl, you got it bad. And that's a good thing.

The menu and shopping only took an hour. Anne fumbled with her keys to deactivate the car alarm while trying not to drop the three bags of groceries in her hands. The alarm chirped and she finally managed to open the passenger side door and plop the bags onto the floorboards. Slamming the door shut, she noticed an envelope under the driver's side windshield wiper.

Oh, Lord, not another advertisement for car detailing. I know my car is a mess, but I'll get around to it soon without spending what I just did for food.

She snatched the crumpled white envelope from its secure place and chucked it into one of the bags. Home again, she staggered into the kitchen and unpacked the food. Finished, Anne was set to stuff the envelope into the trash when she noticed her name was printed on it.

"What the hell." She extracted a note.

Stop asking questions about Fran. It will only buy you trouble. You didn't like her and no one cares anyway.

Naturally, it was unsigned.

Her fingers gripped the cheap, lined notebook paper until it crinkled and tore. Someone had followed her from home to the grocery store. A chill ran up her spine, and goosebumps broke out on her arms.

****

One of Gil's best features was his punctuality. He arrived at six-thirty on the dot complete with a bottle of wine. Anne accepted both the bottle and his kiss on her cheek.

"Something smells fabulous," he said with a grin. "What are we having?"

"Salisbury steak, mashed potatoes with gravy, peas, and a salad."

Gil followed her toward the kitchen like a starving puppy.

"Hi Gil," Lisa said stirring the pan of gravy. "Hope you're hungry. Mom's made enough to feed an army."

"Anything I can do to help?"

"Open the wine and set this on the table," Anne replied handing him the salad bowl. "Lisa, go tell your brother dinner is served."

When they were all seated, she gazed around the table as the dishes were passed. It was nice to be a family again. She'd never realized how much she missed a male presence during meals.

She decided not to spoil the close knit feeling the evening provided by informing anyone about the note.

Telling Gil made the most sense, but if she did that he might instruct her to stop asking questions. And thanks to Susan's accusations, she didn't want to do that. She decided to let it pass for a while.

"So Ken, I hear you are now motorized," Gil said to her son.

"Yep, got my license two months ago."

Anne bit back a groan. Nothing said you're getting old like a child with a driver's license.

"No doubt about it, a driver's license gives you that feeling of independence," Gil replied.

Ken slid a sidelong glance at her. "Sure is nice, but it'd be much nicer if I had my own car."

Anne had been expecting this. "Cars cost money, not only to buy, but to maintain. I suggest a job."

"I'm sixteen and a junior in high school. I can apply in the usual places. I was thinking of doing it this weekend. Can I borrow the car?"

Gil burst out laughing.

Before long Gil was helping clear off the table as the kids went upstairs to finish homework.

He slipped his arms around her waist while she stood at the sink rinsing the dishes before placing them in the dishwasher.

"You have great kids. My brother, Brad, is coming for a visit next week and my daughters will be here for a couple of days. Would you, Ken, and Lisa like to drop by for a barbeque next Sunday?"

She turned and slid her arms around his neck. "I'd like that. I've been wanting to meet your girls. Do you think they'll like me?"

He kissed her hard on the lips. "They'll love you, Take my word for it."

She took a deep breath to steady her fluttering nerves and turned back to the sink.

"Your brother...is he the one who's the geologist?"

"Volcanologist, actually. He's been over in

Southeast Asia for a while. Indonesia, I think. Some volcano erupted a few months ago, so naturally he rushed to the scene. Brad's like that—off at the drop of a hat for an adventure. He loves his job."

"Sounds fascinating. Is he married?"

"Nope. He's thirty-five and hasn't found anybody interesting enough to take his mind off his work. You know somebody?"

"Ninety-nine percent of my friends are writers. I just don't see the two professions meshing."

Gil chuckled. "Opposites attract. Look at us."

"Yeah, just look at us," she drawled. "You thought I'd killed Isadora Powell."

"And I can admit when I'm wrong."

Anne finished the last glass, wiped her hands on a towel, and faced him again.

"Thank goodness for that!"

He pulled her close and kissed her. A moment later a cough had them breaking apart.

"Sorry to interrupt, but I just came down for a bottle of water," Lisa said with an amused expression. She retrieved the bottle from the fridge and looked at them. "Carry on."

Gil and Anne both laughed as her daughter exited the room. Before they could take her advice, Gil's phone rang.

He pulled it from his pocket. "Collins here… That's not surprising." He paused for a long while as he listened. The look on his face turned grim. "That is. What would be the purpose… I have no idea. I'll have to ask the husband. I take this to mean it's official now… Yeah, I never really figured it any other way. I'll get on it first thing in the morning."

He hung up with a frown. "That was Gilson at the lab. The reports came in. The only peanuts found were on Ms. Harrison's food. All the other plates and the breading from the kitchen are clean. And here's an interesting twist. Mixed in with the ground peanuts was a healthy dose of ground lobster shells. She was definitely murdered."

Chapter Six

"Lobster shells!" Anne repeated with a gasp.

"You heard me," Gil said. "It's now an official murder. There wasn't a lobster within sight at that luncheon."

"But why? Good grief, was she also allergic to shellfish?"

"I don't know. Must have been or else why would it be there?" He leaned down to kiss her. "Sorry to cut this short, but I have to go. I need to make some phone calls and set up interviews. The husband is first on the list."

"In that case, you'd better know this." Anne told him about Rose's information concerning Fran and Becky's husband.

"And this Becky person thinks the affair rekindled?"

"According to Rose, she wasn't sure, but suspicious."

"Got a number for her? I'll call and set up an interview."

She pulled up the chapter roster on the computer and gave him the information.

"And don't forget that ghost. Ellie Campion doesn't remember her being at the table after the food was served."

"I'll need to interview that ghost, too."

"Provided we can figure out who it was," she replied.

"Good point. Anything else?"

She told him the theory that Becky could have been the ghost or the waiter.

"Don't worry, we'll check on an alibi."

"Nancy's working on calling the women seated at Fran's table. I'm hoping we can get the names of her critique partners. They must have known about Fran's allergies."

"How so?"

"Whenever I critique, a late brunch or a lunch is usually served, and there are always snacks around during the session. I'll let you know as soon as I have the names."

He turned and walked toward the foyer. Anne followed. So did Bruno. She picked the dog up. Gil kissed her, and then scratched the little shih-tzu behind the ears.

"I'll be in touch."

"Gil, it'll help if we call some of these women, won't it?"

He hesitated. "It might. Just be sure to let me know if something interesting comes up. Do not try to track down clues on your own."

"I won't." She paused. "I suppose you'll be taking another look at the surveillance tapes."

"I wondered when you'd get around to that. I wanted to view them again before I said anything to you. I did see something unusual on the one from that short hallway near the ladies' room where the purse was found."

"And…"

"Around ten-thirty a person who may have been a woman, wearing shorts, a baggy T-shirt, a baseball cap with a large bill, sunglasses, and carrying a huge tote bag entered the ladies' restroom. Five minutes later, our ghost emerged and took the stairs. She reappeared from the stairwell about an hour or so later and reentered the ladies' room. Shortly afterward, the first lady came out and exited into the parking lot."

Anne sucked in a deep breath. "Oh my God, the killer?"

"Possibly."

"Had to be a woman if she used the ladies' room."

Gil shook his head. "Could be the person knew about the cameras and used the ladies' room to throw us off the track. The tape from the second floor shows her popping out of the stairwell at ten-forty and entering again at the right time an hour later. But keep in mind that she could have been a legitimate member who changed here, attended part of the meeting, decided she didn't want to stay, so left."

"Why change into a costume?"

"Ever try driving a car in a costume?" he asked.

"Oh, didn't think of that."

"It might be easier if you and your friends looked at the tapes, too. You may know her. But this time, you'll have to come to the station. My lieutenant reamed me a new one for taking the last batch out of the department for you to see."

"I understand. We can do that. How many tapes are there?"

"A lot. And this hotel hasn't scrimped on surveillance. All cameras were working. As usual, not the best images, but good enough."

"What about Fran's purse? Did you get any fingerprints off of it?"

"Not really. The texture of the material was rough. We even put it through the Super-glue regimen, but all we got were a bunch of partials and a lot of smudges."

"Super-glue?"

"You put the object in an enclosure with a few drops of Super-glue, then seal it up. The fumes from the glue adhere to the prints. In this case we discovered some of what appear to be Ms. Harrison's partials and a couple from an unknown source. Unfortunately, we can't ID them." He kissed her again. "I'll call you tomorrow."

Anne closed the door behind him and hugged Bruno before setting him back on the floor. "Well, Bruno, it looks like the Snoop Group is officially on the job again."

Her first order of business was to call Nancy with the news.

"Shellfish! Was she allergic to that, too?"

"I don't know, but Gil is going to talk to her husband."

"Good idea. They say a spouse is always the first suspect in a murder. So, I take it we are once again going to give Gil gray hair," Nancy commented.

"He's agreed to let us talk to a few people and we can view the surveillance tapes when he's done looking at them. We might notice something or someone he wouldn't." She also told her about what the tapes revealed and about the Super-glue. "The Super-glue thing sounds interesting. So the ghost, if she can be ID'd, looks like the top suspect, at least for doctoring the food. Have you talked to the others at Fran's table yet?"

"Not yet. I wrote most of the afternoon on that work in progress. I do that occasionally, you know."

"Yes, I know, and if this type of stuff keeps happening, I'll have story lines out the whazoo for the rest of my life," Anne replied. "Good thing I switched to romantic suspense."

The conversation ended with Nancy promising to contact the women first thing in the morning.

Anne then relayed the information from Gil to Rose. Her response was much the same as Nancy's.

"Well someone certainly wanted to make sure she died. Talk about overkill."

"And this has to be someone who knew Fran—and knew her well."

"Like a husband? Or a family member?"

"Possibly, but you'd think Fran would notice if her husband or a family member was lurking about."

"True, but she was upset about the election, and then you took her to task about a few things. And don't forget Barb Hamilton. You had to calm them all down. That could have distracted Fran to the point she wouldn't notice who was who. And besides, nobody really pays any attention to waiters or waitresses. They serve you and they leave."

"Hmmm. You've got a point. I'll have to remind Gil about that. He's going to interview the busboy and the waiter who didn't show up for work. I'm looking forward to viewing the surveillance tapes. We might be able to identify the person entering the ladies' restroom."

"All right. I'm interested in the ghost. That should be our priority. Could be our killer. Just give me a day's notice so I can find a sitter for the kids. And speaking of kids, it's time to force them into a bathtub. I'll talk to you later."

Anne thought about the ghost. Obviously, the tape showed it was a woman. Or perhaps not. Gil had said the tape showed a person wearing baggy clothes entering the ladies' room. It could have been a man. The odds of a hotel guest using that restroom were slim on a Saturday.

"Oh well, things weren't clear during the previous murders either," she said out loud.

Her train of thought was interrupted by her phone ringing. She didn't recognize the number, but answered anyway.

"Hello?"

"Is this Anne Jamieson?" a male voice asked.

"Yes, who's this?"

"My name is George Harrison—Fran's husband."

"Oh, Mr. Harrison, you didn't need to call me back." But now that he'd done so, she didn't see the harm in asking a few subtle questions. "I just called to offer my condolences. I believe I spoke with your sister-in-law."

"Yes, you did, and I wanted to thank you for your concern. It's…it's been a trying few days."

"I understand. And I'm so sorry for your loss. Poor Fran. What an awful thing to have happened. I suppose there must have been a mix up in the kitchen. I remember her telling me about her peanut allergy. Was she allergic to anything else?"

"Un…unfortunately, Fran had a lot of food allergies. Made it tough to dine out, although she rarely had a problem. She'd…she'd alert the waiter and he'd tell the kitchen." A sob escaped. "What am I going to do without her? She was everything to me. We'd been married for over twenty years. I...I still can't believe it."

Anne felt like crying herself. "Mr. Harrison, I just don't know what to say. Is there any information on the funeral? I'm sure many of our members would like to attend."

"The arrangements are in place at Matthews Funeral Home. As soon as the coroner releases her...her body..." He choked a bit on the last words. "...we can hold services. I'll let you know."

"Thank you, Mr. Harrison. And once again, my personal and the chapter's deepest condolences."

She hung up and cupped her chin in her hands. The poor man was broken up. His voice had been shaky and his frequent pauses during the conversation suggested he was on the verge of tears.

I guess I would be, too, if I was in his shoes.

She shoved her phone aside, poured a glass of wine, and headed out to the patio to enjoy the cooling night air.

Tomorrow was going to be a busy day.

****

As soon as the kids left for school the next morning, Anne settled behind her desk to plot the next two chapters of her work in progress. A quick check of her voice and e-mails had shown numerous messages. She'd deal with them later. However, images of Fran and the conversations she'd had with others intruded on her work. Eventually, she gave up and tackled her cell messages first. Most were from people wanting information on Fran's funeral or from friends offering support from Susan's posting.

Her e-mails dealt with much of the same. To save time she issued a post saying that as soon as she had information on the funeral, she'd send it out. She also publicly thanked the dozens of members who suggested she ignore Susan.

Let Susan choke on that!

Anne finally decided to call Janine Barrett. She was a fairly new member who, according to Nancy, had had problems with Fran. She couldn't remember if Janine had been at the meeting.

"Janine, this is Anne Jamieson. How are you?"

"I'm fine. What can I do for you?"

"I'll be honest, I can't remember if you were at the meeting or not."

"I was, and sitting as far away from Fran as possible. I was at one of the back tables. It was awful what happened. I feel guilty now for not liking the woman."

"Fran rubbed a lot of people the wrong way, but she was dedicated to the chapter. I understand she hassled you when you first joined."

"I'll say. I joined last November and the first words out of her mouth weren't 'Welcome, nice to see you;' they were 'For which conference committee would you like to volunteer.' When I told her I wasn't ready for that yet, she got rather contentious saying I should show support for the chapter, it was a great way to meet the members, et cetera. Made me feel like a shirker. I may have actually volunteered to help at the sign-in desk if she hadn't been so annoying. Pissed me off."

"I can understand that. I'm sorry she was so insistent. People should volunteer because they want to, not out of a feeling of obligation." Anne paused. "You say you sat at the back of the room?"

"Yes, at the same table as Barb Hamilton. Now there was one pissed off woman!"

"I know. Did you happen to see someone dressed up as a ghost?"

"Sure did. Strange outfit. Looked like she'd tossed a king-sized sheet over her head. I'm surprised she didn't trip on it. I mean the thing was huge."

"Any idea who it was?"

"Not a clue. She never spoke and was up and down a lot. I couldn't help but see every time she left the room."

"Was that often?"

"Often enough. I thought maybe she had bladder problems."

Anne laughed lightly. "Was she there when Fran died?"

Janine was silent for a moment. "No, I don't think so. In fact, she hadn't been around since the salad was served, and I'm not too sure about that either. Why?"

"Oh, no reason. Just curious. Nobody seems to be able to identify her."

"Well I didn't see her face, but at some point I went to her table to talk to Valerie Harding. She was sitting next to her. Maybe Val can tell you more."

"I'll give her a call. Thanks, Janine. I hope you're enjoying the chapter. We really are a nice bunch of people. Have a good one and I'll talk to you later."

She hung up and drummed her fingers on the table top. After consulting the roster, she called Valerie Harding.

"Hello, Valerie. It's Anne Jamieson."

"Hi, Anne. How's it going?"

"It's going. I wanted to ask you about the person dressed as a ghost seated at your table on Saturday. Can you tell me anything about her?"

The woman drew in a sharp breath. "Are you investigating? Oh my God, was Fran murdered?"

Valerie, a longtime member, had been around for years and knew of the Snoop Group's activities investigating other murders. The last thing Anne needed was that information getting out prematurely. Gil would be furious. And Valerie was a notorious busybody who loved gossip. She needed to think on her feet here.

"Good heavens, no. We had a couple of people who didn't pay. We tracked down one of them, but no one knows who the ghost was. She may owe us money. I understand you sat next to her. Notice anything unusual?"

"Only that her costume was ridiculous. She left just prior to the meal being served. At least I was able to nibble something before Fran fell out. Did Fran die of a food allergy?"

"I don't know. I suppose we'll find out eventually. What a way to begin a presidency." They talked for a few more minutes before Anne cut it off. "Well, it's been nice chatting with you, but I have other calls to make. Someone must know who the ghost was. I'll talk to you later."

Anne terminated the call as quickly as possible and crossed her fingers Valerie wouldn't expand on her assumptions that Fran's death was murder.

Remembering her promise to fully report to Gil, she made notes from the people she'd called. A pattern had formed. So far, the consensus was that Fran was pushy concerning the chapter, self-serving considering her role in it, embittered about the election, and not greatly missed by many.

Anne sighed. *Not the best endorsement in the world.* Then a thought occurred to her. *Oh Lord, please don't tell me that as President of the chapter, I'm expected to give a eulogy at her funeral.*

The mere idea sent her into a semi-panic.

"How the hell do I eulogize a woman I didn't like?" she said out loud.

Don't borrow trouble. Maybe the subject won't come up. And if it does, then there must be someone else in the chapter who'd do a more sincere job of it than me.

Shelving that potential problem, Anne called Barb Hamilton. She wanted more information on her issues with Fran.

"Hello, Barb? It's Anne. Have you got a minute?"

"Sure, what do you need?"

"What happened between you and Fran—about the election, I mean? I didn't know anything about it until I got to the meeting."

"Julie Bishop, Carnie Watts, and I were the nominating committee. Fran seemed to be fine with that until your and Rose's names appeared on the ballot. Suddenly, she suggested that the voting be by a show of hands at the September meeting."

"Not exactly a secret ballot," Anne commented.

"Julie pointed that out. I guess Fran's theory was that some of the people who were undecided on who to vote for wouldn't want to raise their hands as being against her or something. When that was vetoed, she demanded that all ballots be cast at the meeting and that

Susan Lynch be the one to actually count them."

"So much for impartial."

"We all three said no to that idea, too. It's no secret Susan is Fran's toady. At any rate, Julie, Carnie, and I decided on our own that ballots would be sent out electronically and could be returned the same way, and that paper ballots be available at the meeting. Fran was not happy, but really couldn't do anything about it."

"So how did you prevent people from voting twice?"

"Once a member clicked on, filled out, and sent an electronic ballot, they were blocked from doing so again. The program sent me a list of who had cast a vote. Then at the meeting I checked that list against anyone who asked for a ballot. If their name was already on the list, I didn't give them one. Those who used a paper ballot checked who they wanted to vote for at the far end of the table and dropped it into a box."

"Sounds like you had it covered."

"I had it covered as best as I could. The only person who tried to vote twice and complained when I refused to let her cast a paper ballot was Susan Lynch."

"Why is it that doesn't surprise me?" Anne said with a sigh.

"She claimed she hadn't voted electronically and was on the list by mistake. I know she wasn't. To be honest, I think this is where the whole 'you cheated' crap began. Not with Fran, but with Susan."

Knowing Susan, that didn't surprise her either. "Well, I doubt anybody took Fran's accusations seriously."

"Is there any way the membership or the board can toss another member out of the chapter? Because Susan

Lynch is becoming a real problem. Her postings on the loop are personal attacks against you. Someone should do something."

"I talked to Georgia Yancey. She sent Susan a warning. Hopefully that'll be the end of it."

"She needs to send her another one," Barb stated. "She's been on again just a while ago."

Anne groaned. "Oh crap. I'd better go see what she's up to now. Thanks, Barb. I'll talk to you later."

Upon hanging up, Anne checked the loop and groaned again. *Susan, Susan, what the hell is wrong with you?*

The message, while not naming her personally, was clearly aimed at Anne.

I don't understand how you people can condone rigged elections, harassment by board members, and turn against me. If you think I'm going to be quiet, you're sadly mistaken. I plan to run for the presidency of this chapter next year and I can guarantee I'll be a damned sight better than what we have now.

Shaking her head, Anne marveled at the woman's thick-headedness. Did she think this kind of rhetoric would win her any votes? The change in Susan since they'd first met was astonishing. A year ago, her former critique partner had not been nearly as vocal as she was now. The conference had changed much of that. Her confrontation with Carmella Radcliff had opened Anne's eyes to Susan's real personality, allowing her and the rest of the critique group to see how manipulative and passive-aggressive she could be. Cutting comments that brought a reaction were met with feigned surprise and the insistence that no offence was intentional.

Plus the woman craved sympathy and pity as was evidenced by her total inability to take criticism of her work—usually in the form of tears. The group had no choice but to ask her to leave. Her negativism brought them all down.

That's when she decided to pal around with Fran. I'm sure much of what is coming from her now, is based on Fran's influence.

Anne scrolled farther down her e-mails and found one from Georgia Yancey.

Anne, just wanted to let you know that I am suspending Susan Lynch from the loop for a month. She replied to my warning earlier with such venom that she left me with no choice. I e-mailed her that the suspension would be lifted immediately if she publicly apologized. If I were you, I'd take care around this woman. I think she's dangerous.

Anne wasn't sure if Susan was dangerous, but she sure was nasty. The passive from passive-aggressive was no longer a factor. At least she'd have a month without having to fear opening the chapter news.

She paused as her phone rang. Called ID identified Gil.

"Hello, Gil. How's your day going?"

"Better now that I'm talking to you."

Anne chuckled. "Same here."

"Can you, Nancy, and Rose come into the station say around nine tomorrow morning to view those tapes?"

"I suppose. I'll call them and get right back to you."

She hung up and placed the calls. Nancy quickly confirmed the time. Rose wasn't sure, but called back a few minutes later with news she had a babysitter until noon, no later.

"Gil, we can all make it," she informed him when she called back.

"Good. It'll mostly be identification of people coming and going on the second floor where you held the meeting."

"Did you ever get a hold of the busboy and the missing waiter?"

"The busboy, Miguel, swears he never served anyone. Film seems to back that up."

"What was he wearing?"

"Black pants and shoes—not unlike the wait staff—but had a gray T-shirt under a black bib apron."

"Darn, I was hoping he was the man Jane says served her and Fran."

"He did mention that he saw a man in dark clothes near the freight elevator as he exited with a cart of food about the time Ms. Harrison died, but couldn't give a description. Said he was walking at a fast clip toward the stairwell at the end of the hallway."

"Well, that's frustrating. So who killed her? The ghost or the man in dark clothing—if it was a man."

"I don't know yet."

"What about the waiter?" she asked.

"Wainwright? Friday night was the last anyone at the hotel saw him. He doesn't answer his door or his phone. A neighbor says she saw him talking with a man in the parking lot when she came home around nine-thirty Saturday night. His car is missing from his parking slot. We're checking phone records."

"So everything's more or less a bust as of now?"

"With Wainwright, yes. We knocked on his door

on Sunday morning and again Monday evening. The neighbor said she'd call if she saw him. Just a minute…What is it, Strock?" A voice she couldn't hear distinctly spoke. "Okay, I'll be right there. Honey, I've got to go. Another case is breaking. I'll see you tomorrow at nine."

Anne hung up and sighed. It sounded like another night without Gil. She glanced at her watch. Not even noon yet.

I'm tired of calling people and tired of my work in progress. Maybe I should visit Candace and tell her what's happened.

The more she thought about it, the better it sounded.

It took almost no time to dash on some lipstick and a splash of cologne before heading for the kitchen and her car keys hanging on a board by the garage door. Bruno stood nearby, his ears up and his tail wagging. He loved car rides, but even though Candace would love to see the little shih-tzu, Anne didn't want to confuse things by letting *him* see his real owner. He'd taken months to accustom himself to a new home almost a year and a half ago.

"Sorry, baby, not this trip," she crooned stooping to scratch him behind the ears. "Next time, I promise."

Traffic was light and she made good time to the prison. These trips were always awkward, but Anne knew Candace enjoyed hearing about friends and the chapter. So, it was the least she could do for the poor woman.

On the drive home, Anne wondered what Candace would do when released. Continue her life in San Sebastian? Start over somewhere else? In spite of having killed Isadora Powell and trying to kill her, Anne had always liked Candace and hoped she could turn her life around.

As she pulled into her driveway, Anne looked forward to tomorrow morning. She'd not only see Gil, but also those tapes.

And who knows, I might see a killer.

Chapter Seven

Anne decided police stations came close to being the most depressing places on the face of the earth. The colors were drab, the lighting inadequate, and the people downright scary—not the cops, but the visitors. Some gazed around the room as if expecting to be shot, while others stared at the floor perhaps in the assumption doing so would make them invisible.

She shifted on the hard plastic chair in the waiting area. Rose and Nancy hadn't arrived yet. Not even Gil had made an appearance to escort her back to his office or the surveillance viewing room.

The main doors opened and Nancy walked in.

"Oh, thank goodness," Anne said with a sigh. "I thought maybe you'd forgotten."

Nancy checked her watch. "You said nine o'clock. It's only eight-fifty-five," her friend replied as she took a seat.

"I know, but I really hate police stations. And I've been in this one way too many times."

"Quit finding bodies and you might not." Nancy smiled to soften the words.

"Technically, I didn't find Fran's body. Everybody at the meeting did."

"From what you said, this looks like murder, too. I know Fran was an irritating pain in the ass, but who'd she piss off so badly that they'd want to kill her?"

Anne shook her head. "Becky Lawrence comes to mind, but she wasn't there—at least not that we know of. I wonder how many other members' husbands Fran tried to seduce."

"Trying isn't necessarily a killing offense. Succeeding maybe. We should be looking in that direction. Does Gil know about our former president's affair?"

"I mentioned the rumor to him and he said he'd check it out."

"Check out what?" Gil said walking up to them.

"Becky Lawrence and whether or not her husband had rekindled his affair with Fran," Anne replied.

"I left a message a while ago. Haven't heard back from her yet. You guys ready to view some tape?"

"As soon as Rose gets here," Nancy said.

At that moment the doors opened again and Rose breezed into the station.

"Am I late?" she asked.

"Nope. Right on time," Gil said with a smile. "Let's get started. There are a lot of tapes."

Gil led them back to a cramped room with several video machines along the walls. VCRs might not be used in homes any more, but they still had a place in police work.

Wonder how long before law enforcement goes digital. Or if digital recording will ever replace tapes. And will shopkeepers, hotels and such will be able to afford to change the systems if they do.

Anne and the others took seats around a monitor. Gil brought them all cups of coffee.

"Before we start, could you give me a quick rundown on the meeting schedule?" he asked.

"Sure," Anne said taking a cautious sip from the Styrofoam container. For machine coffee it wasn't bad. "The meeting begins at ten-thirty in the morning with an informal meet-and-greet session. Those who haven't pre-paid can do so when they arrive."

"Does that happen often?" he asked.

"Not really. Most members send their money in with their reservations via an electronic payment system."

"And who collects the money if they don't use that?"

Rose replied as Anne sipped more coffee. "The treasurer. In this case, that would have been Jane Whittaker. She usually just sits at a table in the room and collects what's due as she checks off names on a list. Past treasurers have set up sign-in tables in the hallway."

Nancy took over the narrative. "Just prior to eleven, the president generally makes a brief welcoming announcement, and then lunch is served."

"After that the president calls the meeting to order. We go over old business followed by new business," Anne said. "As soon as that's done, the speaker for the day is introduced and makes his or her presentation."

"Any time frame on this part of the program?" Gil asked.

Anne shook her head. "Not really. Sometimes the business portions of the meeting take a while, but we try to keep it to less than an hour. Presentations are generally anywhere from forty-five minutes to an hour. The meeting is adjourned around two."

Gil nodded and shoved a cassette into the machine. "This is the main lobby. The tape begins a new twenty-four loop at six in the morning. I've fast forwarded it to ten-fifteen Saturday morning."

He pushed a button and the tape rolled showing people coming and going, including chapter members with some in costume. Anne stifled a yawn. It was boring.

Fran appeared in the film at ten-thirty.

"There's nothing out of the ordinary," Nancy told him. "I arrived at ten-fifteen and went directly upstairs."

"As you can see, I came in at ten-forty," Anne said.

"And I was right behind her at ten-forty-three," Rose chimed in. "Who are all those guys in tuxedos?"

"Some opera lovers' meeting. I guess they all come dressed as Enrico Caruso or something—even the women," Anne replied, shooting a glance at Gil.

He nodded. "They meet once a month, usually on the main floor."

Gil switched the tapes. "This one is the hallway outside your meeting room also beginning at ten-fifteen."

Anne watched the tape, not expecting to see much of anything. Fran, Susan, and Jane arrived within a few minutes of each other. She kept her eyes open for the ghost who put in her first appearance at ten-fifty passing Anne and Rose in the hallway. They watched as the minutes passed. This tape clearly showed the activity between Anne, Fran, Susan, and Barb. It also showed the ghost lifting lids of various meals several times.

"It's almost as if she's peeking to see if it's salad or an entrée," Anne commented.

"Wait for it," Gil responded.

Sure enough, the ghost lifted a lid, moved to and looked around the corner toward the freight elevator, then made her way back to the service cart. She placed two plates off to the side, and moved her hand over one of them before replacing the lid. Next, she once again cast a gaze around the deserted hallway, and then moved quickly down the corridor where she entered the room via the entry closest toward the front. A moment later she slid out by the rear entrance and around the corner never to be seen again. Within a few seconds, a waiter came into view, scooped up the meals set aside, and entered the meeting room. He came out less than a minute later and also disappeared around the corner. The time showed eleven-thirty.

"Oh my God," Rose said with a gasp. "It's a team!"

"A man and a woman?" Nancy speculated.

"Not necessarily," Gil replied. "A stocky woman could have served."

"I wish the tape quality was better," Anne said. "It must be a man. The image shows someone fairly tall."

"Becky is about five-seven," Nancy said.

Anne sighed. "That ghost getup was perfect—no way to discern height or weight. I don't recall any of the waitresses that day resembling the server on tape. Plus, Jane Whittaker definitely claims she was served by a man."

"Or by a woman with really rough dishpan hands," Rose added. "I'm not sure I'd trust Jane all that much. She's not the most observant of people."

"Gil, what does the waiter who was a no-show look like?" Anne asked.

"Six feet, around a hundred and sixty pounds, dark

hair, and still not returning my calls."

"So this could have been him. He sneaks in, serves only two dishes, making sure Fran gets the tainted one, and then leaves again," Nancy surmised.

"And the hall is empty because the real servers are in the room," Rose said. "And because they're busy they don't notice an extra server."

"From the ghost doing his or her thing to the serving, took less than two minutes," Gil replied. "In and out."

"Did they use the freight elevator?" Anne asked.

"Nope, there's a stairwell next to it, and I'll give you one guess where it comes out," he answered.

"That little hallway with the out of the way restrooms," Anne guessed.

"This is from the angle near the remote hallway restroom." Gil once again changed the tapes. The view was from a longer distance since the camera was set up at the junction of the hallways.

This was the tape Anne was waiting to see. At ten-forty-five a person wearing shorts, an oversized T-shirt, a baseball cap pulled low so the bill obscured the face, and carrying a large tote bag walked through the parking lot door and directly into the restroom. A few minutes later the ghost emerged and opened the stairwell door.

"So the ghost is a woman," Rose concluded.

"Not necessarily," Gil said. "Remember what I said about how it could have been a man who knew about the cameras and wanted to throw us off by using the ladies' room."

He fast forwarded the tape to eleven-oh-five. A man—or what looked like a man—dressed in the waiter uniform came in the door from the parking lot. He also took the stairs.

The ghost exited the stairwell at eleven-seventeen and entered the restroom. At eleven-twenty-five, the person with the oversized T-shirt hurried out and into the parking lot. The waiter did the same a few minutes later.

"Wow," Nancy said.

"The point is do you recognize either of them?" Gil asked her.

"Not a chance in hell," she replied.

"Can't even come close," Anne answered.

"Nope," was Rose's comeback.

"You know, something looked odd about Fran in the lobby tape," Anne said. "Can I see it again?"

Gil ejected the last tape and reinserted the first one, and then rewound it to ten twenty-five.

Anne frowned. "Look, Fran's not coming from the entrance, but from another direction. Where was she?"

He rewound the tape several times until she finally showed up at eight o'clock, walking across the lobby and out of frame.

"Eight o'clock? Why so early for ten-thirty meeting?" Nancy wanted to know.

Rose shook her head. "And where was she all that time?"

"What's in that direction?" Gil asked.

"The dining room," Rose told him.

"She was either having breakfast—although why when lunch would be served in three hours—or she went in to do some writing. I've done that before," Anne informed them.

Nancy had continued to watch the screen. "Oh my

God, look. It's Terry Whiting."

The last conference chair entered the lobby and headed for the dining room, too.

Rose sat back in her chair. "You don't suppose they had breakfast together, do you?"

Nancy gave her an astonished look. "For what purpose? They hated each other."

"They did?" Gil said in a quiet tone.

"There were a lot of public accusations and finger pointing regarding the conference last spring. I heard they had to be separated from an out and out cat-fight at a board meeting not long after. I don't think Terry was anywhere close to burying the hatchet," Anne told him.

"Unless it was in Fran's head," Nancy murmured. "Oops, wait a minute, I didn't mean that literally."

"Thought she looked familiar. I remember her from the conference. Sounds like I need to add Ms. Whiting to my list of people to talk to," he said.

"Why don't you let me do it?" Anne suggested. "She was at the hotel, but certainly not at the meeting."

"That you know of," he reminded her.

"True, but if Terry was going to kill Fran, she'd have done it last spring after the conference. Like Nancy said, they had words."

"What kind of words?"

"Fran blamed Terry and another woman for everything. Just let me talk to her."

"She's a possible suspect," he said.

"So, we'll both talk to her."

Gil sent her a long stare, and then heaved a sigh. "All right, but I'll also be interviewing her here."

Rose looked at the clock on the wall. "Damn, it's almost eleven-thirty. I have to get home. Are we done?"

Gil popped the tape out of the machine and put it in a plastic evidence bag along with the others.

"Yes, we're finished. Thank you for your help."

"Somehow, I don't think we helped much," Nancy said rising from her chair.

"Well, you did come up with Ms. Whiting's name," he replied. "Thank you all for coming. Can you find your way out?"

"Sure, we've been here often enough to do it blindfolded," Nancy drawled.

Rose and Nancy walked ahead while Anne lingered. "I'll call Terry as soon as I get home."

"Be discreet. And I thought you'd like to know that we contacted a Doctor Mary Smith in Highcrest. She says she's never heard of the Southeast Florida chapter and can barely write her own name, let alone a book. I looked her up in the AMA membership. There was a photo. She's African-American."

"The woman at the meeting was Caucasian."

Gil leaned down and kissed her. "I was afraid of that. Let me know what Ms. Whiting has to say. Unfortunately, any cameras covering the dining room will have rerecorded. I'll tackle it from another angle."

"What angle?"

He kissed her again and smiled. "Have a good day. I'll call you later."

Anne stood for a moment after he left. The tapes had been enlightening, but she couldn't shake the feeling she'd missed something. It nagged at her, yet no clear answer presented itself. And it was frustrating that the ghost couldn't be identified.

She rejoined Nancy in the waiting area. "Rose gone already?"

"Yeah, she said she wanted to put the sitter out of her misery."

Anne told her about the doctor.

"Maybe the woman wasn't a doctor at all," Nancy said.

"But why say you are when I talked to her earlier, and then try to help when Fran was obviously in crisis?"

"I have no idea. It does, however, explain why she never showed up at the hospital."

"Good heavens, you don't suppose that whoever killed Fran paid off this person to pretend to give CPR and delay any professional medical personnel from doing the real thing, do you? I mean, Fran could have been saved if 9-1-1 had been called even a couple of minutes sooner."

Nancy frowned. "It's certainly something to think about."

"Lunch?" Anne asked.

"Can't today. I've still got to call the women who sat at Fran's table. Maybe tomorrow."

"Eleven-thirty at Rafferty's?"

After confirming the time, both women walked to their cars and left.

On the drive home, Anne formulated what she'd say to Terry. She really hoped her friend had a good explanation for why she had breakfast with Fran—if indeed, she did—but declined to attend the meeting. *I don't think I can stand another friend being a killer.*

****

Anne hesitated, her finger poised over her cell phone as she rehearsed what to say to Terry. There was no way she could let Terry know she'd been seen on surveillance footage or that Gil may want to talk to her.

Kinda like walking on eggs and broken glass at the same time.

Taking a deep breath, she punched in Terry's number and waited through four rings. A part of her hoped Terry wouldn't answer.

"Hello?"

"Terry, it's Anne. Have you got a couple of minutes?"

"Sure. Whatcha need?"

"Well, I was thinking about how the chapter needs a way to generate revenue. Since we no longer have a conference, I got an idea I wanted to run by you."

"Okay, shoot, although I don't think the conference was ever a big money raiser."

"How about if we offer a one-day seminar? We could hold it on a Saturday instead of a meeting. We'd get a good speaker or maybe two. The subject matter could range for something to entice newbies and something for the experienced writers. How does that sound to you?"

"Interesting. We could hold it at the hotel. That way anyone from out of town can stay overnight. We'd also have to deal with a lunch of some sort."

"Of course, but it doesn't need to be fancy. We could offer a morning workshop, break for lunch, and then do one in the afternoon," Anne said liking the idea thought up on the spur of the moment.

"Good concept."

"Would you be willing to organize something along those lines?"

"I suppose I could, although considering what happened the last time I organized something I'd have to ask myself why. And the speakers don't necessarily have to come from out of town. We could make use of our own chapter talent."

"Excellent idea." Anne drew a deep breath. *Here it comes.* "I was going to talk to you about it last Saturday, but you were having breakfast with Fran and I didn't want to interrupt."

Silence greeted her statement before Terry replied in a breathless tone. "What do you mean?"

"Oh, I got to the hotel early and went into the dining room to grab a cup of coffee and a bite to eat. I was in a quiet corner where I could collect my thoughts and organize what I wanted to say. First day jitters, I guess. At any rate, I saw Fran come in and sit at a table, then you joined her. I thought maybe you guys were letting bygones be bygones and didn't want to disturb you."

"Oh, yeah, that. Fran called with just that suggestion. She said something about water under the bridge. I couldn't make the meeting, so we agreed to meet for breakfast."

"So, did you patch up your differences?" Anne asked.

"More or less. Funny we didn't see you there. Our table was close to the dining room entrance." Terry's voice took on a harder tone.

"As I said, I didn't want to interrupt. Plus I was making a list of the meeting agenda. When I looked up again, Fran was alone."

"I had to be somewhere, so I ate light. Uh, look, Anne, I've got an appointment. Let me think this over and get back to you. It sounds like a good idea and won't take as much time or trouble as a conference.

Talk to you later." Terry hung up abruptly.

"Interesting," Anne murmured. "The point is do I believe her explanation of the breakfast? And I doubt she had an appointment."

Fran Harrison held a grudge against anyone who crossed swords with her. And Terry Whiting had definitely crossed swords.

Nope, Terry is hiding something. Whatever it is, she and Fran were not having a talk about reconciliation.

She called Gil, but got his voice mail. She'd try again after lunch. As she ate a sandwich, Anne jotted down notes about the idea she'd pitched to Terry. As an excuse to talk, it had turned out not to be a bad suggestion. She liked the concept.

She did some fast math and speculation. *If we keep the hotel costs down, this could provide another couple of thousand dollars—or more—for the treasury. Holy crap, this is doable.*

It was close to three when she finally called Gil again and brought him up to date on her conversation with Terry.

"What makes you think she's hiding something?" he asked.

"Fran held grudges and loved getting even with people she thought wronged her in some way. She once got on a review site and wrote twenty bad reviews under twenty different identities for a book whose author disagreed with her on some comment left on a blog. So, there is no way she called Terry to put aside their differences."

"Then why were they meeting?"

"I have no clue, but it had to have been at Terry's

request—and like Nancy said, the only place Terry would bury the hatchet was in Fran's head. I don't think she's going to come clean with me or anybody else."

"She might." His tone sounded cryptic.

"How so?"

"After you left the station I went to the hotel and had a chat with the hostess in the dining room. I showed her the stills from the surveillance tape. She IDed both Fran Harrison and Terry Whiting. I also had a chat with the waitress who served them. She said Ms. Whiting ordered coffee only. She *also* said she heard enough to know the conversation wasn't pleasant. They argued in low tones until Ms. Whiting stood and told Ms. Harrison to—and I quote, 'Go fuck yourself and knock it off!' Ms. Harrison laughed as Ms. Whiting left, and then ordered a light breakfast."

"Wow! I take it you're going to interview Terry."

"I called her about fifteen minutes ago and asked that she come in to give a statement at four o'clock. She sounded scared."

"I would be, too. Uh, I lied to her about how I knew she and Fran had breakfast."

"I'll use the surveillance video as my reasoning and what the hostess and waitress said. You're covered."

Anne breathed a sigh of relief. "Dinner here tonight?"

"Can't tonight, sweetheart. I've got more than just Ms. Harrison's case on my desk. I'll be in touch tomorrow."

"Okay. Oh! Did you hear back from the missing waiter yet? What's his name?"

"Jeffery Wainwright and no he hasn't called me

back. His place is locked and his car is still gone. He may have taken off."

"Where does he live? Is there any surveillance?"

"He lives at the Escondito Apartments off San Sebastian Drive. It's a marginal part of town. I asked for tape, but most of the surveillance cameras don't work. However, I do have his license plate and make and model of his car, so I figure to find him soon. Hon, I gotta go, my other line is ringing. Talk to you tomorrow."

Anne hung up and sat back to think. Jeff Wainwright hadn't been seen at work since Friday. Well, not officially at work. He may have been there long enough to serve Jane and Fran. And didn't Gil say something about him being seen by a neighbor Sunday night? Or was it Saturday?

Certainly looks like he ran. But why would a waiter want to kill Fran? And the ghost definitely appeared to tamper with the plate, and then set it aside. Why would he conspire with the ghost? It made no sense.

Anne knew she was missing something, but her mind was on clue overload. Before she could take a moment to get it together, her phone rang. It was Nancy.

"Hey, Nance, what's up?"

"I finally got a hold of the other women seated at Fran's table."

"Anything of interest?"

"I'm not sure. Let me start with Carolanne Rogers. She was definitely irritated with both Fran and Susan. So much so that she nearly called them out on it. The only thing that stopped her was no desire to start another argument. Same goes for Cheryl Johnson. She almost left the table like Ellie. They didn't notice anything unusual with servers or people coming and going. Not much there."

"What about the other two?" Anne asked.

"This is a little puzzling. Olivia said she was talking to Jane when the waiter slipped between them to serve. She seems to think Fran was not at the table but can't be sure."

"That coincides with what Jane said about Fran coming back and eating her salad before beginning on the entrée."

Nancy sighed over the phone and continued. "At any rate, Olivia also remembers talking to Jane when the ghost walked past the table. She doesn't think Fran was there then either."

"Hmmm. I wonder if she has any idea of the time. Fran left the table several times," Anne speculated.

"But this is what's odd. Olivia says the ghost paused by Fran's chair as if she'd dropped something, stooped down, and moved on. That was the last Olivia recalls seeing her. Lynda McIlroy was at the table, too. She confirms the part about the ghost. She was talking to Cheryl and saw the ghost bend down, and then keep going."

"Fran last left the table when I hauled her, Susan, and Barb out into the hall. I'll bet that's when the ghost paused by Fran's chair. Fran was the last one to return."

"Very possible. The food has already been doctored and set aside. The ghost leaves and the waiter arrives before Fran returns. Oh, and I found out Fran's critique group consists of Carla Jeffers, Elaine Graham, and Beth Whisnant. Do we call them, too?" Nancy asked.

"Later. Let's try this on for size. The ghost returns from doctoring the food, maybe sees Fran's purse on the floor next to her chair, pretends to drop something, grabs the purse and leaves, which tells me she knew about the injection pen. No one notices."

"And hangs it in a restroom stall to be found much later," Nancy pointed out.

"Time frame might need some work, but I'll bet that's what happened. I talked to Gil a while ago." She told Nancy about the waiter still being unavailable. "I was wondering if we could help in any way. I mean, he might not have wanted to talk to the cops, but be more receptive to us. I know where he lives."

"You thinking what I'm thinking?"

"Road trip. He might be there, but not answering the door. If nothing else, we can always knock on neighbors' doors pretending to look for him, and then ask questions."

"When do you want to go?"

"Now? It's not quite four. It can't hurt to try."

"All right, I'll come pick you up in fifteen minutes."

Anne hung up and wrote a note to Ken and Lisa saying she was with Nancy and would be home soon.

"So where are we heading?" Nancy asked as they left Anne's.

"The Escondito Apartments on San Sebastian Drive. I don't know the apartment number, but we can look at the mailboxes."

Ten minutes later, they pulled into the parking lot. The complex consisted of three buildings none of which were in good shape. Peeling paint and broken gutters told the tale. A small communal balcony ran the length of the buildings making it look like a cheap motel. It wasn't quite a slum, but was well on its way.

Nancy parked near the first building. A row of mailboxes stood out front like dilapidated sentinels. No Jeffery Wainwright was listed. They moved on to the second building and found his name. His apartment number was two-fifteen. They climbed the concrete steps avoiding touching the rusting handrails. The apartments on either side of Wainwright's had "For Rent" signs stuck in the window. They'd seen several of those on the first building.

Anne paused in front of the door, looked at Nancy, and then knocked. No one answered. She repeated her actions two more times with the same results.

"Jeffrey, Jeffrey Wainwright are you in there?" she called out.

A woman came out of an apartment farther down the balcony.

"You looking for Jeff?"

"Yes, have you seen him?" Anne asked.

"Not recently. Saw him on Saturday night. Car was gone on Sunday morning."

"Uh, thanks, maybe I'll just leave a note."

"Are you really going to leave a note?" Nancy said as the woman walked away and down the stairs.

"No way, but it's obvious he's taken off."

Nancy wiggled the loose doorknob. "Doesn't look too secure. Maybe if we worked it enough, it would open."

"Gil would kill us."

"Yeah, but we could always say it was unlocked or not latched properly. I wonder what the legalities are with private citizens doing something like this."

"Probably the same as a burglar. It's called breaking and entering. I seem to recall we got into a lot of trouble doing the same thing at Dorie's."

"I suppose you're right." She frowned and felt the door. "That's funny, the door is cold."

Nancy manipulated the doorknob again and leaned against the cracked wood. The lock sprang and opened a few inches. Cold air rushed out.

"On my God, what is that smell?" Anne clasped a hand over her nose.

"Something dead," Nancy replied choking. "I think we may have found Jeffrey Wainwright."

Chapter Eight

Nancy called 9-1-1 while Anne ran down the steps to barf into the nearby bushes. It didn't take long for six police cars, two fire rescue trucks, and an ambulance, all with lights flashing, to crowd the parking lot. Curious neighbors stood in groups talking amongst themselves. Crime scene tape cordoned off the area around Wainwright's apartment. Anne and Nancy gave their names and addresses along with a preliminary statement to one of the policemen first on the scene, and now stood off to the side at the bottom of the stairs.

"This is four, isn't it?" Nancy asked.

Anne still fought her rebellious stomach. The flashing lights from the vehicles didn't help the situation any. "What?"

"Bodies. This is the fourth body you've found in a little over a year. Five if you count Fran."

"I don't keep stats like that," Anne said with a groan. "And I didn't find Fran. She kind of found all of us."

Her attention was diverted from talk of bodies when Gil drove up. He exited his car and walked over to them. The look on his face told her they were in trouble.

"What the hell are you doing here?" he demanded.

Anne sighed. "Well, we thought…"

He cut her off. "Never mind. Save it for the police

station. I assume you've already spoken with an officer."

Anne nodded. "Just the basics."

"I'll need statements from both of you. Stay here until I get back."

He walked away with a strong, angry stride.

"I don't think he's too happy with us," Nancy said.

"Offhand, I'd say he's downright furious," she replied.

Gil spent the next twenty minutes upstairs behind the tape with the rest of the law enforcement people before rejoining them. He stared at the women for several long seconds.

Unnerved by his scrutiny, Anne shifted from foot to foot before breaking the silence. She spoke in a hurried voice.

"I Googled the Escondito Apartments. We came because we thought we could help by asking him questions. Just because he didn't answer his door, doesn't mean he wasn't here. The neighbor told us she hadn't seen him or his car in several days. We kind of jiggled the doorknob. I guess it wasn't latched properly, so it opened. Then we smelled him." She paused to take a breath. "It is Jeffrey Wainwright, isn't it?"

"It is. His driver's license was in his wallet." He continued to glower at them.

"Don't give me that stare," Anne said. "We found him for you."

"Anne, this isn't the time to get confrontational," Nancy whispered in her ear.

He glared at her. "Don't push it, honey."

Nancy cleared her throat. "How was he killed?"

Gil's eyes shifted to Nancy. "Don't know yet.

Found a bag of what looks to be coke in the kitchen along with a powdery residue on the counter. Could be an overdose."

"How long has he been dead?" Anne asked.

"Long enough to stink. I'd say at least three days, but it's hard to be accurate without an autopsy," he replied. "The air conditioning was turned down as far as it would go. That would help retard decomposition. Now, I want both of you at the station immediately. Give your statements, and then go home. I'm going to be here for a while."

"I doubt I'll be having an early night. Drop by if you can or give me a call…please," Anne begged.

His expression softened. He leaned down to kiss her lips lightly. "All right. Now, get going."

Neither of the women hesitated, but turned and walked quickly to Nancy's car parked several yards away. They both sat for a moment staring at the scene in front of them. Dusk was falling and the shadows gave the place an eerie look.

Anne heaved a sigh. "Okay, according to the neighbor, she last saw Wainwright on Saturday night. Maybe someone came by with a bag of cocaine."

"But why turn down the air conditioning?"

"The visitor could have been his supplier. Maybe Wainwright owed money and the guy killed him. Or maybe, it was a friend with a new score and came by to share. They snort up. Wainwright ODs, and the other man wants to be long gone, so he turns down the thermostat and boogies."

"In that case, where's Wainwright's car?"

"Maybe the visitor took it."

Nancy shook her head. "Why?"

"Perhaps he intended to make a night of it and someone dropped him off," Anne suggested. "Or he came with Wainwright."

"And when his friend checked out permanently, he takes the keys and leaves."

"Sounds reasonable to me."

Someone rapped on the window causing Anne to jump. It was a scowling Gil. She lowered the window. "Don't do that! You scared me."

"Why are you still here?" he demanded.

"We were talking." She told him about her and Nancy's theory.

"Do your talking down at the station. Now go!"

"The least he could have done was say thanks," Nancy mumbled as he turned and stalked away.

****

It was after nine o'clock when Anne stumbled through her front door, exhausted. The police had taken their own sweet time taking down hers and Nancy's statements. As they were leaving the station, the neighbor they'd spoken with entered. She eyed them with a suspicious stare, then moved on to an interrogation room.

Lisa greeted her. "Good grief, what took so long? Ken and I were beginning to worry." She stood on the balcony overlooking the two story foyer.

During the drive to the station, she'd called saying she and Nancy had some writing business to discuss. Anne didn't like lying to her kids, but neither did she want to burden them with the truth. Dead bodies didn't make for good dinner conversation.

"Oh, you know writers; once we get started it's hard to stop."

Ken came down the stairs. "Mom, are you all right? You don't look so hot."

"I'm fine. Just tired. It's been a long day. So I think I'll grab a quick bite to eat, and then go to bed. What did you have for dinner? Is your homework finished?"

"Yeah," Ken replied. "We both got done a while ago."

"And we had some leftovers," Lisa added. "Are you sure you're okay?"

She waved a hand. "I'm good. But right now, I'm hungry."

Ken looked up at his sister who shrugged before moving off down the hallway toward her room. Ken climbed the stairs to follow.

Anne wasn't in the least bit hungry. *Finding a ripe, three or four-day-old body tends to destroy one's appetite.* Still, she had to eat something. Dumping her purse on the counter, she headed for the fridge. A simple toasted cheese sandwich and tomato soup sounded as good as anything.

After eating, she made her way upstairs to her bedroom, closed the door, and immediately called Rose with the news.

"Oh my God! Do you think that whoever arranged Fran's death killed the waiter, too?"

"I never thought of that angle. Yet it seems that Wainwright must have been in contact with the fake waiter at some point in time."

Holy cow, what if the cocaine was the payoff for not showing up at work? She needed to run this by Gil.

Rose was still talking. "And I had a panicked call earlier from Jane Whittaker. It seems members are asking for a refund from the meeting of death. She claims the bank account will be severely drained if she does that."

"How can that be? According to the last treasurer's report we had over twelve thousand dollars on hand. We should be able to cover the hotel and refunds."

"Unless Jane is using some creative bookkeeping," Rose said.

"Damn, just one more thing for my to-do list tomorrow."

She hung up and immediately called Jane.

"Jane, can you come to my house tomorrow around ten o'clock?"

"Can't. I'm busy most of the day."

"How about later in the afternoon? Say around four?"

"Four? I guess so. Why?"

"I need to take a look at the books."

Jane drew in an audible breath. "Why?"

"Because I'm the president and need to see what our financial situation is, especially since we'll be refunding the cost of the luncheon."

"You talked to Rose, didn't you?"

The time for diplomacy was over. "Yes."

"All right, I'll be there at four or a little after."

Anne didn't bother to say goodbye. She was too angry. *If Jane has screwed up our finances, I swear I'll demand she resign.*

Gil had not called. She contemplated calling him, and then put the phone down. Even though he'd kissed her goodbye in the parking lot, he'd been more than displeased with her and Nancy's actions. Best to let him cool down.

She tried writing on her work in progress, but

finally gave up. It was after eleven when she slipped into bed. What she wouldn't give for a normal day.

****

Gil called shortly after nine the next morning.

"Hi, Gil, how's everything?"

"Could be better. Look I'm sorry I was so angry yesterday, but dammit, Anne, you shouldn't have been anywhere near Wainwright's apartment. Suppose he had been inside—alive? What would you have done then?"

She sighed. "Questioned him, I guess."

"That's not your job! I don't mind you talking to your writer friends about things, but under no circumstances do I want you going to a suspect's house and playing detective. I don't care what you see on TV, it just isn't procedure."

"I'm sorry, Gil. Really, I am. It won't happen again."

"It better not."

Anne bit her lip. She deserved the dressing down.

"Did you find out anything about the poor man?"

"Turns out Mr. Wainwright is no stranger to the San Sebastian Police Department. A couple of DUIs, petty theft, possession of marijuana for personal use, and one bust for possession of cocaine three years ago. And one of the neighbors saw a man coming around the corner of the building around nine-thirty. Wainwright met him, they climbed the stairs, and entered Wainwright's apartment. "

"Do you think this man is connected to Fran's death?"

"I have no idea, but it's possible. Now do you see why I was so upset?"

"I do, and you were absolutely right." She told him about her latest theory of the cocaine being a payoff.

"We'll check it all out." His tone had turned testy.

"Would you like to come over for dinner tonight?" she asked in a conciliatory voice.

"How about we go out. My brother, Brad, is due in later this afternoon. I thought maybe you'd like to meet him."

"Love to. What time?"

"Six all right with you?"

"Six is fine."

She hung up in a happier mood. Gil was no longer angry with her—well, at least not as angry as earlier— and seemed eager to have her meet at least a part of his family.

Downstairs, she made a pot of coffee and contemplated her upcoming meeting with Jane. This encounter was not likely to be a pleasant one. While it brewed, Nancy called.

"Hi, Anne, how did you sleep?"

"Not bad considering. How about you?"

"The same."

Anne repeated what Gil had said about Wainwright's police record and her conclusions.

"Well, at least we found him. After I got home last night, I called Fran's critique partners. All of them said there was no trouble in the group. Fran was bossy and dictatorial, but listened to what they had to say. Elaine also told me that Susan wanted into the group, but that all of them, including Fran, put the big kibosh on that. She had the feeling Susan was sucking up in hopes they'd change their minds."

"Sounds par for Susan's course."

"Beth Whisnant didn't have time to talk much, but said she wanted to get something off her chest, so I agreed to meet her later this afternoon."

"Any idea what she meant?"

"Not a clue. I've got a dentist's appointment in a while. I'll talk to you later."

She had barely hung up when her phone rang again. This time it was Ellie Campion.

"Am I interrupting?" she asked in a hesitant tone.

"Not at the moment."

"I had a call last night from Mary Anderson, one of my critique partners. She wants out of the group. I later talked to Patty Webster and Gay Mackey. They're in Susan's group, too. All of them want out. Would it be unethical for the three of us to just start meeting without telling Susan?"

Honestly, why ask me this, Ellie? Anne sighed and tried to reply diplomatically.

"I imagine you can do anything you want. Sounds as if you all are dumping Susan." *Certainly won't be a new experience for her.*

"Yeah, I guess it is. I've had several beginning writers and a few experienced ones showing interest in critiquing. I was thinking of asking one of the experienced to join us. Susan's not going to be happy, but honestly, what does she expect after the things she posted on the loop?"

Anne half-tuned out Ellie's talk and glanced at the clock on the kitchen wall. If she got to work immediately, she could get that chapter finished. And if she did meet that goal, she *might* post something positive on the loop about next month's meeting. *And when was the last time I was on any of my social media sites? I've got some serious updating to do.*

"Is there anything new about Fran?" Ellie asked.

The question brought Anne out of her thoughts. She liked Ellie—thought she'd make a good board member—but had no intention of imparting privileged information.

"Just that it was a reaction to her peanut allergy. Ellie, you said you noticed the ghost walking around on several occasions. Did you see her stop by Fran's table?"

"Not specifically, but I do seem to recall she stooped down as if she dropped something, and then headed out the door at the back of the room. Whether or not it was by Fran's table I don't know."

"Okay, thanks. I need to get back to work. I'll talk to you later."

She hung up, poured a cup of coffee, and hurried upstairs to her office. The ghost was looking better and better as the killer. But who was it? *Could have been anybody.*

Five hours later, she staggered down the steps, mentally drained, but with a chapter finished and two scenes of another written. Not wanting to interrupt the flow, lunch had consisted of a PBJ. Now, she was starving. With a light dinner the night before, Anne wondered how much snacking she could do and still eat dinner tonight.

Settling on a bag of corn chips and some salsa, she posted a positive message on November's chapter meeting and hit her social media sites with comments on her writing adventures, which were nowhere near as adventuresome as reality.

She finished with the internet and was thinking

about what to wear for her night out with Gil and his brother when the doorbell rang.

Jane Whittaker stood on the doorstep, her arms cradling several manila folders.

"Jane, come on in."

Jane entered and thrust her cargo at Anne as she entered. "Here are all the bank statements for the past year, along with the checkbook. I think you'll find everything in order."

The treasurer had practically thrown them at her. Anne struggled to keep the folders from falling to the floor.

"Oh, thanks. Would you like a cup of coffee?"

"No thanks," she replied in a stiff tone. "I assume you want to go over them now."

"No, that's all right. I'm going out tonight. I'll take a quick look at things tomorrow, and then call you if I have any questions." Anne had the feeling she'd have a lot of questions.

Jane seemed taken aback, as if expecting to explain something and now having to wait.

"Well, if you have any questions, give me a call."

Without any further conversation, the treasurer left. *Well, that was short and sweet.*

Anne took the folders upstairs and set them on her desk. They represented another chore for tomorrow morning. She just hoped she didn't find anything too horrible.

A glance at the clock told her she needed to start dinner for the kids.

Ken and Lisa came home from their after school meetings and sniffed the aroma of garlic and onions.

"I've been thinking about spaghetti and meat sauce

all day," Lisa said with a grin.

"I could wade into a couple of plates," her son added.

"You'll be doing it alone. I'm going out with Gil and his brother."

"Ah, finally meeting the family, huh?" Lisa commented. "Dress nice and make the most of it."

"I intend to, and now, if you will make the salad, I can go shower and change by six."

Dressing in a pair of navy blue slacks and a pale yellow silk blouse, Anne was just coming down the stairs when the doorbell rang. Gil was early. She took a deep, only slightly nervous, breath and opened the door.

It wasn't Gil, but Nancy. She rushed in, and then stopped to take in Anne's garb.

"Are you going somewhere?"

"Dinner with Gil and his brother. What's up?" she asked leading Nancy into the living room. "Have a seat."

Nancy sat on the sofa while Anne chose a chair.

"I just had a cup of coffee and a long talk with Beth Whisnant. She told me things had been going fine with the critique group, but that Fran was acting very strange since the conference last March."

"Strange how?"

"Well, for starters, she wasn't her usual self when offering critiques. I guess normally Fran would get nit-picky about details."

"Happens to us all the time," Anne said.

"Agreed, but here's what's odd. Beth claims that Fran hadn't submitted anything for critique the last couple of months. Beth put it down to the election. I guess their last meeting was nothing more than Fran blasting you and demanding the rest of the group vote against any proposals you might make."

"That doesn't surprise me. She was damned upset. Anything else?"

"Last May she asked Beth for a loan—a personal loan—of three grand."

Astonishment jabbed her in the chest. "Three thousand dollars! What for?"

"Beth said Fran explained it as having overspent her credit cards and didn't want her husband to know."

"Did she pay it back?"

"Yes, in August. Beth had no idea if she approached anyone else in the group. Personally, if I was having financial problems, my critique partners would be the last people I'd beg."

"Same here. Of course, that group has been together a long time."

"Oh, and Beth said that Susan called her yesterday saying that since Fran was dead, she'd be happy to take her place in the group. Beth told her it was too soon to think about that."

"Apparently not to Susan."

"At any rate, the more Beth thought about the loan, the more uncomfortable she became. Said at the September meeting, Fran needed to talk to her—badly. Beth suspected she was about to get hit up again and avoided her." The doorbell rang. "Oh goodness, here I am yammering away and Gil's here."

Anne hurried to the front door and opened it. Gil and his brother walked in.

"Anne, I'd like you to meet my brother Brad. Brad this is Anne Jamieson."

Brad Collins looked nothing like Gil. He stood

nearly six-one and appeared like he'd spent most of his life in the great outdoors. His dark hair was on the long side and his hazel eyes twinkled. He extended his hand.

"Anne, Gil's been talking about you for ages. Glad I can finally meet the real thing."

She shook his hand. "Same here. Are you in town for long?"

"A couple of weeks. I'm between volcanoes at the moment."

"Volcanoes?" Nancy said from behind Anne having followed her into the foyer.

"Helloooo there," Brad drawled. "I'm Brad Collins."

"I'm Nancy Carlyle and just leaving. Hi, Gil. I didn't mean to interrupt your night out. Just had something to discuss with Anne."

Gil shot her a look. "Discuss?"

She waved her hand. "Writing stuff. Look, I'd better get going. I'll talk to you later, Anne."

"You hungry?" Brad asked with a devastating smile.

"What?" Nancy said giving him a surprised look.

"Why not join us? I'm a third wheel and would like the company, not to mention the conversation, of a beautiful woman."

Anne shot a glance at Gil who shrugged. "By all means come along, Nancy."

"Oh, I don't think…"

"It's no problem. Really." Anne turned to Gil. "Where are we going?"

"I was thinking The Jigger and Keg. It's a sports bar, but a nice one."

"But I'm not really dressed to go out," Nancy

replied with a gesture toward her jeans and Miami Dolphins t-shirt.

"You look fine to me," Brad said in a cheerful tone. "Although we do have to discuss your choice of football teams."

Then Nancy did something Anne hadn't heard in a long time. She laughed.

"Very well, Mr. Collins, but I warn you; I'm a good debater."

"So am I, and it's Brad."

Anne and Gil had little to say on the way to the restaurant. Instead they were subjected to the promised debate.

"The *Patriots*? The *New England Patriots*? Are you kidding me?" Nancy said in a loud voice. "You do realize I have to hate you now."

"Convince me otherwise."

By the time they arrived at The Jigger and Keg, Anne was stunned at the byplay between the two in the backseat. Brad was definitely flirting, but what astonished her was Nancy reciprocated.

"Enough about football. I want to know more about this volcano thing," Nancy said as they were seated at a table.

"I'm a geologist who always loved volcanoes. It's nature at its fiery best. We can learn so much about the earth from them—the natural heating and cooling cycles, the age, and much more."

Anne leaned over next to Gil. "I think they're getting along more than well. Whodathunkit?"

"Certainly not me."

During dinner, Gil and Anne discussed the upcoming family get-together at Gil's while Nancy and

Brad didn't miss a beat in their conversation either. At some point, the talk had switched to writing. Brad seemed dutifully impressed and swore he'd read one of Nancy's books soon.

"I'll bet he hasn't read anything other than a science journal since college," Gil said to Anne in a low tone.

"Amazing, frankly amazing," she replied.

"So, Nancy, how would you like to have dinner and take in a movie tomorrow night?"

"Are you asking me out on a date?"

"Sure, why not?"

"How old are you?"

"A very sophisticated thirty-five." Brad assured her.

"I'm forty."

"So what? I've learned that age differentials are merely a nanosecond in the geological world."

"Oh my, you're good, you're very good. It's a date."

Back at the house, Nancy smiled and waved at them as she drove away.

"Congratulations," Anne told him. "She's a hard nut to crack."

Brad raised his eyebrows and grinned. "And I'm just the nutcracker that can do it."

"All right, Lochinvar, let's go home. I have to be in the office early in the morning," Gil said rolling his eyes. He leaned down and kissed Anne. "I'll be in touch."

She watched through the open door until the brothers drove down the street.

"Wow."

****

After seeing the kids off to school the next morning, Anne got down to the business of reading the financial files Jane had dropped off. It didn't take a genius to see Jane was in way over her head. A simple family checkbook was more her speed. A non-profit organization was another story. Rarely did the bank statement coincide with the checkbook. The treasurer's report listed any discrepancies as "miscellaneous expenses."

What really disturbed her were the August reports. According to Jane, the chapter had over twelve thousand dollars in the checking account, but the bank statement showed only nine thousand. The September statement was missing, yet the treasurer's report showed a little under eleven thousand dollars in the account.

"Something isn't right," she muttered out loud.

Wanting to look at the numbers with a fresh eye, she moved on to credit card statements. The chapter had a credit card to pay for things such as travel expenses and hotel rooms for outside speakers. The president and the treasurer were the only two authorized to use it. The card had a limit of two thousand dollars.

She riffled through almost a year of receipts. The card had been maxed out after the conference.

So Fran and Jane paid the hotel with a credit card. Did they pay the balance over time by check?

Anne pulled the folder with the printouts of the checkbook activity across the table and opened it. She scanned the checks, but found nothing out of the ordinary until late July.

Sheer anger pulsed through her veins. There in

damning black and white was a check made out on July 28th to Frances Harrison in the sum of three thousand dollars—and signed by Jane.

Chapter Nine

Anne paced around the kitchen taking deep cleansing breaths and trying to get her temper under control before she called Jane. Finally deciding close counts, she dialed the chapter treasurer.

"Jane, it's Anne. We need to talk. Now."

"Oh really? What about?" Her voice held a tone of fear.

"I think you know. Come on over to my place," Anne said.

"I can't...not right now. I...I...I've got a doctor's appointment in less than an hour."

Anne inhaled a deep breath. She couldn't very well demand the woman cancel, but the hesitation and desperation in Jane's voice suggested she was lying.

"Well, I guess I could call an emergency board meeting for later in the day when all of us can be here."

Silence greeted her words. "I can be there in fifteen minutes."

"I thought so. I'll be waiting."

She hung up with a hard thumb press on the end talk button, and then reread some of the statements and treasurer reports.

I wonder how long she's been faking it. Should I call for an audit? Of course I should. And how bad is it really? Will the IRS be knocking on our door?

Anne gritted her teeth. As a non-profit

organization, the government scrutinized the details, but being the government maybe they had overlooked the inconsistencies. She had the mind-numbing feeling the chapter was about to get grilled. Either way, they were in trouble. *And what will be the reaction of WAA?*

The doorbell rang. Anne hurried to answer. Jane stood on the front porch shifting her weight from foot to foot and refusing to make eye contact.

"Come in, Jane. Let's go into the kitchen."

She turned and led the woman down the hallway. Once there she indicated Jane have a seat at the table now strewn with sheets of paper. She didn't offer the woman anything to drink. The hell with hospitality.

"I think you know what this is all about, don't you?"

Jane bit her lip. Her eyes welled until a tear trickled down her cheek.

"The minute you said you wanted to see the books, I knew you'd find it. That's why I dumped the files on you yesterday and ran. I was scared. I'm sorry, really I am."

"The chapter treasury is not a bank. We don't make loans, especially something as big as this. And even if we did, the board would have to be in on the decision. What the hell were you thinking?" She pulled out a chair and sat.

"It started with the conference last spring. We owed the hotel and they didn't want to take a check for the full amount, so Fran put part of the cost on the credit card, and we paid off the rest by check over the next couple of months. The credit card was finally down to a zero balance in early July."

"I don't see any that reflected anywhere in the

treasurer's report."

"Fran told me to keep it under the rug. She didn't want the membership to know exactly how much we lost."

"And exactly how much was that?" Anne asked in a tight voice, her temper once again rising.

"We admitted to four thousand dollars, but the real number was closer to six grand. We took a hit financially, but not enough to bankrupt us."

"Oh, God. Why did you go along with it?"

"Fran assured me everything would work out. She…she counted on getting reelected. Then last July, Fran came to me and said she needed a favor. She needed to borrow some money."

This is my worst nightmare. "What for?"

Jane shrugged. "She never actually came out and said."

"You loaned her chapter money with no explanation, no collateral, or even a signed promissory note?"

"She said she had a personal problem and that she'd have it paid back in a couple of months. All I had to do was make sure the treasurer reports didn't show the three thousand dollars. I was to pretend the money was there. That way when it was replaced the books would gibe with the bank statements. No one would know. I…I didn't feel comfortable about it, but Fran was insistent."

"Oh God," Anne murmured again. "Where's the September bank statement?"

Jane reached into her purse and produced the missing statement. "I took it out when you called yesterday. If you asked I was going to say I couldn't find it, but would get it to you as soon as possible." Jane looked up at Anne for the first time. Tears ran down her cheeks. "I told Fran at the meeting that the money had to be put back immediately. With you as the new president, I knew you'd eventually ask something like this."

"And what did Fran say?"

"She told me to stall if you asked to see the books, and that she'd get the money by the end of the week."

"And then she died."

"And then she died. How much trouble am I in?"

"Legally? I don't know. What you did was fraud. But you are in big trouble as far as the chapter is concerned. I have no choice but to ask that you resign. I don't care what reason you give. I'll have to find someone to take over immediately. I just hope I don't have to initiate an audit."

She wasn't sure if she had the authority to make such a request without first discussing it with the entire board, but figured Jane wouldn't know either. As for the audit, she was certain it needed to take place as soon as possible.

"I swear, Anne, this is the only time it happened. I know I made mistakes here and there, but they were honest mistakes."

"Here and there? Try every month. You counted some receivables twice to cover up the losses. According to the bank statements, we have around nine thousand dollars in the account. Yet your reports show closer to twelve. And you never even presented a budget for this year."

"Fran told me not to. She said it would all work out after December. We'd present a budget and make it look good. I'm not a bad person," she sobbed.

"I know you're not, Jane, but there's nothing honest about any of this. You manipulated the books. People go to jail for that."

"Jail? Are you going to tell the police?" she wiped her cheeks with her fingertips. New tears flowed.

Anne heaved a deep breath slid a blank sheet of paper and a pen toward the woman. "I don't know. I'll have to discuss it with the board and see if there is some way we can fix things without it becoming common knowledge to the membership, at least not right away. Now, if you would write out a simple resignation letter that will make it official. As soon as I find someone to take over, I'll announce it on the loop."

Anne wasn't sure she had the authority to do this without full board approval either. Did the entire membership need to know? Probably. But maybe it could wait a few months until the mess was sorted out. Maybe just saying Jane had been under a lot of stress and made too many mistakes. But as of now, she just wanted the woman gone.

"All…all right. Whatever you say."

Jane quickly wrote two sentences, signed it, and then rose. "I'm sorry, Anne. I really am."

"I know. Oh, and Jane, don't talk about this to anyone."

"I won't. I promise."

After Jane left, Anne sat down at the table and stared at the financial mess in front of her, then called Rose.

"Why the hell would Fran need three grand?" she demanded upon hearing the news.

"I have no idea, but she also borrowed three

thousand dollars from Beth Whisnant last spring. All I know is the chapter is short. We have to replace Jane as soon as possible. I'm not even sure I know how to go about it."

"Let me look at the bylaws and get back to you."

Anne hung up and held her head in her hands. Rose was good with things like by-laws. Maybe she could find a solution. The chapter just might be on the brink of disaster, especially if an audit discovered more missing money. Then another thought occurred to her.

I only have Jane's word that Fran said she'd pay it back. Maybe it was an ongoing thing between the two of them. Suppose my election upset their little apple cart. What if Jane demanded the three thousand be replaced and Fran told her to stuff it?

"Jane would be in a world of hurt, and Fran could say the check was a forgery or something," she murmured out loud.

And we also only have Jane's word that she spoke to Fran at the meeting. Suppose the two had talked earlier. What if Jane was so scared and angry about possibly taking the fall, she decided to do something about it? I wonder if she knew about Fran's allergies.

****

"Actually, we only have one option," Rose said when she called back with the interpretation of the bylaws. "If the President resigns, then the Vice-President takes over, but for all other board positions a special election must be held within sixty days of the resignation. An interim board member can be appointed until said election."

Anne groaned. "I was afraid of that. Looks like Fran ignored the by-laws when our last Secretary resigned and moved. She just appointed herself, with no input that I know of. She took a chance, but then not many people actually read by-laws. The point is how much do I have to tell the membership?"

"Well, for now all you have to say is that Jane resigned for personal reasons. Then I'd suggest we call in an expert to untangle the mess and find out how much financial trouble we're in. I seem to recall that Mavis Holloway's son is an accountant. Maybe he'd do it for a reasonable price."

"I hope so. Oh God, what a mess."

Rose sighed. "One ray of sunshine is that while quarterly board meetings are open to the membership, there's nothing that says a special session has to be announced. It's a loophole, but one that might work. I mean, I can just see Susan Lynch showing up."

"Heaven forbid! Now, I have to talk someone into dealing with our finances for a couple of months."

"How about Nancy? She's good with numbers."

Anne hadn't thought about her critique partner. "That might be a good idea. Any way you look at it I have to call an emergency board meeting."

"The sooner, the better."

"Thanks, Rose. I'll get back to you with the time."

Anne hung up and slowly gathered the financial papers from her kitchen table. Nancy made sense as an interim treasurer. First off, Rose was right—the woman had a good head for numbers. Second, she was always supportive of the chapter and her critique partners. And third, Anne trusted her.

With a long sigh, she picked up the phone, called Nancy, and told her the whole story.

"Oh Lord, what was Jane thinking? Unraveling this

badly knitted sweater could take forever."

"I know, but if we hire an accountant like I want, then the pressure will be off the treasurer. Naturally, it will have to be put toward the membership for a vote. In the meantime, you'd only be stuck with the job for a couple of months."

"I'll do it, but only until the election. No way do I want the job any longer than that. Besides, three of us from the group on the board might not sit well with people."

Anne breathed a sigh of relief. First hurdle cleared.

"I'm going to call an emergency board meeting for this afternoon. Can you make it say around three?"

"I suppose so. But it is Friday. Some people may not be available."

Hanging up from Nancy, she realized she only needed to call two other board members. Rose would certainly be here, and even though Luella's position was non-voting, she still had to be notified. She didn't know Luella that well, but the woman struck her as the kind that would demand some kind of legal action. Anne didn't want to get into that if possible.

Maybe all I need to say is that Jane resigned. She called, told her that, and breathed a sigh of relief when Luella said she couldn't attend.

Kathy and Ellie, however, needed to know the whole gruesome story. She called, told them Jane was no longer on the board and asked if they could drop by briefly at three o'clock. Both expressed surprise at Jane's resignation, but promised to be there.

Rose arrived first complete with a toddler and the baby. "Sorry, but I couldn't find a sitter on such short notice. This won't take long and once we vote, I can scram."

Anne didn't mind. The baby was sound asleep and Graham, an active two-year-old, had a small backpack full of toys.

Nancy arrived next. "This better not take long. I've got a date tonight."

During the crisis with the bank accounts, Anne had forgotten to delve further into last night's dinner.

"A date?" Rose said with arched eyebrows.

"You heard me, a date, with a man. This doesn't happen often, so I want to make the most of it."

"Who is it?"

"Gil's brother, Brad," Anne answered as the doorbell rang.

It was Ellie closely followed by Kathy.

Anne didn't waste any time, but led them into the living room and told them the hard facts in blunt terms.

"How much trouble are we in?" Kathy asked.

"Don't know yet. Rose said Mavis Holloway's son is an accountant. I'll call and see if he can help."

"I can't believe Jane would do something like that," Kathy said. "I know she isn't the brightest bulb in the pack, but this was just plain stupid."

"Oh, I don't know," Ellie replied. "Fran could be damned persuasive."

"That's the bad news. The good news is Nancy has agreed to step in as interim treasurer. Is that all right with everyone?"

Everyone agreed. Then Kathy brought up the subject of telling the other members.

"They have to know," she stated.

"Can we give it a month or so?" Anne asked. "Perhaps we can just explain that Jane resigned for personal reasons and didn't pay as close attention to her position as she should have, thus mistakes were made. That's why we're having an audit done."

"That might work," the vice-president said. "But the sooner we do it, the more transparent it will look."

"Okay, I'll announce the resignation and special election at the next meeting."

"Too long," Kathy said. "I'd look for a permanent replacement immediately."

The meeting was adjourned having taken only fifteen minutes. While Kathy and Ellie left, Rose lingered.

"Gil's brother?" she said with a twinkle in her eye.

Nancy gave her a look. "Yes, Gil's brother. He's a geologist who studies volcanoes. We're going out to eat, and then to a movie. Now, if you'll excuse me, I have to get ready."

Nancy sailed out of the door with her head held high.

"This is interesting." Rose gathered up her kids and the toys.

"I'll say. I haven't heard from Gil all day. Think I'll give him a call. Maybe he has some more information on Fran and Jeffery Wainwright."

As Rose left, the mention of the dead waiter brought the murder of Fran back to the front of her mind. Disaster was piling up on disaster.

Reality sucks.

****

Gil arrived at seven complete with a large pepperoni and mushroom pizza. Anne had the Chianti open and ready.

"Welcome. Just you and me tonight."

His eyebrows rose. "Yeah?"

"Kids are at a football game and will be going to a school sponsored dance later."

"Time enough to have our own dance," he said with a suggestive smile.

"We can always reheat the pizza." She grabbed the box from his hands and set it on the kitchen counter, then led him upstairs.

An hour later, they were back in the kitchen.

"Have I told you how much I like dining at your house?" he commented.

Anne sipped her wine and gazed at him over the rim of the glass. "I'm the perfect hostess who always sees to her guests' wants and needs."

Gil laughed and took a huge bite of pizza while she contemplated telling him about Fran's financial activities. If they weren't related to her murder, then he had no reason to know. She decided to wait until he'd had his fill of pepperoni and Chianti.

"Any more news on Fran or Wainwright?"

"I talked to Mr. Harrison and her sister this morning. They said Ms. Harrison had numerous food allergies besides peanuts, including strawberries, raw tomatoes, plus some citrus fruits. And of course, shellfish of all kinds."

"Someone who knew her well had to kill her."

"We're checking out the family now. Her friends are next."

"I think most of her friends were writers. We've talked to some people like her critique partners who probably knew about her allergies," she said. "Did you talk to Becky Lawrence and Terry Whiting yet?"

He nodded. "Both. Ms. Lawrence says she just

didn't feel like dealing with Ms. Harrison, so stayed home. Her husband was at work, so there's no corroboration. Ms. Whiting said she and Ms. Harrison had words about the conference and met to patch things up for the sake of the chapter."

"Yet the waitress said Terry left in a huff."

"She claimed Ms. Harrison made a snide comment. That's all. I also showed a still of the waiter from the surveillance video to one of the women serving the meeting. She said it kinda looked like Wainwright, but wasn't sure."

"Any news on Wainwright?" she asked.

"Preliminary tox screen shows he was coked up pretty good when he died."

"The mystery man in the car. A deal gone bad?"

Gil frowned. "Possible, but if a dealer wanted to off a guy for non-payment, doing it this way is an oddity. You kill him and leave the body in a remote area."

"Maybe he's sending a message."

"It just doesn't feel right." He shook his head.

Anne realized that while she wasn't sure if Jane and Fran's business transactions related to the case, Gil might.

"Gil, I don't know if this is relevant, but our treasurer, Jane Whittaker, resigned this morning at my request. I found she was being less than truthful about the books."

She told him all she knew about the situation and her thoughts on Jane's explanations of when she and Fran had spoken.

"I'll have to have a chat with Ms. Whittaker again."

"Will she get in trouble for what she did?"

"Only if the chapter presses charges."

"I don't think it'll come to that. I'm not even sure who, if anybody we can go after for the money. Fran borrowed the same amount from one of her critique partners last spring. Told her it was to pay off credit cards before her husband found out, but you know, now that I think of it, that doesn't sound like Fran. She was great at spending other people's money, but tighter than a virgin's ass with her own."

"And she borrowed the same amount from the chapter a few months later? Who is this woman? Sounds like I may have to talk to her, too."

"Beth Whisnant, but she said Fran paid her off in August," Anne said slowing her words. "Do you think she may have used Beth's loan for whatever reason, and when she didn't have the money to pay it back borrowed from the chapter?"

"We're checking the finances of the Harrisons. Something may come up." He leaned over to kiss her. "There really is something to you and your friends investigating, after all."

"Even when we do it wrong?"

"Let's not go there."

"And speaking of going places, what's with your brother and Nancy?"

Gil shrugged. "I have no idea, but all Brad could talk about last night and today was Nancy. Asked me all kinds of questions—most of which I couldn't answer."

"I'll pry it out of Nancy at some point in time." She laughed.

The front door slammed indicating Ken and Lisa

had returned.

"Hey, thought you were going to some dance after the game," she said as they walked into the room and greeted Gil.

"It was lame," Ken said. "No upper classmen at all. Just freshmen. Boring!"

"And the only guys there were total geeks," Lisa added.

"Who won the game?" Gil asked.

"We lost, 38 to 20," Ken said with a grimace.

"I guess I should be going," Gil commented as he rose from the sofa.

"Not on our account," Lisa told him with a smile.

"Naw, just time I got home. You all are coming on Sunday to my place, right?"

"Wouldn't miss it," Anne replied as she let him out the front door.

****

Nancy dropped by the following morning to pick up the financials.

"I may as well jump into this now." She crammed the papers into an accordion folder. "Any idea when the shenanigans began?"

"As close as I can figure, just before the conference from hell. We had good attendance, but spent a lot on comps, the hotel, and food. Terry overestimated how many hotel rooms we'd need. The hotel wasn't a sellout for that weekend, so the chapter had to cough up almost four thousand bucks to cover the contract. I found the invoice in the files. Jane wrote it off as editor/agent expenses and miscellaneous items. Naturally, there are no receipts."

Nancy groaned. "Oh God, what a mess. I'll get

right on this and see how much trouble we're in. Did you call about a real accountant?"

Anne nodded. "This morning. Mavis said she'd ask her son if he could take us on at a reduced rate."

"Thank goodness. I can unsnarl some of this, but a professional is the only answer."

"I just hope the IRS doesn't come after us."

"They will. They always do."

"Uh, how was your date last night?"

"He took me to Giovanni's."

"Good choice. Shows he's trying to impress you. What movie did you see?"

Nancy shot her a sidelong glance. "What is this—the third degree?"

"Just curious, that's all."

"Well, if you must know, we never got around to going. We ended up at my place."

Anne folded her arms across her chest and repressed a grin. "Your place? Good grief, did you sleep with him?"

"*That* is none of your business!" she exclaimed, not making eye contact.

"Oh my God, you did, didn't you?" she replied with a laugh.

"I said it was none of your business!"

She laughed harder remembering the jibes she took from her friends when she first started dating Gil. "Was he good?"

Nancy's right eyebrow rose while the left corner of her mouth slipped into a half-smile, giving her a sly expression. "Damned good."

"Bully for you! Care to discuss the details?"

"No. Besides, I'll see you tomorrow at Gil's. Right

now, I need to get started on this mess you've handed me."

With her head held high, Nancy walked out the front door. Anne chuckled again.

Nancy and Brad? Her mind asked a lot of questions—like what if their relationship progressed as well as hers and Gil's? She'd never thought of her critique partner as potential sister-in-law material—assuming, of course, that she and Gil went that route.

She climbed the stairs to her office, still in a good frame of mind. That ended when she pulled up her e-mail.

"Oh, geez, not Susan again." She groaned.

She'd rather walk barefoot on ground glass than deal with her paranoid former critique partner, but opened the e-mail anyway.

I talked to Jane last night and she says she resigned. I don't buy her excuse of personal reasons. What did you do to her? She was an excellent treasurer. Who's going to take her place? Another one of your friends? Since that bitch Georgia Yancey has banned me from the loop, I am left with no choice but to contact you for an explanation. Can you tell the truth for a change?

Anne sighed and tamped her anger at the belligerent tone. She'd specifically told Jane not to discuss this with anyone. Before answering, she forwarded the message to Jane with the admonition not to discuss it again.

She was tempted to ignore Susan altogether. It was never a good idea to reply or comment on anything while emotional. However, and against her better judgment, she ignored her instincts and answered.

Jane's decision to resign is not up for discussion. It has nothing to do with you or anybody else. Nancy has agreed to step in on a temporary basis until a new treasurer can be elected. I was waiting until after the weekend before making the announcement. And if you don't think I tell the truth, why bother to ask me for details?

She hit the send button with more force than usual ruing the day she'd ever met Susan Lynch.

Writing was out of the question. Her mind was too focused on Jane, Susan, and the chapter in general. To keep busy, Anne committed the particulars of the case into a special folder on her computer. Maybe the repeating of the incidents and the facts as she knew them would help her find solutions to the crimes.

An hour later, she was no closer to anything except frustration. It was obvious the man and woman seen in the surveillance video on the main floor were involved in Fran's death in some way, but identifying either was next to impossible.

And could it be that one or both of them had an accomplice or accomplices already in the room? Like a fake doctor?

She sighed and logged back into her e-mail, wincing when she saw a reply from Susan.

And under whose authority did you appoint Nancy Carlyle as our new treasurer? That should be a decision made by the membership. You're trying to pack the board with your little friends.

Anne took a deep breath. Once again, the smart thing to do would be to ignore Susan, but her temper was up and she fired back an answer.

Susan, according to the by-laws, the board may

appoint a replacement on an interim basis until a special election can be held to elect a new member. This election is to be held no later than sixty days after the resignation is accepted. And before you ask, the board may appoint said interim member without holding an open discussion. Treasurer is an important position and needed to be filled immediately. Nancy has no intention of running for the office. I hope this clears up any misconceptions you may have regarding the situation.

She sent the e-mail. To cover her backside, Anne forwarded the entire series of e-mails to the rest of the board hoping this was the end of it. No such luck. Her former critique partner answered back almost immediately.

I think you're trying to pull the wool over our eyes. I won't let you get away with it. Consider this official. I nominate myself for the now open position of treasurer.

"Oh great, just what I need," Anne said out loud in an aggravated tone.

The problem was she might pull it off if a more qualified candidate didn't come forward. The land line ringing brought her out of her depressing thoughts.

"Hello?"

"Uh, Ms. Jamieson? This is Pamela Waters, Fran Harrison's sister. I just wanted to let you know that the funeral has been scheduled for Tuesday at eleven o'clock. Everyone is invited here afterward for coffee and cake." She gave Anne further details.

"Oh, thank you for letting me know. I'll post it on our chapter news loop immediately. How's Mr. Harrison doing?"

A huge sigh came over the line. "Not good. He's

still in shock, poor man. Apparently, Fran's death was not an accident. None of us can imagine who'd want to murder Fran."

Anne bit her tongue. "I'm sure the police will find the killer soon."

"I certainly hope so. George mentioned something about you coming over to collect some of Fran's papers concerning your group. Would the day after the funeral be all right?"

"Yes, that's fine. And again, please accept my deepest condolences."

After hanging up, she tapped her fingers against her lips. *Chapter business is one thing, but I wonder if I can snoop enough to find personal correspondence, too.*

Fran borrowed money for a reason, and Anne was determined to find out why.

Chapter Ten

Ken parked in front of Gil's house. She'd allowed her son to drive. All in all, she had little to criticize. He drove the speed limit, used his turn signals, and generally did a good job.

The babble of conversation and the aroma of burning charcoal told them the festivities had already begun. They followed their noses to the back yard.

"Anne," Gil called out from the patio. He walked toward them, then leaned down to lightly kiss her cheek. "So glad you could make it. Nice to see you, too, Lisa and Ken."

"Thanks for inviting us," Lisa replied.

He smiled at Anne. "Can I get you something to drink? Wine? Beer? Soft drink?"

"I can handle a glass of wine," she answered.

"I'm good for a soda," Ken chimed in.

"Soft drinks and water are in coolers next to the house. The wine's inside. Come on over. There are some people I'd like you to meet." His hand clasped hers.

Anne took a deep breath and strolled side-by-side with him.

"By the way, you look gorgeous," he said.

She glanced down at the black denim Capri pants topped with a bright purple, form fitting, t-shirt. The color set off her auburn hair to perfection.

"Thanks. I was so nervous I barely saw what I grabbed from the closet."

Gil chuckled. "Don't give me that. You spent hours trying on and discarding clothes."

"Busted."

They paused near a group of people sitting in lawn chairs on and near the large flagstone patio. She was certain Gil felt the nervous tremors rippling through her body to her extremities.

"Caroline, I'd like you to meet someone," he said.

A petite blonde separated herself from a conversation and advanced. Her blue eyes crinkled when she smiled.

"Anne, this is my oldest daughter, Caroline. Cari, this is Anne Jamieson."

The girl extended her hand. "Anne, I'm so pleased to meet you. Dad's spoken about you a lot."

She accepted the handshake. "I've heard a lot about you, too. You're in college, right?"

"Florida State."

"How do you like it up in Tallahassee?"

"I wish it was closer so I could get home more often, but I do get to see Mom every couple of months."

"I seem to remember Gil saying she lived in Tampa?"

"Yes. Dad said something about your kids being here today."

Anne called Lisa and Ken over to introduce them. Another young woman with light brown hair and blue eyes joined them. Without waiting for a prompt from Gil, she held out her hand and smiled.

"Let me guess—you're Daddy's Anne."

She had to laugh as she returned the handshake.

"Guilty as charged."

"Oh, good heavens, don't say that in a policeman's house. Someone might get the wrong idea."

Gil chuckled. "This is my other daughter, Barbara. She's in her sophomore year at the University of Florida."

"I'll bet football season is interesting in this house," Anne said.

He rolled his eyes. "Oh yeah."

Over the next fifteen minutes, Gil introduced her to most of the people there, including his aunt and uncle, and several neighbors. By now, Anne had found a seat and sipped wine Caroline had presented. Ken was playing a game of H-O-R-S-E with other teens at a basketball hoop set up near the far end of the yard. Lisa was talking to Barbara and another young lady. For the first time since arriving, Anne relaxed.

"Brad! I was beginning to think you weren't coming," Gil called out.

Anne turned to see Gil's younger brother step through the patio doors with Nancy. Her friend wore a pair of light blue shorts, white sandals, and a white sleeveless blouse. But what caught her attention was Brad's arm firmly around Nancy's waist, and the fact that Nancy was laughing—almost as if she'd been flirting.

I'm not sure how to react to this. It's so out of character for her.

Nancy joined her after Brad had introduced his date to various people.

"You look…nice," she said as Nancy took a seat.

"You mean different, don't you?"

"I've never seen you wear anything except skirts

and the occasional pair of slacks."

"Maybe this cougar thing has me thinking in younger terms."

Brad brought Nancy a beer and kissed the top of her head. "You okay for a while?"

She waved a hand and smiled. "I'm fine. Go say hi to your friends and play basketball."

"Beer?" Anne questioned as Brad hurried off. "I am seeing a whole new you."

"I know. I kind of like it. I was going to spend the day writing, but decided to bag it. This sounded like more fun. Can you imagine me kissing off writing for even a day?"

"No. Not in a million years. This might not be the time to bring up the subject, but have you had a chance to do anything with the financial mess I dumped in your lap?"

Nancy took a swig from the bottle and sighed. "You're right, it's not the best time, but yeah, and it isn't pretty. The treasurer's report says we have oodles of money in the bank, but according to the bank statements, we don't."

Anne's stomach clenched. "I only had time for a quick glance. How far off are we?"

"I'd say several thousand dollars."

"Oh my God."

"And I found something else interesting—checks for varying amounts made out to cash. They coincide with our meeting dates."

"What the hell?" A vision of the IRS knocking on the chapter door flashed before her eyes. "Cash? Varying amounts?"

Nancy nodded. "All the way from two hundred

dollars up to a thousand. I called Jane just before Brad picked me up. She says Fran told her those were speaking fees commanded by the speakers. Jane claims Fran said the speakers preferred to be paid in cash."

Astonishment almost left Anne breathless. "But that's crazy. I've never heard of anybody who presented a meeting workshop getting paid anything other than travel fare and hotel accommodations when needed. Members who presented charged us nothing and the chapter picked up their lunch tab."

"I went back over statements from a couple of years ago. No such checks were ever issued until Fran became president and Jane treasurer. I think good old Fran was bilking the chapter. I can't decide yet whether Jane was an accomplice or just plain stupid."

Anne sat back and gulped her wine.

"And this'll frost your balls," Nancy continued. "I found the chapter credit card receipts from the last national conference. Fran attended with conference fee, travel, and hotel room paid for by the chapter. That's SOP. But she also took along her husband and another couple as guests. She put everything on the credit card and as far as I can tell never repaid the chapter."

"Did you ask Jane about it?"

"Yep. She said Fran told her the extra couple of thousand dollars was for miscellaneous entertaining expenses to boost the chapter's image."

"And Jane paid up without any investigation, itemized receipts, or questions? Can this get any worse?"

"I don't know. All I do know is that this is going to take an expert to untangle. I don't think the chapter is in going-out-of-business trouble financially, but God only knows what kind of mess Jane got us into with the government regarding taxes and such. Whoever takes over this job is in for a hell of a ride."

"You're just full of good news today. I've got some for you. Susan is throwing her hat into the ring for treasurer," Anne told her.

Nancy rolled her eyes. "If no one else steps up, I'll do it. Can't you just see her handling money?"

The problem was Anne could. The thought scared the crap out of her.

Brad returned and claimed Nancy for a game of ring-toss. Gil sat in her vacated seat.

"So, are you having fun?" he asked.

"I am. Lisa and Ken seem to be talking to your family and friends, and I'm starving. When is master chef Gil Collins going to begin working his culinary magic?"

He laughed and pulled her to her feet. "Right now, and I need a sous chef."

An hour or so later, Anne was stuffed with burgers and hot dogs, and a determination to sweet talk Gil's Aunt Betsy out of her recipe for potato salad. She never did find out who baked the brownies, but managed to eat three of them.

"So, did you guys enjoy yourselves?" she asked her kids on the way home—Ken driving, of course.

"I had a great time," her son answered. "The food was fab and I played basketball with one of Gil's neighbors who played for the University of Miami a few years ago. He made All-American, but didn't make the pro ranks."

"Caroline and Barbara are so nice," Lisa said. "Barbara invited me to visit her in Gainesville if I wanted to go to school there. She also said she hopes her dad doesn't screw things up. She thinks you're a keeper. Mom, you made one hell of an impression."

She ignored Lisa's word choice, but glowed in the second hand praise. It was a huge hurdle to meet Gil's daughters and friends. This day boded well for their future.

"I was kind of surprised to see Mrs. Carlyle there with Gil's brother," her daughter commented.

"They're seeing each other for the time being. I guess Brad's schedule depends on when the next volcano blows up."

"Wow, can you imagine being a volcanologist?" Ken said in an awe-filled tone. "That must be fascinating."

"All I keep visualizing are the movies, *Dante's Peak* and *Volcano*, not to mention the reality of the geologists killed when Mt. St. Helens blew," Anne replied.

Once home, the kids went upstairs to finish any homework, while Anne poured a glass of iced tea and fired up her laptop.

The conversation she'd had with Nancy reminded her she needed to inform the membership of Jane's resignation. But first, she e-mailed Jane to give her a heads up before getting down to business. It took her a few minutes to frame the news into a diplomatic message. She didn't want to alarm the membership with too much of the truth so soon after Fran's death. Anne saw no need to raise the specter of the IRS quite yet. She'd wait until the results of the audit.

It is my unfortunate duty to inform you all of the resignation of our Treasurer, Jane Whittaker, due to personal reasons. She was a valued member of the board and worked hard in her post.

As per the by-laws, the board met yesterday and appointed Nancy Carlyle as interim Treasurer. A special election will be held prior to sixty days from yesterday for the position. Details will be forthcoming. Anybody who is interested in filling the role can contact me privately.

She added her e-mail address and hit the send button. Now, she hoped someone with a modicum of sense and a strong moral code would step forward.

Anybody but Susan Lynch. The chapter can only take so many disasters in a year.

****

Anne dressed carefully for Fran's funeral trying to set a dignified image in a navy blue suit with a light blue blouse. If she wasn't chapter president, she'd have skipped the whole thing. But as it was, she had no choice, especially since Fran's sister had called and asked her to speak on behalf of the organization.

Monday had been relatively quiet giving Anne time to actually write. Mavis Holloway's son had called to say he'd be glad to take on the job of accountant for the chapter at a reasonable price. She told him the basics of their problems. When he agreed to take them on anyway, she gave him Nancy's number. So far, she hadn't heard from either of them.

However, she did hear from three other members expressing interest in the Treasurer's position. Two of them actually had accounting experience. Anne had breathed a sigh of relief. She was certain any of the other candidates could beat Susan Lynch in the election.

The parking lot at the funeral home was almost full when Anne arrived, but she finally found a spot near the back. Rose and Nancy were waiting for her on the front porch.

"Looks like a good turn-out," she commented as she climbed the steps.

"I've seen a lot of members going in," Rose said.

Nancy heaved a sigh. "I just hope the service is short. I need to get back. I'm in the middle of a turning point in my story."

They entered the foyer of the establishment and were greeted by the funeral director.

"Are you here for Mrs. Harrison?" he inquired.

"Yes," Rose replied.

The man gestured to the left. "Right this way."

Another man met them at the entryway. "There aren't many seats left or perhaps you are members of the family."

"No, I'm the president of the local writers chapter and these ladies sit on the board," Anne explained.

He consulted a list on a clipboard. "Ah, you must be Mrs. Jamieson, one of the speakers. Follow me. Your seats are reserved."

"This is a first," Rose whispered. "I've never had a reserved seat for a funeral before."

"Maybe it's a board member thing," Nancy commented as they marched behind the man and took their seats in the second row. Kathy Samuels was already seated there.

Anne glanced around and made eye contact with Jane Whittaker and Susan Lynch. Both women averted their heads. Ellie Campion sat several rows back with some friends, but nodded and smiled at Anne. She assumed the first row was for family.

"Excuse me, but I think I should introduce myself to Fran's husband and sister," she said rising. "I'll be back in a moment."

She made her way forward and stopped in front of a man with thinning brown hair. He wiped his eyes with a tissue.

"Mr. Harrison? I'm Anne Jamieson, the chapter president. I just want to extend my deepest condolences to you and your family."

The man sniffed. "Thank you. This is Pam Waters, Fran's sister," he said indicating a dark-haired lady to his left.

Anne murmured more condolences.

"Thank you for coming and for agreeing to make a few comments to the assembly. We appreciate it," she said.

"Glad to do it," Anne lied.

"I believe you're scheduled to talk after the last family member. We had so many people who wanted to say kind things about Fran, but had to keep the list short or we'd be here for hours. You will be coming to the house afterward for some food and talk, won't you?"

She would rather skip the whole thing, but nodded anyway.

"Of course. Thank you for inviting me."

Pam waved her hand. "I know you writers are a close knit bunch. I'm sure many will attend.

Anne returned to her seat. "Are you guys going to the house afterward?"

Rose shook her head. "I can't. The baby has a doctor's appointment at one, and I have to take Bethany to her dance class after school."

"Not a chance in hell," Nancy replied in a low tone. "I don't even want to be here."

"I wonder who's going to speak," Rose said.

Anne relayed the sister's comments.

"Lord, I hope Susan isn't one of them," Nancy whispered.

A man stepped up to the podium and bowed his head. "Let us pray."

The service began with the minister saying what he had to say followed by Pam Waters praising her sister. She in turn was followed by several other family members doing the same. The husband sobbed as did many in the assemblage. Anne sneaked a peek over her shoulder at Jane and Susan. Both were blotting tears from their cheeks.

Then it was her turn. The minister introduced her to the crowd and she took her place at the podium. She stared out over the rows of chairs and took a deep breath. Susan, with a mutinous expression, glared.

Anne kept her comments short, praising Fran's writing and her dedication to the chapter. She even threw in compliments for the last conference and how well Fran had handled a chaotic situation. She felt like a hypocrite since most of what she said was insincere. She returned to her seat ten minutes later.

The rest of the speakers, including Fran's critique partners and Jane, also kept their comments short. Still Anne fidgeted and let her mind wander to her latest work in progress.

The service finally ended and the funeral procession wound its way through the streets of San Sebastian to the cemetery. After a few more brief words and it was over. Rose practically ran to her car in order to make it to the pediatrician's office. Nancy also left.

Fran's house was packed with mourners. Anne spoke to many chapter members, avoided Susan and Jane, and left as soon as was decently possible.

"I'm so glad you could come," Pam said. "And thank you for the kind words you spoke."

"As I said, I was glad to do it. Um, is it all right if I come back tomorrow morning to see if I can find those papers we need?"

"Yes, of course. We haven't been in her office since she died. Poor George just can't face it. He's so broken up he's been sleeping on the sofa in the den. I guess I'd have a hard time sleeping in the bed, too, if I'd lost my husband."

Anne murmured something she hoped was appropriate and left. She was almost to her car when a voice hailed her.

"Anne, wait up!"

She turned to see Ellie trotting her way.

"I heard you talking to Fran's sister about coming back tomorrow. Do you mind if I tag along? I can help with some of the paper sorting."

Anne liked Ellie, but didn't feel comfortable with her suggestion.

"Thanks, Ellie, but I think I can handle it."

"Oh. All right. I didn't mean to be pushy. I just wanted to help—as a board member, you know."

"That's okay. How is the critique partner match-up going?"

Ellie smiled. "Great! I've had fifteen people contact me so far. I'm asking for experience levels, comfort levels, and genre specifics. You know, are you offended by explicit sex scenes, how long have you been writing, are you pubbed, things like that."

"Good job. I'm sure you'll do fine."

"Well, I've got to get home. If I can help with anything, please let me know."

Ellie left, but before Anne could get into her car, Kathy Samuels walked up.

"Thank God, that's over," she said. "I hate funerals. I never know what to say."

"At least you didn't have to give a eulogy even though you knew her better than I."

"Not really. I'm not sure anybody knew Fran all that well."

"Still it was a nice turn-out," Anne said.

"I can tell you who wasn't there—Terry Whiting and Becky Lawrence. I talked to Becky last week and she said she'd rather have root canal than listen to praise for Fran Harrison. Terry just said no, she wasn't coming."

"Hard feelings from both ladies."

"I can understand, I suppose. Fran had a fling with Becky's husband, and Terry's hubby wasn't immune to Fran's come on either from what I heard. Nasty business. Well, I'd better be going. See you at the next meeting."

Anne stared as Kathy walked away. She knew about the brief affair with Becky's husband, but Terry?

Curiouser and curiouser.

****

Funerals always sent Anne into a funk. A glass of wine helped put her in a better mood. Gil calling to say he'd treat all of them to take-out Chinese food almost made her forget the morning's activities. Almost.

In spite of the friendly bantering between them all

during dinner, something nagged at her.

If Fran was having affairs that appeared to be common knowledge among many chapter members, how could her husband not know about it? Was he that dense? His tears and broken-hearted reactions said he truly grieved. Still, it seemed odd. Perhaps she could discreetly delve into the family relationship when she returned to the house tomorrow.

After dinner, with the kids upstairs finishing homework, Gil and Anne cuddled on the sofa.

"Gil, may I ask a personal question?"

"Of course. What is it?"

"Did…did either of your ex-wives ever cheat on you?"

He drew in a deep breath. "I suspected my first wife, the girls' mother, may have been seeing someone just before we split, but I was never sure, and frankly, didn't want to know. The marriage was over, so what did it matter? Why?"

"But suppose the marriage wasn't over, at least not yet. How would you have reacted?"

"Angry, hurt, disappointed, wondering what I could have done to be a better husband. Why?" he repeated.

Anne told him of the gossip about Fran and other men and her thoughts about George Harrison.

"There are two thoughts that come to mind. First, if his wife was discreet, he may not have known a thing. Second, he knew and didn't care."

"But is it possible for a spouse *not* to know? I know Kenneth never cheated on me—he told me that and I believed him. That wasn't his style."

"There's a sixth sense that tells you when things

are wrong. Like I said, I suspected Laura of seeing someone, but never pursued it. Sometimes, ignorance *is* bliss."

"I can't imagine knowing your spouse was cheating and not caring," she said shaking her head.

"May have been an open marriage or he simply loved her so much he turned a blind eye."

Anne had a hard time imagining anyone loving Fran.

Gil's cell rang. "Damnation, now what...Collins here." He listened for several seconds. "Okay, I'll be there in fifteen minutes. Any witnesses...Keep 'em separated."

"Trouble?" she asked.

"Armed robbery at a convenience store. Perp shot the clerk. He's on his way to the hospital." He rose, pulled her up with him, and then leaned down to kiss her. "I'll call you tomorrow."

Alone again, Anne poured another glass of wine and resumed her seat on the sofa. What Gil had said about cheating spouses made sense, yet she had trouble believing anybody would condone affairs.

If Kenneth had done that to me, I'd have killed him. Suddenly, she sat up straight. *What if? Oh no, that's a stretch. If George was anywhere near Fran at the meeting, she would have known, said something, introduced him—anything.*

Unless he was wearing a ghost costume.

179

Chapter Eleven

Anne rang the Harrison's doorbell at precisely ten o'clock the following morning. She'd spent most of the night tossing and turning as her newest theory refused to leave her mind. Could George Harrison have killed his wife? Had all those tears been faked? And if he had posed as a *waiter*, why didn't Fran recognize him?

Because Fran wasn't in the room when the waiter served the dishes.

Dumb luck or did he watch as his wife paced in the hallway, slip in, and place the tainted food at her place? And the person who came and went as a ghost from the downstairs restroom was almost certainly female. At least, she thought it was, but with that crummy tape quality, who knew?

Unless, Harrison dressed as the ghost and Wainwright served after all. Or vice versa.

After three cups of coffee, Anne decided the whole concept was too far-fetched to be believable. Perhaps the poor man really was blissfully unaware of his wife's roving eye.

The door opened and she stared at a tall, very thin man staring back at her. It was George Harrison.

She heaved a mental sigh of relief. No way could this man have been the same one seen on the surveillance tapes from the hotel. That image had been of a much heavier person.

"Mr. Harrison, I'm Anne Jamieson—from the Southeast Florida chapter of the Writers Association of America. We spoke briefly at the funeral yesterday."

"Yes, of course, please come in." He stepped aside allowing her to enter. "Thank you so much for the kind words you said about Fran. She was such a loving, giving person."

"Uh, yes, yes she was," she stammered. Fran was anything but that.

"I just don't know what I'm going to do without her." He blinked rapidly. "Pam said something about you needing some papers Fran had regarding the chapter."

"Yes, she gave me almost everything right after the election, but you know how it is with a change in administration—always a few things left undone."

"No problem. I'm sure you can find what you need in her office. She was highly organized." He led her down a hallway and opened a door. "Here it is. Nobody's been inside since… I'll tell Pam you're here. She can help if you need it."

"Thank you."

He hesitated as she entered as though reluctant to leave her alone. "Well, I guess I'll leave you to it. It's time for my morning walk. Take one every day. Sometimes Fran would join me. Excuse me, I'll go get Pam."

Anne's heart went out to him as he left. *Poor man. How could I have ever suspected him of killing his wife? Even though she was a bitch, he loved her.*

She looked around the room. Converted from a bedroom, the spacious area held a large desk, several file cabinets, two bookcases, a sofa, and a couple of end tables. She saw no sign of a computer. *Maybe the police confiscated it.*

Sighing, Anne opened the top drawer in the desk. It contained the usual pads of paper, pens, and sticky notes. The next drawer held reams of copier paper. The bottom one had mailing supplies, although nowadays most authors just e-mailed submissions.

She turned her attention to a file cabinet. The first drawer held personal data like tax returns and business expenses. As much as Anne would have loved to sneak a peek, she refrained. The second drawer possessed much of the same. She quickly moved on to the next cabinet.

Ah, this is more like it. Inside were manila folders dealing with chapter business. She pulled several and set them on the desk. *It'll take forever to go through everything here. I'll take them home, see what I need, and then return the rest.*

"Good morning. I see you're finding things all right."

Anne turned to find Fran's sister, Pam Waters, smiling in the doorway.

"Yes, I think so. It was nice of Mr. Harrison to let me do this so soon after the funeral, but there is some material I need immediately. Same with our new secretary. Fran took over that job when the last secretary moved a couple of months ago."

"Yes, my sister often did other people's jobs."

Anne caught the slightly sarcastic tone and wondered how close Pam and Fran had been.

"Do you need any help?" Pam asked. "Fran kept every slip of paper known to mankind in here. Have you looked in this cabinet?"

Anne nodded. "Yes, it's all personal stuff."

"In that case, let me look in this one over here," she said indicating a three drawer metal cabinet in the corner. "It'll make things go faster. I'm sure you don't want to spend all day sorting through my sister's compulsive habit of hoarding."

What an odd thing to say. Doesn't sound like they got along that well. Maybe I can ask a few discreet questions about Fran and other men.

She cast a glance at Pam. The family resemblance was slight. Fran had been medium height, thin as a reed and had short, light brown hair. Her sister, while the same general size, was heavier and sported much darker, longer hair.

"So, are there any other brothers or sisters in your family?"

"We have a younger brother in California. He and Fran hadn't spoken in close to fifteen years. Fran disapproved of his lifestyle. He's gay."

Startled by such personal information, Anne could only stare. "Oh, I'm sorry—uh, not that he's gay, but that they didn't get along."

"Fran was a hard person to get along with. She always had to have things her way. Made for a lot of friction growing up. I'm younger by two years, so she often made my life a living hell, if you get what I mean."

Why is she telling me this? It's none of my business and I really don't need the details of her childhood.

Pam, however, rambled on. "And God forbid anyone else should have something she wanted. You wouldn't believe how many of my clothes ended up in her closet. Oh, here's something marked "chapter bills" with this year's date."

"Just add it to the stack," Anne said gazing around the room. "I don't see her computer."

"Police took it. Checking e-mails, I guess. They said they'd return it soon. I'll let you know as soon as they do in case anything pertains to your writers group."

She was still uncomfortable with listening to Fran's shortcomings, but determined to probe anyway. *Might as well take advantage of the situation.*

"I appreciate that. Uh, I know what you mean about older sisters getting their own way and such. I have an older sister, too," Anne lied. "She was just a little smarter and a little prettier than me. She never had to lift a finger to get a date—ever. Men just flocked to her. Was Fran that way, too?"

Pam sniffed. "I'll say. Never understood it considering the personality."

"My sister never out-grew her obsession with men. She has three divorces to prove it."

Pam straightened and glanced toward the open doorway before lowering her voice.

"You didn't hear this from me, but Fran was a man eater. She liked nothing better than other women's husbands or boyfriends. Even came after my husband. Jack and I ended up getting a divorce over it." The bitterness in her tone came through loud and clear.

"Oh, I'm so sorry, I didn't mean to open old wounds."

Pam waved a hand and resumed flipping through folders in the bottom drawer of the cabinet. "Not to worry. It was a long time ago, and to be honest, she did me a favor because Jack couldn't stop skirt-chasing either. I guess I shouldn't be saying bad things about the dead, especially my own sister, but it was hard to hear all that praise yesterday at the funeral. Just brought back not so fond memories."

Anne wondered just how much she hated her sister.

"I feel sorry for Mr. Harrison. I mean, he was so heartbroken over Fran's death."

"I could never figure out if he knew about her flings or loved her so much, he ignored the obvious."

Anne looked around the room. "This is a big house. Will George be staying on or selling it? What does he do for a living?"

"He was a CPA for years, but now does the books along with the buying for their antique store. He's also there for all the deliveries to make sure nothing's been damaged in shipment."

"That's right, I remember Fran saying something about owning an antique store. I didn't pay much attention since I'm not into antiques."

"It's called Fran's Fabulous Finds. She also does—did—a brisk online business with old stuff like that. Personally, I never liked that kind of thing either. Oh, George! You scared me. Back from your walk already?"

Anne jerked in surprise. She hadn't heard him at all. How long had he been standing there? And what had he heard?

George stared at her, and then smiled. "Yes, just walked in the door. How's it going? Are you finding what you needed?"

"Yes, thank you."

"Ah, here's a folder that says 'chapter correspondence.'" Pam pulled it out. "And two more titled just 'correspondence.' I'll add them to your pile. George, is there a box in the garage, Ms. Jamieson can put them in?"

"Sure, be back in a jiffy."

Anne closed the drawer in her cabinet. "I think that's it."

"Same here. I hope you've got everything you need. Can I get you something to drink before you leave? Coffee, iced tea, soft drink?"

"Oh, no thank you. I should get home. I've got a lot to do."

George returned carrying a box with a popular wine logo on it. "Here. Will this do?"

"It's fine." She dumped the pulled folders into the box.

"Let me get that for you," Fran's husband said.

After thanking Pam for her help, Anne left with George following.

"I hope you don't take everything Pam says as gospel," he commented. "She had Fran had a grudge match for years. I'm afraid Pam was jealous of her sister most of her life. I guess this is her way of getting even."

So he did overhear some of what was said.

"I understand, but it's really none of my business. Well, thank you for letting me retrieve the files. You've been a great help, and once again, I'm so sorry for your loss."

Anne slid behind the wheel and waved as George headed back into the house.

What an interesting hour. She'd come away with needed files, learned that Fran had likely been having multiple affairs, and that Pam Waters had hated her sister's guts.

Hated enough to kill?

****

Anne picked up lunch at a fast food drive-thru on the way home. By the time she pulled into her driveway, the morning was shot and the afternoon didn't look good either.

She was in the middle of her second taco when her cell rang. Caller ID showed it was Jen.

"Jen, how's your mother?"

"Doing great. She's out of the hospital and coming along so well Dad is ready to take over. I should be home on Friday. My question is what's going on there? Any more about Fran?"

Anne spent the next twenty minutes bringing Jen up to date on events.

"So, Fran was whacked with both peanuts and shellfish? Someone really wanted to make sure she was dead. And you and Nancy found the waiter's body? You guys have been busy. What else have I been missing?"

Anne explained about Jane Whittaker and the problems with the finances.

"Holy crap! Are we broke?"

"No, but Nancy and Mavis Holloway's son think they can straighten it all out.

"Lord, let's hope so. Go on. Any more cheerful news?"

She told Jen about her trip to Fran's house and her conversations with George Harrison and Pam Waters.

"I'd heard whispers about Fran and her affairs," Jen said. "I didn't know about Becky or possibly Terry's husbands being involved, but at the last holiday party she was flirting hot and heavy with Jane Whittaker's spouse. Jane, dolt that she is, laughed it off. I have no clue if anything came of it. I also saw Fran batting her eyelashes at—oh, what's her name, the new board member's husband, too."

"Ellie Campion?" Anne's voice rose in surprise.

"Yeah, I think so. They left the party early. Maybe Ellie didn't appreciate the president of the chapter hitting on her hubby."

"I didn't attend the party. Did you know Fran had an antique store?"

"Yeah, it's over off Main Street in the old part of town. The stuff was nice, but expensive, and Fran refused to dicker on price, the cheap-ass."

"Can you remember when you went there?"

"Hmmm, in the spring, I think. Wouldn't surprise me if she strong-armed friends and relatives to keep the place afloat. Kinda like highway robbery. Any other fun stuff to report?"

"Not yet. Look, Jen, I've got to read those files. Call when you get back in town. We'll all go have lunch."

"Will do."

Anne hung up and dumped her now cold taco into the trash, then headed upstairs with the box of folders. So both Jane and Ellie's husbands had been on Fran's hit list. Ellie hadn't said a thing. And how mad was she?

Mad enough to leave the party early.

And Jane had just laughed? She wasn't the most observant of people. Could she have written it off as a joke or having had one too many?

Or did she laugh to mask a deep-seeded anger?

And had she been angry enough to do something about it?

****

At the end of two hours, Anne was ready to pull her hair out. Fran kept damned near every piece of paper concerning the chapter—most of which was non-essential. So far, the contents were business related, not personal.

She pitched the last folder onto the top of the file cabinet. Gary the Gargoyle stared back at her from his perch on the shelf over it.

"Gary, not only was the late, unlamented Fran a pain in the ass, she was also massively OCD," she told him. The inanimate stone figure's smirk mocked her.

Five folders marked "correspondence" still sat in front of her. The temptation to turn it all over to Rose was strong, but Anne wasn't above being slightly OCD herself. As chapter President, she felt it was her duty to at least scan the stuff.

The first two files contained e-mail hard copies—many with hand written annotations by Fran. Most of her comments were not pleasant, especially if the sender had been critical of the chapter and her running of it.

The next two folders dealt with vendors' correspondence like the hotel where meetings were held and the San Sebastian Inn, scene of the last conference. One letter clearly stated the hotel would not be willing to host another chapter affair anytime soon. Fran's reply was pithy and to the point—the hotel security sucked and the chapter should have a reduction on the bill because of it. On this, Anne agreed. Several letters were exchanged, but in the end, the hotel got their money.

The last folder surprised her. It was personal correspondence, and had obviously been misfiled. While none of her business, she couldn't resist looking at it.

Many dealt with the antique store. Fran leased out space to various other dealers—at an exorbitant price. She required a year's commitment from the seller and treated the contract like that of an apartment—the first and last month's rent up front. A couple of letters were downright nasty concerning Fran's business practices. Apparently as store owner, Fran had also taken a twenty percent cut of anything sold. One unhappy vendor accused her of pushing one dealer over another. Fran's reply had been sarcastic and rude, in the category of prove-it-if-you-can.

The ghost at the meeting popped into Anne's head. Could it have been someone from outside the chapter? Someone Fran had swindled? But would that person have known about her allergies? Or about where and when the meeting took place?

They would if they were also a writer—or a critique partner. Perhaps even a chapter member. It was something to think about.

Also in the folder were long lists of items from all over the country. *New stock, no doubt, bought by George Harrison.* She wondered if he'd take over the store now.

The last item in the folder gave Anne the answer to one mystery—why Fran needed three grand.

It was an invoice, dated the end of May, from a lawyer delineating the initial cost of his services. Attached was a business card of a private investigator.

She recognized the law firm. They specialized in divorce.

****

After dinner, Anne sat at the kitchen table with a notebook. The kids were upstairs finishing homework or messing around with computer games. She picked up a pen, sipped from a glass of white wine, and settled into the chair.

Time to make a list of suspects.

At the top she simply wrote "the ghost." Underneath that she added the names of Becky Lawrence, Terry Whiting, and just to be thorough, George Harrison.

She also made a notation of "vendor from antique store" at the bottom. She'd go to the store and ask around as soon as possible.

Anne included the names of Jane Whittaker, Barb Hamilton, and Ellie Campion to the list. None sounded remotely capable of pulling off Fran's murder.

Fran's critique partners were next. For all she knew, Fran had been hitting on their husbands, too.

She also added "wait staff" to the list. Any one of them could have doctored Fran's food, but how they'd know about the allergy was still a mystery. The surveillance tape, however, rather ruled out that theory. Plus, Jeffrey Wainwright, the waiter, was very dead. She had no clue if the deaths were related.

By the time she finished, Anne had a column of names, a column of motives, and absolutely no connection between any of them.

She shoved the notebook aside and polished off her wine. *That was a useless endeavor. I'm no closer to figuring this out than I was when it happened. I need to take a look at Fran's Fabulous Finds.*

Anne headed upstairs to her office. She hadn't even bothered to check her e-mail today—not that she wanted to. Everyone in the chapter had an opinion about everything and had no problem with telling her. Some ideas made sense. Others were sheer nonsense. And what was worse, all deserved a reply.

Anne pulled up her e-mail. Luckily, only the Southeast Florida chapter digest had any she needed to answer.

After an hour, the list was whittled down to only four. The next one she opened, however, sent a chill up her spine.

I guess the note on your windshield didn't get through to you. STOP INVESTIGATING FRAN'S DEATH!!! What does it matter if she was murdered? She's dead and that's what counts. Butt out or you'll regret it!

Anne sucked in a deep breath and looked at the sender's name—"joeblow" from a popular e-mail provider. She clicked on the name. Four items appeared: copy address, new message, search for messages from…, and add to contacts.

Well, that's a lot of help. Then a thought occurred. *What if this is Susan? Sounds like something she'd do out of spite. I wonder if she's also responsible for the note. She could be more than just paranoid—maybe borderline total whacko.*

Anne didn't want to deal with her, but rather than delete the message, she saved it. She tapped her fingers on her desk. She'd call Gil first thing in the morning.

Anne finally drifted off to sleep only to dream of tripping over bodies while walking through an antique store with Fran, Becky, Terry, and Jeffrey Wainwright.

****

Gil arrived shortly after the kids left for school. He frowned at the e-mail message. "And you say you also got an anonymous note?"

Anne handed it to him. "It was tucked under my windshield wiper while I was at the grocery store last week."

"Why didn't you tell me right away?"

"I should have, but things piled up and I forgot. It seemed kind of childish to me." She told him of her suspicions the writer and sender of the e-mail was Susan Lynch.

"I don't care who it was, they followed you."

"That creeped me out, too. I couldn't get any info from the e-mail address."

"Doesn't take a Rhodes scholar to set up a dummy e-mail address. Anything else I should know about?"

She didn't like his sarcastic tone, but let it go. Besides, she kind of deserved it. She told him about the personal correspondence that she accidentally picked up at Fran's.

"She had an antique business downtown. The folder contained invoices, letters, and lists of merchandise. I was going to return it to her husband. Plus I found an invoice from a law firm whose specialty is divorce. There was also a business card from a private investigator attached to the invoice."

Gil frowned. "Who was it?"

"I can't remember offhand. I just glanced at it. Why?"

"Some attorneys hire PIs to look into things for clients. The investigator bills through the lawyers. Are the letter and the card in the file?"

Anne bit her lip. "No, since it was in her personal correspondence, I set it aside. I didn't want to return it to her husband. Fran was dead and he was pretty broken up about it. Why destroy his illusions at this point?"

"Let me have the file and the invoice. I'll take a quick look and see if there's anything of a suspicious nature."

"Is that legal?"

He shrugged. "I may not be able to use anything I find, but it'll give me an insight to look into her personal affairs."

"Affairs being the operative word here. Fran played around a lot."

She ran upstairs and returned with the business folder and the letter.

Gil glanced at the latter with a frown. "This puts a whole new light on things. I'll contact the attorneys and the PI, see if they can give me anything."

"I thought there was a confidentiality thing with them."

"There is, but since the lady in question is dead, the PI might divulge some information."

She told him about the harsh words between Fran and some of her leaseholders.

"We'll check on it."

Anne hesitated. "Actually, I was going to go to the antique store and ask a few questions. I mean, Fran had to have an assistant to cover days she wasn't there."

Gil's eyebrows rose. "You get an anonymous note and a threatening e-mail and you're going to ask questions? I really wish you wouldn't."

"I'll be fine. I'll nose around the store, make a few

comments, and listen. It's not like I'm skulking in the shadows and eavesdropping."

"Annie…"

"Gil…"

He threw his hands up in the air. "All right. I couldn't stop you anyway, but for the love of God…"

"I know…Be careful," she finished for him. "Any news on who killed Jeffrey Wainwright?"

"Not yet."

"Do you think it's connected to Fran?"

"Maybe."

She heaved an exasperated sigh. "Is 'maybe' the only thing you can say?"

He shrugged as his lips curved into a small smile. "Maybe."

"Oooo, men! Dinner tomorrow night?"

The smile turned into a chuckle. "Let's go out. Thai all right with you?"

"Sounds wonderful."

After Gil left, Anne tried to put the pieces of the puzzle together. On the surface, Wainwright's murder and that of Fran had no connection. Yet her intuition told her otherwise. Now if only she could figure out how they connected.

And what about Becky and Terry? They had the motive, but not the means or the opportunity. Unless one or the other was the ghost, which meant they had the opportunity. But the means? Did either of them know about Fran's allergies? And how could she ask them such a question?

But first she needed to go to Fran's shop.

If nothing else, the threatening notes said someone was nervous.

Chapter Twelve

A little bell tinkled above Anne's head as she pushed open the door to Fran's Fabulous Finds. To her right was a large counter with a computerized cash register, several business card holders, and free notepads bearing the name of the shop. They reminded her of the kind of freebies set out on tables at conferences. Behind the counter sat stacks of boxes and bags in varying sizes along with reams of tissue paper.

A short woman with gray hair and wearing glasses glanced up from rearranging items in a display case filled with jewelry.

"Good morning, how may I help you? Are you looking for something specific?" she asked.

"Oh, no," Anne replied. "I've never been in before and just thought I'd look around."

"Be my guest. All booths with a number are leased by other dealers. If you find something you like, just let me know. Many of the vendors will negotiate on price. Everything else is store owned by the proprietor and the price is usually firm."

Anne thanked the woman and turned to the left. It didn't take long for her to discover the aisles were cleverly set up in a maze that directed the customer to the larger, more expensive items like furniture, paintings, and silver up front.

The farther she walked, the smaller the items and

prices. She rounded a corner and stopped to admire a quilt draped over a quilt stand. Three large armoires formed a wall between the next stall. Two hutches formed the remaining two walls making a cozy area. The hutches contained china figurines. A small needlepoint boudoir chair invited the customer to have a seat, pick up the old book on the table next to it, and read. She sat and closed her eyes, easily envisioning a late Victorian lady indulging in a leisurely moment.

The effect was spoiled by a door opening nearby and the sound of voices.

"I suggest you go home and try to calm down," a man's voice said in a stern tone.

"Oh God, I wish I'd never said anything!" a woman replied, her high-pitched voice shaky.

"But you did. Now go home and don't contact me again. Understand?"

The rush of feet down an aisle told Anne the woman was leaving. She rose, but the configuration of the booth prevented her from seeing who spoke. By the time she made her way out into the next aisle the bell over the door jingled lightly. The woman was gone.

She rounded another corner in the maze of aisles. To her right was a partially open door with a plaque on it that said, "Office." Anne stopped to listen as the man was now obviously talking on the phone.

"Yes, that's right, I'll be taking over the business. I'm sure you'll find the transactions much smoother… What do you mean? It'll be business as usual, of course. We can double the shipments and as soon as these leases run out we can add more merchandise that's ours alone… I'll hire someone I trust to deal with customers and our commodities. Don't worry, I've got this all figured out. We'll be making more money than ever before. Now, I'm going to start taking inventory. I'll be in touch."

Anne whipped back around the corner when conversation ended, and then turned as the man exited the office. He stopped to stare.

"Oh, Mr. Harrison, how are you?"

"Mrs. Jamieson," he replied with a wary glance around the aisle. "What are you doing here?"

"Just having a look around. I had forgotten Fran ran an antique store until yesterday when your sister-in-law mentioned it. I must say, there are some lovely items here at very reasonable prices," she chattered.

"Yes, there are." His facial expression bordered on glacial.

Anne looked up and down the aisle. "I have to admit, though, I'm a bit lost. These aisles remind me of a maze."

"That was Fran's idea to keep customers in the store longer. The longer they're here, the more likely they are to buy."

Almost like holding them for ransom until they did.

"Yes, I can understand that. Could you possibly steer me in the right direction to the counter?"

"Follow me. I was just on my way out."

Anne trailed him through twists and turns until finally coming out near the front door.

"Thank you so much," she said in what she hoped was a calm tone. Getting caught eavesdropping made her nervous.

"Are you leaving now?" he asked.

"In a moment, I want to just look at the jewelry. Please, don't let me keep you."

He nodded, and then looked at the clerk. "I have some errands to run, Miriam. Should be back by two o'clock."

"Yes, sir." The woman turned her attention back to Anne. "What can I show you? We have some lovely filigree rings, bracelets, and brooches in sterling silver and eighteen carat gold."

"I'll just look through the glass if I may." She peered at several items on the top shelf. "What a lovely ring. Is that a real diamond?"

Miriam removed the ring and set it on a black velvet pad. "Yes. It's small—only about a quarter-carat, but the workmanship is exquisite."

Anne asked to see several items, and while the prices were high, the merchandise was first class. She requested a price on an Art Deco silver cuff bracelet. Two hundred dollars was a lot, but the symmetrical design done in marcasite made it hard to refuse. She offered a hundred and fifty.

"Well, this is a store owned item, so I really shouldn't, but Mr. Harrison told me this morning that he wanted to move items, so I guess it's all right."

They dickered for several minutes before settling on a hundred and seventy-five. Ann flipped out her credit card.

"It was so sad about Mrs. Harrison," she said as the clerk rang up the sale, wrapped the bracelet in tissue paper, and put it in a small bag. "Had you worked for her long?"

"About three years. She was exacting, but always dealt fairly with me."

"Well, Fran believed in speaking her mind."

"That she did," Miriam replied in a dry tone. "I

take it you knew her."

"Yes, she and I go way back. I suppose Mr. Harrison will be taking over now."

"That's the impression I got, although today was the first day since his wife's death that he's been in."

"He always struck me as kind of a cold, standoffish person."

"To be honest, he was rarely in here unless a shipment of new merchandise had arrived. He'd stay in the back with the items to make sure they hadn't suffered any damage during transport. He didn't often say much other than hello."

Anne looked at her watch. "I must be going. Oh, a little while ago, I saw a lady hurry out. I only glimpsed her from the back, but she looked like a friend of mine. Do you know who she was?"

"Can't say that I do. She was in a couple of times to talk privately with Mrs. Harrison. I don't know what they talked about, but the woman always left in a huff or on the verge of tears. I think she may have been a former vendor who felt the store owed her money."

"I see. Well, thank you for your time. I'll be back."

Anne walked slowly to her car. The woman's voice had sounded vaguely familiar, but she couldn't pin it down. *Or maybe I just think it sounded that way.*

And her encounter with George had been uncomfortable. She suspected he knew she'd overheard his phone conversation and wasn't too happy about it. *He certainly isn't shedding any tears over Fran today. Or maybe just trying to move on.*

She was just sliding behind the steering wheel when her phone rang. Caller ID showed it was Rose.

"Hey, girl, what's up?"

"I know this is short notice, but Nancy's here and we wondered if you'd like to come by for lunch—nothing fancy, just sandwiches."

"I can do that. I've also got those correspondence files I picked up at Fran's in the car. "

"Oh, good. We were talking about the chapter and have some ideas for future meetings."

"Would you like me to bring anything?"

"No, that's all right. Come on over."

Anne hung up and headed for Rose's. Ten minutes later she pulled into the driveway behind Nancy's car.

Nancy answered the door. "Rose is in the kitchen. How was your morning?"

"Very interesting," she replied heading for the back of the house. Once there, she told them of her experience at Fran's shop.

"Doesn't appear you learned much of anything," Nancy commented.

"Other than the fact Fran's husband is taking over the business. Sounds as if Fran had him relegated to a minor role—you know, buying merchandise, unpacking it, that sort of thing," Rose said.

She also told them about the anonymous note and e-mail along with her suspicions of the sender.

Rose snorted. "I can see Susan doing something like that."

Nancy shook her head. "I don't know. If she was going to threaten you even in a minor way, she'd do it to your face. Anonymity isn't her style."

"You could be right, but I can't think of anyone else who'd be so threatening. Typical passive aggressive behavior—manipulate from a distance," Anne replied.

They discussed chapter business over lunch, coming away with some good ideas. Anne closed the small notebook she carried everywhere and shoved it into her purse.

"I'm glad we had this little get together. Rose, I like your idea of holding a workshop after meetings. A simple hour-long interactive session would help new writers tremendously."

"And the extra ten dollars a person won't do the treasury any harm either, considering the circumstances," Nancy added.

Rose opened her mouth to reply when her phone rang. She answered as she walked into the dining room.

"My God, is she going to be all right?" Several long seconds went past as Rose listened. "We had no idea she'd react like this. I mean nobody knows why she resigned... Yes, I'll tell Anne. Thanks, Ellie."

"What was that all about?" Nancy asked.

"That was Ellie Campion. It seems Jane Whittaker tried to commit suicide."

"What!" Anne and Nancy exclaimed simultaneously.

"Ellie had called about an hour or so earlier asking Jane for some things regarding the chapter. Jane told her she was out, but would be back by eleven. When Ellie got there the front door was ajar, so she walked in and found Jane on the kitchen floor with a bottle of pills of some sort scattered all over the floor."

"Good God, I hope this hasn't got anything to do with her resignation," Anne said.

"Me, too."

"How do they know it was suicide? She could have had a reaction to medication or something," Nancy commented with a frown.

"According to Ellie, she left a note. Ellie said she called 9-1-1 immediately."

"Lord above! What did Jane have that Ellie would need?" Nancy asked.

"I have no idea," Anne replied. "Is Jane going to be all right?"

Rose nodded. "Ellie apparently got there not long after she took them."

Anne shook her head. She knew Jane had been upset over the resignation and the irregularities in the books, but suicide? No one outside of the board knew the truth.

She followed Rose and Nancy back to the kitchen when a thought struck her. The woman's voice, even thought high-pitched and clogged with unshed tears, in Fran's store had sounded familiar.

Good God, could it have been Jane? And what had she said that caused her to be so sorry now? And why was George so cold and almost angry?

Rose's eyebrows drew together. "I can't believe it. "She didn't do anything bad enough to warrant this."

"Guilty conscience, maybe?" Nancy said.

Anne shook her head. "I'll swing by the hospital on my way home," Anne replied. "I feel just awful that my demand she resign could have led to this."

Nancy waved her hand in dismissal. "Don't beat yourself up over it. It's not your fault."

"I think I'll give Ellie a call. See if she has any more details." Anne pulled out her cell, scrolled down her directory, and then dialed. It rang three times before Ellie answered.

"Ellie, it's Anne. I just heard about Jane. What the

hell happened?"

"Oh, God, it was awful. I'd gone over to pick up some information about critique groups. She used to be in charge of them, remember?" Ellie gave her the same info Rose has passed along. "I could see she was alive, so I called 9-1-1. Hope you're not upset that I called Rose and not you, but her name pops up in my directory first. I was kind of rattled."

Anne jumped in when Ellie paused for breath. "Good grief, don't worry about that. Did Jane say anything?"

"Not really. She was mumbling between moans. Something about secrets always get out and humiliation. Didn't make much sense to me. I followed the ambulance to the hospital. She's up in ICU."

"Rose said something about a note?"

"It was on the island. Just said she was sorry for everything."

"Thanks, Ellie. Don't say anything about this to anyone else, okay? I'm sure Jane wouldn't want to be the object of speculation from other chapter members."

"My lips are sealed. Promise."

"Are you still at the hospital?"

"No. Her husband and a couple of other people were there, so I came home."

"I think I'll stop by and try to see her."

Anne hung up and relayed more of the story as per Ellie.

"Lord, what a turn of events," Rose said.

"Wonder what kind of pills they were," Nancy asked. "If they'd been sleeping pills, she'd have most likely been in the bedroom."

Anne shuddered. "Well, whatever they were, they

didn't have much time to act. She may have gotten dizzy and fallen. The hospital's not far out of my way. I'll drop by on my way home."

"If she's in ICU, visitors will be restricted," Rose replied. "Assuming, of course, she's still in ICU. This happened several hours ago, so they pumped her stomach immediately. She may be in the psych ward under suicide watch or something."

"I can almost guarantee she is and will be for at least three or four days," Nancy replied. "Maybe released to a mental health facility for a few weeks after that depending on her state of mind."

"I'll give it a shot," Anne said slinging her bag over her shoulder. "See you all later."

The hospital parking lot was almost full, but she finally found a spot not far from the main entrance. A ledger board in the central hallway showed the Intensive Care Unit was on the third floor. Anne made her way to the reception desk.

"Hello, I was wondering if I could see Jane Whittaker."

The receptionist consulted her computer. "I'm sorry, but she's not allowed any visitors except immediate family."

"I see. Would you know if any of the family is here at the moment?"

"You might check in the waiting room."

"Thank you."

Anne made her was down a hallway to a large room with comfortable chairs. She glanced around at the dozen or so people present before seeing a man who fidgeted in his chair and kept glancing at his watch. She walked over.

"Excuse me, but are you here for Jane Whittaker?"

The man looked up from his book. "Yes, I am. I'm Bill Whittaker, Jane's husband."

"I'm Anne Jamieson, the chapter president of Southeast Florida Writers Association. I can't begin to tell you how sorry and shocked I am at this."

He indicated she should sit in the chair next to him. "Aren't we all? Thank God her friend didn't just walk away. I should have seen this coming. She was terribly upset at what happened with the chapter."

Anne sat. "Yes, I know, and I feel badly."

He shook his head. "No need. What she did was highly irregular. I don't mean to speak ill of the dead, but that Fran woman was a tyrant. Bullied Jane. Jane didn't have the expertise to be treasurer and relied on her way too much."

"I suppose she thought the president would have more knowledge about how things worked," Anne replies as diplomatically as possible. "Still, I didn't expect something like this."

"Neither did I. She was very upset last night by a phone call. Said she'd go see whoever had called in the morning."

That coincides with what Ellie told Rose about Jane not being at home when she'd called.

"Have you talked to her since they brought her in?"

"Just a little. They pumped her stomach so she was pretty groggy. Said she was sorry, it was a stupid thing to do, but she didn't think she could take the humiliation. Luckily, she only took about four or five anti-depressants before the effects made her dizzy and she hit the floor."

Anne rose. "Well, please tell Jane the board is

thinking of her and wishing her a speedy recovery. And tell her that neither this news nor the information regarding her resignation will be made public for any reason."

"Thank you. I appreciate that."

Back in her car, she tapped her fingers on the steering wheel. So Jane had a call last night that upset her. She must have confronted the caller this morning, not gotten a good answer, and flipped out.

I wonder if her caller was George Harrison.

****

Anne was putting the finishing touches on her make-up for her dinner out with Gil when Rose called.

"Did you read the stuff in these files?" she asked.

"Some. Fran kept every scrap of paper that came her way and then some. I didn't have time to go through it all. Why?"

"Most of it is pretty cut and dried, but then I got to the letters and e-mails concerning the conference."

Anne stopped applying eye shadow. "Anything unusual?"

"Well, for starters, there are several e-mails from various agents and editors stating they would not be returning to another conference due to the lack of security at the hotel."

"That's not surprising. I'd heard those comments before the conference had even ended."

"Then I came across more e-mails from attendees demanding a full refund, including expenses of getting there. Some claimed they were traumatized by the murders. Others said the deaths of two agents had robbed them—meaning the attendees—of a chance to submit their work, thereby suggesting the chapter was perpetrating a fraud. One even threatened legal action if she wasn't repaid."

"Any idea how Fran responded?"

"She apparently sent out a form e-mail saying the hotel was responsible for security, and that the chapter was sorry some attendees felt traumatized, but once again it was a situation beyond our control. Then she said that all material requested by Carmella and Alan was being forwarded to other agents within those agencies, so their work was being seen. No fraud was involved."

"Sounds like she was covering the chapter's ass pretty well," Anne said returning to her make-up.

"There were also some personal things at the back of the folder."

"Personal?"

"From what I can gather, she and Terry Whiting exchanged more than a few heated e-mails each blaming the other for a lousy conference."

"That's not fair. It wasn't anybody's fault two murders occurred—well, other than the murderer's."

"She also got e-mails from chapter members complaining of her tactics on running the chapter. I don't know if she answered directly, but you should see some of the handwritten comments she made on the hard copies. Not nice at all. But there was one I found very interesting."

"Interesting how?"

"It was from Wendy Travers, the person in charge of the editors and agents. It wasn't addressed to Fran, but to Jane Whittaker. In it she suggests that Fran submitted fraudulent receipts and invoices for the conference and for chapter business. She asked Jane to verify if all those things were legit. I can only assume Jane either forwarded the message or printed it out and gave it to Fran. There's no sign if Fran answered or not."

"You think Fran may have been embezzling from the chapter?" she asked remembering Nancy's comments about random checks made out to cash.

"I have no idea, but I think it might be a good idea to let Nancy see if she can find anything in the Treasurer's files."

"Oh, brother, this is getting worse and worse. Poor Jane, if Fran told her to do something, she did it. I wonder if that's what caused her to try to kill herself."

"Did you see her at the hospital?"

"No, but I talked to her husband. He said she was upset by a phone call last night and was going to see the caller this morning. He didn't know who it was. She's going to be all right, but still..." Anne's voice trailed off.

"So, do I keep the nasty stuff in a separate file?"

"Do we have to keep all of that?" Anne asked.

"I don't think so, but..." Rose paused.

"But what?"

"She exchanged e-mails with board members after the election trying to get them to go along with her and declare it fraudulent."

"And?"

"Well, the exchanges are all on one big e-mail, nobody bothered to truncate it, but Madge Conway, the other secretary candidate, was the only one to agree with her. Jane was noncommittal as usual, Ellie said no, but Kathy Samuels told her in no uncertain terms to get over it, to which Fran replied—and I quote—'I will remember this. You should have more loyalty to me and to the chapter. Anne Jamieson is a troublemaker and her involvement in the murder of Dorie Powell shows she has no business even being in the chapter. I suggest you rethink my suggestion of declaring the election null and void. It only takes three of us. I can talk Jane into it.' Kathy replied no again. Then Fran calls her a disloyal bitch."

"I don't think we need to keep that in the files. It's petty and does no one any good."

"I agree."

Anne swiped her lipstick over her lips. "Besides, I don't think that part about only three board members need to declare the election void is right. The rank and file membership would also have to okay it."

"You're probably right. And this from a president who made herself secretary last year when the woman who held the position moved."

"She sure didn't follow the by-laws, did she? Keep what you think is relevant and dump the rest."

"Will do. Have a good evening."

She laughed. "I intend to. Gil and I are going out to dinner."

Rose hung up with a chuckle.

Anne rose, smoothed a hand over her hair, and headed downstairs. *Is there no one whom Fran didn't insult or piss off?*

Gil arrived as she hit the foyer. He whistled when he saw her.

Suppressing a giggle, she twirled allowing the full skirt to billow. "I felt like dressing up tonight. I've been thinking about Thai food all day."

"Well, in that case, let's not linger." He smiled,

crooked his elbow, and tucked her hand in the bend.

"So, how was your day?" she asked as they drove to the restaurant. "Did you find out anything from the file I gave you?"

"Some. The store's finances are in good shape. The Harrisons cleared in the high five figures a year in sales from it."

"Fran's sister said George used to be a CPA, but now does the buying for the shop." She paused. "Come to think of it, they lived very well for income from an antique store. I guess her husband did well in the accounting business."

"This is just preliminary. I'll dig deeper if I have to."

Gil swung into the parking lot of Thai-Thai, a popular restaurant not far from the beach. They were seated immediately. After ordering wine, they read the menu before deciding on chicken with spring vegetables for her and chicken in red curry sauce for him—both dishes Thai hot.

When their drinks arrived, Anne told Gil about her day at the antique store, Jane's attempted suicide, and her talk with Jane's husband at the hospital.

"And you think Ms. Whittaker was the woman you overheard in the shop?"

"I'm not sure, but it makes sense."

"How?" Gil asked.

"Maybe Jane went there to ask George to put the money Fran borrowed back in the chapter's account and he told her no."

"But she'd already resigned, so what would be the point?"

"I don't know, maybe to help repair her reputation

and avoid possible criminal charges." She sighed heavily and leaned back. "Yet, her husband said she'd had a phone call last night that upset her and she planned on talking to that person this morning."

"And you think that person was George Harrison?"

She heaved another sigh as the waiter served their food. "What I can't figure out is why Fran's husband would call Jane with something that upset her. Unless, of course, the caller was someone else and she saw them first, and then went to the store to ask for the money."

"What was the woman's demeanor in the shop?" Gil asked as he dug into his curry.

Anne took a bite of her super-spicy chicken and let the heat roll around on her tongue before answering.

"Her voice was kind of high-pitched, and she was on the verge of tears—you know that sound; kind of a breathless, slightly gasping quality."

"My guess is Ms. Whittaker was not in the shop. You heard someone else."

"And did the conversation have anything to do with Fran?" she mused. "For all I know it was a vendor."

"Don't see things that aren't there," he warned.

The waiter stopped by and they asked for refills on their wine. The drinks arrived and for a few minutes they concentrated on the food.

"So, did you talk to the lawyer and private investigator?" she asked when she finished her meal.

"Attorney hasn't gotten back with me yet, but the PI called late this afternoon."

"Did he have anything important to say? I'm curious. Fran contacting a divorce attorney looks like trouble for George."

"The law firm of Crocker, Ryan, and Montgomery not only litigates divorces, but other things as well. They just settled a big case out of court concerning fraudulent advertising. A well-known car dealership was forced to cough up a bundle. Seems their used cars weren't quite what had been advertised or represented to buyers."

"What did the PI have to say?"

Gil looked her straight in the eyes. "He spoke in generalities, but the gist of it was he was asked to investigate certain offshore banks in the Bahamas, Panama, and the Cayman Islands—by Fran Harrison."

Chapter Thirteen

"Offshore banks? That's where criminals hide their ill-gotten gains," Anne said thinking of Isadora Powell.

"Not necessarily," Gil replied taking a sip of his wine. "Sometimes people are considering a move to a foreign country and want some insight into the banking system. It helps if there's easy access to banks here in the States."

"But I never even heard a whisper that Fran and her husband were thinking of moving out of the country."

"Maybe she never discussed it with anybody other than her husband."

"Or maybe she didn't plan on including George in the move." Anne sipped from her wine glass. "But why go through an attorney to hire a private investigator? Why hire a PI for that matter? Just get online and Google what you need to know."

Gil smiled. "You are beginning to think like a cop, my love. The same question popped into my head, too."

She swirled the wine in her glass and thought. Something didn't sound right.

"It doesn't make sense. Fran was a logical person and a good businesswoman—greedy, but good. And why borrow three grand from the chapter to cover the cost of the investigator? Unless..." she interrupted herself to stare at Gil.

"Go on, keep working on it."

"Unless, she didn't want her husband to know what she was up to."

"If you ever want to quit writing and become a detective, let me know." He leaned forward. "I've already requested more financial and phone records. Plus, I think it's time to have another talk with Mr. Harrison. I'm meeting him tomorrow morning at Fran's Fabulous Finds. And before you ask, no you can't go."

"I wasn't planning on asking. Besides, he wouldn't say anything important with me around anyway. Probably won't say anything important to you either. I wonder if Fran was thinking of taking off with another man. The question is, did good old George know or suspect anything? If he did, that makes for one hell of a motive, plus he put on one smashing performance at the funeral. No, I think I need to dig deeper into these rumors of Fran's numerous affairs."

"Be discreet."

"I'm always discreet." She ignored him rolling his eyes and continued. "Jen is a fountain of information regarding rumors. She's due back tomorrow. I'll see what else she may have heard. In the meantime, I'll make a list of members whom Fran may or may not have wronged." She shot Gil a keen glance. "The family is usually at the top of the suspect list with something like this. How about George Harrison? Are you investigating him?"

"We are. He claims to have been at home all morning working on spreadsheets concerning store inventory and expected shipments."

"So nobody can verify that."

"We could always get a warrant to look at his

computer, but as of now, there's no probable cause. And we still have no motive as to why he'd want his wife dead."

"Unless like I said, he got wind of her actions about the banks. Perhaps he discovered her affairs. And maybe those attorneys were gearing up for a divorce."

"Let's see what the attorney has to say when he calls me back. I may be able to persuade them to divulge information."

"Gil, I never noticed, but what was the date on that invoice from the attorneys?"

"May sometime. Not sure of the exact date."

"And Fran borrowed three thousand dollars from Beth Whisnant in May. Oh, boy."

The waiter stepped up to the table casting a glance at their empty plates.

"May I get you some coffee or dessert?"

"Anne?"

She shook her head.

"No, thank you. Just the check."

The server removed the dishes and returned a minute later with the bill. Gil added the tip, refigured the bill, and tucked his credit card into a slot in the folder.

"Let me know what you find out from the so-called wronged women," he said as the waiter disappeared. "However, I do think this is deeper than a love triangle. Something else is going on. And I have a feeling the answer lies in the financial statements."

"Anything more on the dead waiter?"

He shook his head. "The surveillance cameras are set up on the corners of the buildings and near the outside stairwell entrances. Some of them even work.

The witness's statement is corroborated. A guy wearing a hoodie and a baseball cap pulled low, comes around the corner, meets Wainwright, and they go up the stairs at nine-thirty. He's carrying what looks like a small brown paper bag. The clothes are loose-fitting and conceal weight. Although he looks to be on the tall side, he walks bent over in an attempt to disguise his height. He comes out again at eleven-thirty—minus the bag and moving fast. The camera just catches him getting into Wainwright's car and driving off."

"So, he's the killer. The drugs may be in the bag he's carrying. They—or maybe just Wainwright—take a hit or two of weed or coke. The bag is either in the trash or his pocket when he leaves. Does that sound logical?"

"As logical as anything else about this, especially if he was Wainwright's supplier. It may have been a routine they followed. And there was no brown paper bag in the trash."

"But why kill him?" Anne asked.

"Maybe he owed money to the seller or he talked too much in public about his connection."

"Do you think it's in any way connected to Fran's death?"

Gil shook his head. "Hard to say, but I don't like coincidences."

"And why take a dead man's car? Where's his?"

"He's first seen on another surveillance camera coming across the lot from the direction of a house next door. We checked. That house has been unoccupied for months. He could have been a squatter, but that's very convenient, and like I said, I don't like coincidences."

The server returned with the finalized bill, wishing

them a good night.

"Nightcap?" Anne asked as they pulled into her driveway.

Gil shook his head. "Not tonight. I have some paperwork at the station that needs to be cleared up before I have my chat with Mr. Harrison tomorrow at ten. I'll call you in the afternoon."

He walked her to the door, gave her a toe-curling kiss, and waited until she was inside before driving away.

She leaned back against the door and sighed, then pushed herself upright. *Time to start another list of suspects.*

Upstairs, she checked on Ken and Lisa. Ken barely looked up from his computer game, but said his homework was done. Lisa replied the same as she watched some reality show on her TV.

Satisfied, Anne pulled out the chair at her desk in the office and started the list of possible Fran-the-man-eater haters. She hoped the pen didn't run out of ink.

****

Anne sat in a silent kitchen sipping her third cup of coffee and reading the list she'd compiled the night before. Nothing new jumped out at her. She sighed. Why can't things ever work out to a logical conclusion the first time?

Her cell ringing interrupted her thoughts.

"Hello?"

"Uh, is this Anne Jamieson?" a hesitant male voice asked.

"Yes, it is."

"Oh, good. This is Bill Whittaker, Jane's husband. We spoke yesterday at the hospital."

"Yes, Mr. Whittaker, how's Jane?"

"Doing much better, thank you. She's been transferred to a private room in the...that is in another wing of the hospital."

He didn't need to mention the words "psych ward." She assumed that was standard operating procedure for attempted suicides.

"I'm so glad to hear that. Is there anything I can do for you?"

"Actually, yes there is. Jane would like to speak with you whenever you have the time. The doctors have cleared her for limited visitation. Would...would you have time today?"

"Yes, of course."

He heaved a sigh. "Oh, thank you. She's very anxious to talk to you. How about you drop by around one this afternoon?"

"One is fine."

"She's in room 312 of the psychiatric wing. Just go on up and check in with the receptionist. I'll see to it your name is on the list of approved visitors."

"I'll see you then."

She hung up wondering what Jane could possibly have to say that necessitated an immediate audience.

****

"You will have exactly fifteen minutes to talk with Ms. Whitaker," the receptionist at the entrance to the psychiatric wing told Anne. "Her doctors want her to remain as calm as possible for the next couple of days."

"I understand," Anne replied.

"I'll let you in through the double doors. The check-in desk is just down the hallway."

Anne nodded and stepped away toward the large

steel doors with the thick and what she assumed was bulletproof glass windows. As she approached, they swished open, no doubt activated by a button at the reception desk.

"May I help you?" a nurse at check-in asked.

"Yes, my name is Anne Jamieson and I'm here to see Jane Whittaker. I believe her husband, Bill, has put me on a list of some kind for visitors."

The nurse gazed at her computer screen and scrolled. "Yes, ma'am, I see your name here. Please be seated in the waiting room. Someone will be with you in a moment."

Anne turned and walked twenty feet down a corridor into a large area. Several people sat on sofas and in chairs reading magazines or books. She took a seat and tried not to stare. Bill Whittaker was not in attendance, but she supposed he may have been with Jane.

Ten minutes later, a nurse walked in and scanned the group. "Anne Jamieson?"

Anne rose. "Yes, I'm Anne Jamieson."

"Please follow me."

She trailed the woman down another corridor and turned right before stopping at room 312.

"I'll be back in fifteen minutes."

"Thank you." Anne took a deep breath, knocked, and opened the door.

The room looked like any other hospital room if you ignored the bars on the window. Jane lay in the bed with the head propping her up in a semi-sitting position. The television was tuned to some old comedy show. Jane ignored it and picked at the blanket covering her. She looked up when Anne entered. Her face was pale and pinched looking.

"Anne, I'm so glad to see you. Please sit down."

She pulled a chair up to the side of the bed. "I'm glad I could come. I hope you're feeling better."

Jane attempted a smile. "Taking a bunch of pills was such a stupid thing to do, but I was so upset and so afraid."

"About what? Hon, no one on the board would *ever* reveal the reason for your resignation."

"I know that. No, I was angry with and afraid of Susan."

"Susan? Susan Lynch? Whatever for?"

Jane sighed and turned her head to gaze out of the barred window in silence. The quiet lasted almost a full minute before she answered in a low tone. "Susan knew about the loan to Fran."

Anne sucked in her breath in astonishment. "What? How? Did Fran actually tell her?"

"No. Remember when I told you I asked Fran to replace the money immediately after the election? Well, I'd pulled her into an empty meeting room to discuss the situation. Apparently, Susan saw us enter. I thought I'd closed the door, but guess I didn't. Susan eavesdropped." She swung her gaze back to Anne. "You're going to have real trouble with Susan."

"How?" Anne had no problem seeing the paranoid Susan listening in on a private conversation. She dismissed the fact *she* had done the same yesterday.

"I know she's been banned from the chapter loop for a while, but she's making phone calls trying to drum up support for a recall election."

"That'll never fly."

"I told her that when she called me the other night.

Then she told me she knew the things Fran and I had done. She insisted I come to her house the next morning to discuss the matter."

"Discuss the matter?" she prompted when her friend hesitated.

Once again silence reigned as Jane seemed to gather her thoughts. "I got there around ten-forty-five. It was short and not so sweet. She said if I didn't support her recall bid and her campaign to be your replacement, she'd tell the entire chapter what we'd done. I panicked, drove home, and did what I did. I vaguely remember Ellie calling me as I drove, but can't remember what she said. I…I guess I owe her my life." She sniffed and dabbed her eyes with the edge of the sheet.

Loathing and disgust at Susan's actions clawed deep in Anne's gut. *That bitch! How dare she do this? The woman is a cancer in the chapter. The problem is how do we cut it out without killing the patient?* She leaned forward and patted Jane's arm. "That's one of the most despicable things I've ever heard. And you can be sure that if Susan Lynch ever breathes a word of this to anyone, the entire board will deny it and call her a liar to her face—in public!"

Jane actually smiled. "Thank you. I just feel so foolish. I walked into the kitchen wanting to die. The humiliation, the contempt my friends would feel for me pushed me over the edge. I've been taking anti-depressants for several years. I stared at the cabinet where I keep them for the longest time. It seemed like the best way out. I wouldn't have to endure the pain of seeing friends—people I'd known for years—turning away whenever I walked by. I wrote some kind of note, filled a glass, and started taking them. I don't know how many. I kind of remember getting dizzy. Then I woke up in the emergency room. Now, I'm in the nut ward. Who knows when I'll get out?"

"I doubt they'll keep you much longer." Anne wasn't really sure about this, but Jane needed some encouragement. "You regret what you did, and I'm sure with the proper treatment, you'll be fine. And don't worry about the chapter. Let me take care of that."

"Thank you, Anne. I told my husband the whole story last night. I had to beg him not to go to Susan's and wrap his hands around her neck until her beady little eyes popped out. What's wrong with her? Why is she so nasty?"

"I don't know, but she obviously has her own set of problems."

"She should be the one in here, not me."

Anne nodded in agreement. Somehow the chapter had to deal with Susan Lynch—and fast.

The door opened. The nurse stood there. "Time is up, Ms. Jamieson."

Anne rose and squeezed Jane's hand. "I've got to go. Let me know when they spring you and we'll have lunch, okay?"

"I'd like that."

As Anne left, she had a whole new set of problems to think about. Mostly Susan. The woman loved to create trouble. She remembered when Susan had first joined the critique group, appearing quiet and shy. Her inability to take criticism showed early and by the time the group had asked her to leave, her galloping paranoia had taken hold. Then she began hanging around with Fran creating a perfect storm of manipulative, nasty personalities.

But one question had been answered. No way was it Jane Whittaker she'd overheard in the antique store.

So who was it and did it have anything to do with Fran's murder?

****

Anne leaned back in her chair and dropped the thick packet of papers on her desk. She'd read the by-laws twice and at no point did they cover the suspension or out-and-out dismissal of a member of the chapter. Board members, yes, but not a word concerning the general membership.

So, now what? And is Susan's behavior even a reason for such action? All she's doing is circulating a petition. There's no way her conversation with Jane can be made public.

She picked up her cell and called Rose, but had to leave a message in voicemail. She then tried Nancy.

"Hi, Anne. What's up?"

She explained what Jane had told her and the ambiguity of the by-laws. "So, any ideas?"

"If the by-laws don't specifically cover it, then I'd have to say our hands are tied unless the national organization has rules covering this," Nancy responded. "I can't believe Susan tried to blackmail Jane. Yet, on the other hand, I can see it perfectly."

"Have you heard anything about a recall petition?"

"Not a word, but then I'd be one of the last people she'd call. Have you talked to the other board members?"

Anne sighed. So far, her presidency had consisted of a murder—two if she counted the waiter, Jeffrey Wainwright—and a lot of libelous innuendo.

"Not yet."

"You know, she may not contact any of them because if she's trying to get the election declared null and void, then a couple of them would have to be included in the purge, not just you."

"I never thought of that."

"Personally, I wouldn't worry about Susan. She'll never get any more than a dozen signatures. And a dozen out of a membership of almost a hundred and thirty will be an embarrassment."

"I suppose you're right. Look, I'm at loose ends tonight. Gil's working and the kids are at a school function. How about we meet somewhere for dinner?"

"Uh, I can't tonight. I've got plans."

"With Brad?" Anne asked in a teasing tone.

"As a matter of fact, yes. He's renting the movie *Volcano*, so he can show me all the mistakes made describing what a volcanologist does. I'm even making dinner for him."

"You're cooking?"

"Hey, I can cook pretty damned good," Nancy replied with a laugh.

"Well, have a good time and I'll talk to you later."

Anne chuckled as she hung up. Nancy and Gil's brother were rapidly becoming more than just a brief encounter.

It was too early to eat, but she decided a trip to the mall sounded sensible. She needed to get her mind off her problems, Fran's death, and the chapter for a while. Besides, the Hungry I was located in the mall. She'd eaten lunch there on several occasions, so why not give it a try for dinner?

After texting her kids of her plans, she drove to the

shopping center. Anne enjoyed just wandering around people watching and looking at merchandise. She was about to enter The Sound of Music store when she literally bumped into a familiar face.

"Becky, I'm so sorry. I didn't mean to run you over."

Becky Lawrence looked surprised, and then laughed. "No problem. I wasn't watching where I was going."

Anne hadn't had a chance to talk to Becky about Fran. Maybe a casual conversation over a glass of wine—or better yet, dinner—would yield some information.

"Neither was I. Would you like to get a glass of wine or some dinner?"

"I can't do dinner. Jim's expecting me home, but a glass of wine would be nice."

They walked over to The Hungry I. The hostess seated them immediately and a waiter took their order.

"So, what did you buy today?" Anne asked.

"Nothing much for me, but Jim's birthday is next week, so I managed to get him a couple of hard to find CDs." She took them out of the bag and showed them off.

"Operas?"

"Yes, Jim loves it. His mother is first generation Italian and loves all things Italian, including music. She instilled the love in her son, too."

"How about you? Do you like it?"

Becky shrugged. "It's all right. I can listen to it on the CD player as background when I read, but find sitting through a live performance a bit tedious."

Anne read the titles. "*Rigoletto* and *The Best of*

Enrico Caruso. Wasn't Caruso a tenor?"

"Yes, Jim just loves him. I paid an arm and a leg for the Rigoletto thing. Caruso plays the Duke. It's a toughie to find."

Anne handed the CDs back to Becky and remembered the surveillance tapes of the opera lovers' meeting at the hotel the day Fran died.

"Is he a member of that opera group that meets at the hotel?"

"The Opera Lovers of San Sebastian? Lord, yes, but he hasn't been to a meeting in several months. His work has kept him busy."

The waiter brought their wine and as they sipped, Anne thought. How hard would it be for Jim Lawrence to wear a tux jacket, close it up to the throat to resemble a waiters' uniform, and sneak into the writers' meeting?

"So, is there any word yet on what happened to Fran?" Becky asked.

"Nothing other than she died from anaphylactic shock after accidentally ingesting peanuts." She didn't mention the shellfish angle.

"Do the police have any clues yet?"

"Not that I know of, but I think they're looking for someone who came dressed as a ghost."

Becky shot her a surprised look. "A ghost? Why?"

"Apparently, this ghost was caught on surveillance nosing around the food carts in the hall, then disappeared shortly before the entrée was served. Nobody knows who it was. He or she never spoke or removed the headpiece."

"How odd." Her voice now had an element of fear in it. She stroked the stem of her wine glass and stared into the liquid. "I think we'll discover it was a silly mix up in the kitchen. Hotels are so careless about stuff like that. I once ordered unbreaded eggplant parmesan and got a load of tasteless crumbs on my dinner. I heard you were investigating, too."

"Well, as president I feel it's my duty to give as much assistance to the police as possible. And besides, my name came up as possible poisoner."

"Susan Lynch? I heard about that and read the loop. Pay no attention to her. She's a bona fide whack job."

Anne sipped her wine and took a shot at getting Becky to talk.

"I know Fran and I didn't see eye-to-eye on things, but her death was such a shock."

"She was a bitch," the other woman said with still downcast eyes. "I suppose you've talked to Rose about Fran and Jim."

"She told me. I'm sorry."

Becky cleared her throat and took a large sip of wine. "The affair didn't last long and has been over for a while, but I didn't trust her. I tried to keep clear of her at chapter meetings. Terry Whiting and I were thinking of starting a support group for wives wronged at the hands of Fran Harrison."

Strange. Becky told Rose she suspected the affair had rekindled.

"I heard a rumor that Terry's husband might have been on her hit list."

"Terry was convinced there was something going on, but had no real proof. She didn't like Fran before the conference, but afterward it turned into out and out hatred. And Terry said she'd never attend another special event as long as Fran was around. I'll tell you,

Fran loved those Christmas parties. They were a hunting ground for her. All that booze loosening up inhibitions was like an aphrodisiac."

"I kind of remember that you haven't been to a meeting in a while."

"Like I said, I try to keep clear of her whenever possible. Maybe now, I can attend without wanting to throw up. I wouldn't be surprised if Terry didn't do a happy dance when she heard the news Fran was dead."

Since Anne had gone this far, she decided to go further.

"And another odd thing. It seems a waiter for the meeting was AWOL, yet Jane Whittaker swears a man served her." She leaned forward as if telling a secret. "The real waiter was later found dead of a drug overdose."

"How… how awful," Becky said with a strange expression. She looked at her watch and gulped a large portion of wine. "Wow, it's after five. I've got to get out of here. It was nice seeing you, Anne, and thanks for the drink. Maybe I'll make the next meeting."

She gathered up her purchases and left.

Anne watched until she lost her in the crowd. Fine at first, Becky had become more nervous the longer they talked. Her departure had bordered on panic driven.

She's hiding something. Like maybe she has no idea where her husband spent Saturday morning? And could the ghost have been someone working with Jim Lawrence to eliminate a pest? Someone like Terry? Or Becky herself?

She hadn't really gained much information about the affair. And if Becky suspected the fire had been rekindled, she wasn't admitting it. However, other information was useful.

So, Jim Lawrence is a member of the Opera Lovers club. He could have disguised himself, but what would be his motive for killing his former lover, Fran Harrison?

She sipped her wine. Unless, Fran was pressuring him to begin seeing her. *Maybe the affair had heated up again. Maybe Jim wanted to break it off and Fran threatened to tell Becky.*

She remembered Gil telling her Becky's husband had been at work the morning of the murder. *But what if he wasn't? And what if Becky knows where he went and why?* Then another thought struck her. *Suppose Becky had heard about Fran's allergies, dressed like a ghost, doctored the food, and then her husband served it?*

She shook her head. Wouldn't Fran have noticed her lover serving her? *But Fran wasn't in the room at the time.* And what part did the dead waiter play in all of this?

Anne ate a light dinner and arrived back home before seven. Once inside, she looked at her cell and realized she'd missed a call from Jen. She replied immediately.

"Hi, Jen, are you home?"

"Got in a couple of hours ago. I tried calling, but didn't bother to leave a message."

"I was at the mall. Ran into Becky Lawrence and we had a drink. Guess the background noise drowned out my phone ringing. How's your mother?"

"She's going to be fine. Dad is playing chief nurse and she loves it. Anything happening on this end?"

"Boy, I'll say." Anne filled Jen in on the latest developments, especially with Jane.

"She actually tried to kill herself?" Jen said in a shocked tone. "And Susan is responsible? God, what is wrong with that woman?"

Anne also told her about the petition that might be circulating.

"If it's a recall, then she'd have to have some kind of cause, wouldn't she? And if she's trying to void the election, then she has a problem with those board members, like Rose also elected. Nancy's right about that. Gets awfully sticky. Nancy's also right that you shouldn't worry. Susan is her own worst enemy."

"I guess what you're saying makes sense. I need to let it go."

"Oh, and I don't know how important this is, but when you mentioned Fran's shop, I remembered something odd from the day I was there. I was talking to Fran when this guy comes in, doesn't look at anybody, but heads straight for the office. He doesn't knock or anything, but just walks right in. A few minutes later, he walks back out cradling this really ugly urn-like thing in his arm. He gets to the front door when Fran runs after him, saying something like, 'You need to pay for that' and the guys says, 'I settled up with the man in charge' and waltzes on out."

Jen stopped to take a breath. So did Anne.

"The man in charge? I'll bet Fran loved that."

"Are you kidding? Her jaw clenched and her eyes practically shot sparks. She turned to me and said something like 'I've got to talk to George. Look around all you want. If you need help ask up front.' Next thing I knew she stomped off. I looked around for a while when Fran came back out. I heard her tell the salesperson at the counter that she didn't feel well and was going home."

"I suppose the customer could have put in an order for some kind of special merchandise Fran didn't know about."

"I guess."

She needed to think and couldn't do it with Jen yammering in her ear.

"Look, Jen, I've got to go. I'll talk to you later. Glad you're home again."

Anne hung up and tapped her fingers against her lips. In spite of her explanation to Jen about the customer with the urn, she had her doubts. And why would the customer refer to George as the person in charge? According to Fran's sister, George was only there occasionally to inspect deliveries and do the books. Fran ran the day-to-day operations. On the other hand, maybe George liked to give the impression he owned the business, perhaps to the extent that he made deals on the side without informing his wife. And keeping the proceeds for himself.

That explanation was possible, but was it probable?

I'm missing something here, but damned if I know what.

Chapter Fourteen

Saturday morning was a busy time in downtown San Sebastian. Anne had to circle several blocks before finding a parking space. Luckily, it was only a short walk to Fran's store and only a little farther to the farmer's market.

She'd tossed and turned all night, her head spinning with theories about Fran's and Wainwright's deaths, plot lines for her current work in progress, and Jen's information about her experience at the shop. To be honest, she wasn't sure why she was returning to the place.

Anne switched her tote bag from her right to left shoulder and followed two other shoppers into the store. The salesperson, a man, turned to her when the ladies stated they were just browsing.

"How 'bout you? You need help?"

"I'm afraid I'm the browsing type this morning, too," she said with a laugh. "I was in here the other day and bought a lovely bracelet, so decided to come back for another look around. I believe a lady helped me."

"Yeah, well, she ain't here no more."

She was taken aback by the lack of good grammar. Come to think of it, the man himself looked rough around the edges. His long black hair was slicked back into a ponytail and his clothing consisted of jeans and polo shirt with a recent coffee stain on the front.

The bell over the door tinkled again as another customer arrived. "My goodness, you seem busy this morning."

The man shrugged. "It's Saturday."

"I'll bet you miss having help. I mean, I'm sure the other lady knew the merchandise so well. I was under the impression she worked here for quite a while."

The man sent her a piercing look, his narrowed dark brown eyes making her want to take a step back.

"Too long, I guess. The new owner wanted someone up front who could deal with shoplifters." He eyed the tote bag. It contained her wallet amongst other things.

"Oh, my, was that a problem?"

"Yeah."

His brief answer left her with little else to say. "Hopefully, that will be a thing of the past. I understand Mr. Harrison taking over?" Anne probed.

"Yeah, he's taking over."

Anne took another tack by gazing at the items nearby. "I'll say this, Fran did have some nice merchandise."

"Some of its good stuff, some I can't think why anyone would want to lay out the bucks for."

"Um, yes, I suppose it's all a matter of taste."

George Harrison walked down the aisle. "Carlos, I have to take my sister-in-law to the airport. Keep your eyes on things here for an hour or so. Hello, Mrs. Jamieson. Back again?"

"Yes. Fran had such nice things I just had to return for a second look."

"I'm the one responsible for the nice things. If you look closely, you'll see a lot of it is not antique, but merely second hand. That's why we never mentioned antiques in the store name. You get what you pay for."

"Uh, yes, I guess you're right," she replied, once again taken aback by the critical words.

"Now, if you'll excuse me, I must be going."

"Tell your sister-in-law it was a pleasure meeting her and I hope she has a safe trip home."

He nodded and pulled Carlos aside to speak softly to him. Anne turned away and pretended to inspect a set of old china.

So Pam Waters is leaving. A thought crossed her mind causing her to pause. *Pam had no love for her sister. Suppose she didn't arrive just for the funeral. Suppose she came a day or so earlier to visit? Maybe she and Fran argued—argued enough to spawn murder. And Pam would certainly know about Fran's allergies. Could she have been the ghost?*

George Harrison left and the new clerk returned. "You sure I can't help you find something, lady?"

"Maybe later. For now, I'll just walk around."

Two more women came in the door. The man approached them, and then led one of the ladies to some items across the room.

Anne wandered down the aisles taking a second look at the merchandise. George had been right. Some was good, high quality while others were not so nice. Fortunately, the new man stayed out of her sight. His appearance and demeanor didn't suggest he had any experience in the world of retail or antiques. In fact, he was downright rude.

So why would Fran's husband suddenly let the other lady go and hire this man? Looks like he picked him up off the street corner. And while shoplifting was always a concern for store owners, the really valuable things were too large to just carry out or were kept under lock and key by the front desk.

Nor did she like the tone George had used regarding the merchandise. *He* was the one responsible for the nice items? George Harrison was a snob and full of crap. *That, however, is not a crime.*

She peeked around a corner to see the salesclerk still busy with a customer. Satisfied, she headed toward the office with no idea what motivated her actions.

Anne paused in front of the closed door and looked toward the ceiling, but saw no cameras. Not expecting the door to be unlocked, she turned the knob anyway. To her surprise it opened. Casting a quick look over her shoulder to make sure no one saw her, she slipped inside.

The desk was tidy. A small stack of manila folders sat off to one side. A sticky note was attached to the top one—*Carlos, shred and toss.* Anne quickly flipped through them. Inventory of merchandise and delivery receipts. The bottom one held several sheets of paper with columns of names and items. The heading on the tab merely said, Special Orders. She moved on to the file cabinets hoping to find something financial. A fast glance showed nothing of that sort.

Probably at the house.

She was about to leave when a door in the back corner of the room caught her eye. She opened it and walked into the warehouse area. Furniture and shipping crates were strewn about the space.

Unable to resist, Anne inspected a large secretary with intricate scrollwork. Admiring the workmanship, she wondered at the price. *Probably more than I can afford, but I'd love to have this.* A quick search revealed more of the same. Nice items that would fetch a good price.

She glanced at her watch. She'd been here for over half an hour. Since the new clerk stayed near the front of the shop, it was obvious he knew she was still in the store.

Time to get out of here.

She slipped back into the office and hesitated. Another rapid look at the top folder on the stack on the desk showed a computer printout of the inventory. Without stopping to think, she grabbed the folders and shoved them into her tote bag.

Opening the office door a crack, Anne peeked down the aisle. No one was around, although she heard voices from the front of the store. With more confidence that she felt, she opened the door and walked out closing it behind her. The folders in her tote seemed to weigh a hundred pounds. She hustled through the maze and made for the exit noting there was a camera covering the front of the shop.

The clerk was now at the counter ringing up a sale. Another shopper was near the door.

"Hey, you. Lemme see what's in that shopping bag," Carlos said in a loud voice.

"What?" the woman replied in an outraged tone.

Anne's heart almost stopped. She used the woman as a shield and hurried onto the sidewalk before ducking into another store in case the clerk came looking for her, too. Ten minutes later, she exited and headed straight for her car. The farmer's market could wait another week.

****

Once home, Anne hurried upstairs to her office. Why on earth had she taken those folders? It was so stupid! Gil would be livid. *And what could I possibly glean from anything in them? Giving in to impulses is never a good idea.* Her actions could have put her in a lot of trouble if the clerk had searched her bag. The only excuse she could give was an intense dislike of Fran's husband and his new clerk.

She plopped into the chair at her desk, removed the folders from her tote bag, and sat back to read them again. The inventory involved expensive items that had arrived in the past month. She recognized the description of the secretary she'd admired in the storeroom. Delivery receipts were all from the same company, Rodriguez Moving, with a Miami address. The names of the customers in the last folder marked 'special orders' had been compiled in the past month also. A sheet of paper at the bottom of the pile held the most interesting information. It was a list of money being paid and received over the past three months. That was all. Just a list. No names or merchandise description.

Anne sighed. This had been a useless endeavor. She had no idea what it was she just read. The only question in her mind was why a note instructing the new clerk to shred them? The information was fairly recent. She shook her head and rose having no clue as to what to do with the folders. Returning them to the store was not an option. And they couldn't have been important or the note wouldn't have said to destroy them.

In the end, she tossed them into her paper recyclable bin. The trash guys were due on Monday anyway.

With the kids spending the weekend with their father, Gil was coming over at seven o'clock for dinner.

She spent the rest of the afternoon writing and menu planning. It was close to five when she decided a trip to the grocery was in order. With a list in hand, the task didn't take any more than forty minutes.

Anne walked in and dumped the grocery bags on the kitchen counter, then headed for foyer, her mind busy with making sure the bedroom and bath were presentable. The first thing she noticed was Bruno hiding under the end table in the living room.

"Bruno, what's wrong, sweetie?" The little shih-tzu shivered and stared at her with mournful eyes. She reached down and pulled him out, then cuddled him in her arms. "Goodness, you are in a state. What frightened you?"

She made her way back to the kitchen and set him on the floor. It took her a moment to realize the sliding glass door was ajar. The hair rose on the back of her neck. She hadn't used that door since yesterday. *And it sure as hell wasn't open this morning.*

She scooped the dog back up, grabbed her cell, and exited the house through the open door. A few seconds later, she was in her driveway and on the phone to Gil.

"I'm not sure, but I think I had an intruder in the house," she told him giving him the details.

"Where are you now?"

"In the driveway. I have no idea if someone is inside or not and I sure as hell wasn't going to look. Thank God, the kids are in Orlando this weekend."

She hated that her voice shook. She didn't resent being scared, but sure resented some stranger having this kind of control over her.

"You did the right thing. Now go to a neighbor's and wait for me, I'm on my way."

He hung up and Anne hurried across the street to stand in her neighbor's driveway. The Sampsons were out of town, but it put some distance between herself and whoever was inside—if anybody.

Gil's car screeched around the corner ten minutes later. A patrol car pulled up behind him.

"Stay put," he ordered when she walked to the curb.

Anne obeyed. Bruno, no longer shivering wiggled in her arms. She put him down on the grass where he immediately lifted his leg on a tree.

The officers from the other car joined Gil as they split up with guns drawn. One policeman went around the back of the house. Gil and the other man entered the front door. Five minutes later, the men returned.

"No one's inside, but your office is a mess. Papers tossed everywhere. The intruder also gave your dresser a good going over, too," Gil informed her. "They got in through the sliding glass door. Probably lifted the door until the lock released. I hate sliding glass doors. Just too easy to break in."

The other officer called for backup on his radio. For the next hour or so, police swarmed throughout the house dusting for fingerprints. By the time Anne was allowed back inside, dinner was a vague memory. Luckily, nothing was taken from her dresser. Her jewelry box was intact. It would take her a while to decide if anything was missing from her files in the office.

"This doesn't make any sense," Gil said. "Someone

breaks in, but doesn't take anything."

"Kids maybe just wanting to create a mess and scare the crap out of me?"

"Possibly."

"Wish old Gary here could talk?"

"Gary?" he asked gazing around the paper-strewn floor.

She nodded toward the stone figure on the shelf over the file cabinet. "Gary the Gargoyle. He was a gag gift from the kids ages ago. Sometimes I talk to him."

He gave her a strange look, but refrained from saying the obvious. "What kind of stuff did you have up here?"

"Notes on my books, publishing things like contracts and such, chapter business—certainly nothing worth stealing—unless…"

"Unless what?"

"I had a bunch of Fran's stuff. I picked it up the other day from her place." No way would she confess to her lapse of common sense regarding the folders from the store. "Most of it was chapter related. She had several hard copies of e-mails from the past year, along with dealings from vendors and the hotel. Nothing earth-shattering. I gave it to Rose yesterday. I did, however, accidentally pick up a folder or two of her personal things having to do with her antique business."

Gil picked up several sheets of paper and put them on her desk. "Are they still here?"

"No, I chucked them into the car. I was going to return them, but forgot." She paused. "I guess I should put the groceries away. I'm not sure I can cook chicken parmesan right now."

"We can go out or order in."

"Order in. I don't feel right about leaving the house tonight. Plus poor Bruno was scared to death. I'm not far behind him."

"I'll stay the night, but I doubt whoever did this will come back."

Chinese was the order in consensus. They were well into it when Anne thought to ask, "So, how did your interview with George Harrison go yesterday?"

"Pretty much as expected," he replied before eating another forkful of chicken in garlic sauce. "He told me he would be taking over the store and when I asked about how he and his wife got along, he swore everything was fine. Claimed he had no idea who'd want to harm her. Thinks it was a mix up in the hotel kitchen and that they got rid of the evidence before we could analyze it."

"Do you buy it?"

He shrugged. "No reason not to at this stage, but to me it seems odd that a CPA would suddenly want to run an antique shop."

Anne answered without revealing she'd been to the shop that morning. "I heard he bought some items for the store and did the books."

"Not all the financial information has come in yet, but I did get some information on Jeffrey Wainwright. Cause of death was definitely a massive overdose of cocaine. He had enough in his system to down an elephant. And the remaining amount in the baggie we found came back from the toxicologist as being ninety percent pure."

"I'm not too up to date on the drug world. Is that good or bad?"

"For Jeffrey Wainwright, bad. The cocaine that

comes into this country from Central and South America has that purity."

"Ninety percent? Why not a hundred?"

"The raw product has to be processed. It loses some of its intensity. Once it's sold here, the dealers cut it to make it go further. They use anything from baking soda, to powdered milk, to even talcum powder. That brings the purity level down to anywhere from fifty to thirty percent. That's generally what's sold on the streets. And then there's crack, another form of cocaine. It's nasty and highly addictive. Wainwright showed no signs of being a crack user, however, and we found no such paraphernalia in the apartment."

"So someone used to snorting thirty percent and suddenly gets ninety is likely to overdose?"

Gil nodded. "Especially if he's not a regular user and not expecting it. He thinks he's got the thirty and blasts a large line of ninety up his nose. It feels so good, he does it again and again. His heart starts racing to the point of arrhythmia. His body temp rises sharply along with his blood pressure, and he can pass out."

"And with no one calling 9-1-1, he dies," she finished.

"That's about it. Once the victim has passed out, he'd still be breathing very fast. It's not a stretch to imagine someone holding that little baggie under his nose so he'd inhale more."

"Is that what happened?"

"Don't know for sure. All we do know is that bag was almost empty."

"What about the car?"

"Haven't found it yet. Probably in some canal."

Anne agreed. But a suspicion that the dead waiter

was somehow connected to Fran's death still nagged in her mind. It was just too much of a coincidence. Yet she couldn't reconcile the why.

Let's assume the mystery waiter at the meeting bribed Wainwright to not show. Would Wainwright even connect the death of a woman at a writer's meeting with the man who'd paid him to not show up at work that day?

No mention of Fran had made the television news and as far as she knew nothing had been in the paper about it other than the obituary. And the waiter likely didn't know Fran's name or the real name of the man who'd bribed him. Plus, Wainwright had died on Saturday night or close to it. Why kill him?

Because the killer is one careful son of a bitch. The deaths have to be connected. A lot of supposition going on here, but I can't see any other explanation.

Anne sighed. She was tired of thinking about Fran, the waiter, and the whole mess.

"You're awfully quiet," Gil said as they finished the meal.

"Can't keep things out of my mind. How do you do it?"

"I learned how to turn my mind off a long time ago. How about we watch a movie, and then go to bed?"

"How about we forget about the movie and go to bed?"

Gil laughed as he grabbed her hand and led her upstairs.

****

Gil's phone rang as they were finishing brunch the next morning.

"Collins here…Oh, really? Any ID…Okay keep them busy and I'll be there shortly." He hung up and turned to Anne. "Seems they found Wainwright's car around three this morning."

"Where?" she asked.

"A couple of patrol officers caught it running a red light and ran the plate. The two kids in the car were arrested and have been in jail since then. I've gotta go, hon. Will you be all right?"

"I'll be fine. Lisa and Ken are due home this evening. Did the kids say where they got the car?"

He shook his head. "I'll find out when I get to the station and talk to them. If it makes you feel better, I'll have a cruiser drive by every once in a while."

"Thanks, I appreciate it." She waved goodbye as he left, then shut the door behind him.

Even Gil's presence last night hadn't eased her nerves. Every little outside noise or creak in the house snapped her out of whatever sleep she had attained. She hadn't fallen in to a deep slumber until just before dawn.

Determined not to let the events of yesterday control her, Anne did household chores, and then wrote on her work in progress. Gil had helped clean up the mess from the night before, but in her mind's eye, she still saw the paper-strewn floor in vivid images.

Two hours later, she deleted all she'd written. It was garbage, total garbage. The break-in and her experience at the shop kept intruding on her concentration.

She finally gave up. The kids would be home in a few hours. *Might as well make the chicken parm I didn't last night.*

As she assembled the ingredients, Anne couldn't keep her mind off those folders now resting in the blue recyclable bin in her garage. Something about them seemed off.

She retrieved the folders and sat at the kitchen table to read them again beginning with the one marked "Inventory."

Once again, nothing seemed out of place. The items listed ranged from large pieces of furniture to old trunks. Then something near the bottom drew her attention—6 Grecian urns with lids. One Grecian urn she could understand, but six? Granted she knew little about antiques, but it seemed to her that the scarcer the item, the more valuable. She could find six or more inexpensive urns at the local craft store.

Puzzled, Anne closed the folder and opened the one titled "Deliveries."

This list covered the past ten months. Notations beside each delivery date included numbers, each one different. She had no clue what they meant. The number of items delivered, maybe? And the same delivery company was used—Rodriguez Moving out of Miami.

I could swear someone told me that George traveled all over the state and elsewhere to find merchandise. So why would a moving company out of Miami be delivering something bought in Northern Florida or out of state?

Her sense of logic and order said they wouldn't.

The last folder contained the "Special Orders" list. Just names and items—Roscoe Larkin, 2 steamer trunks; Armando Sanchez, urn; Willie Sanders, urn; Chico Diaz, bookcase.

Okay, I suppose it must have made sense to someone.

Still it was odd.

Anne picked up the sheet of paper at the bottom of the pile. The heading merely said "Received" and "Paid" along with a list of numbers she assumed were prices and costs. The date on the print out showed it had been rendered a week ago. *Right after Fran's death.*

"Six thousand in, six hundred out; four thousand in, four hundred out; ten thousand in, one thousand out," Anne repeated out loud, reading from the list. "Ten percent each time."

She closed the folder and tapped her fingers on the table, then rose and went into the garage where she slid them under the driver's seat in her car along with the other folder from Fran's house. After the break-in, she didn't trust her office.

Maybe I'll tell Gil about them. I could always say I got them at Fran's with the rest of the chapter business. That way, he won't get mad at me again even though swiping the files was stupid.

The front door opened and closed again with a thud. Anne's heart rate accelerated until she heard Lisa call out.

"Mom, we're home."

She hurried into the foyer to hug her kids. "Goodness, you're home earlier than I expected. Is your father coming in?"

Ken shook his head as he turned for the stairs. "Naw, he and Paula wanted to get back to Orlando."

"Did you have a good time?"

"It was a quiet weekend," he answered. "We went to a museum yesterday and took in a movie last night."

"That sounds like fun." She gazed at her daughter. "Are you all right? You look a bit pale."

Lisa shrugged. "My nose is all stuffed up and I've got a little sore throat. A lot of kids at school have colds or the flu."

"Oh dear, do you feel like eating dinner? I was going to make chicken parmesan."

"Yeah, I'm hungry, just tired."

"Okay, you guys unpack and bring down your dirty laundry while I get dinner started."

Anne was making the salad when Ken came into the kitchen with an armload of dirty clothes and headed for the laundry room. A moment later the sound of water gushing into the washing machine made her grateful she'd taught her kids how to do things for themselves.

"So, how did your weekend go?" Ken asked as he returned and grabbed a bottle of water out of the fridge.

She hesitated. Should she tell them about the break-in? She didn't want to worry her children, but at the same time they had a right to know.

"Not the best," she replied and told him the details of Saturday evening.

"You're kidding? Was anything taken?"

"As far as I can tell nothing is missing. Since they only hit my office and bedroom, I have to assume the thieves were looking for jewelry or cash. Most of my good stuff is in the bank and as we all know, I have no cash on hand."

"I'll bet it was a bunch of punks from the area who know who lives here. They also know Lisa and I have nothing of value and made straight for your rooms. The Johannsons over on Seabreeze Drive were burglarized about a month ago. Come to think of it, one of the kids at school said they'd had an incident of someone stealing stuff from their garage."

"I never thought to ask Gil if there'd been a rash of break-ins in the neighborhood. Certainly, I never heard of any."

"Never heard of any what?" Lisa asked walking by with her laundry. She dumped it on the laundry room floor and also snatched a bottle of water from the fridge.

Anne told her what had happened.

Lisa's reaction was immediate. "Oh my God! My jewelry! I didn't think to look…"

"Relax, they only tossed Mom's room and office. Besides, who'd want that junk you wear?"

"It is not junk. Some of it's kinda nice."

"Gimme a break."

"Whoa, time out, you two. Gil said he'd have a patrol car cruise by every once in a while. I'm sure it was just kids. Probably saw me leave, came up, rang the doorbell, and when no one answered, took advantage of the situation."

"How'd they get in?" Lisa asked.

"Jacked up the sliding glass door. Gil put it back on track, but I have to call the repair man in the morning. The lock is damaged, plus I'm going to have a pin installed at the top."

Both of her kids' heads swiveled to the breakfast area.

"Geez, it doesn't look any different," Ken said.

"I didn't see anything wrong when I came in from the garage with the groceries, either. Now, do you have any homework to finish? If so, then I suggest you get it done before dinner."

Ken and Lisa left the room, giving Anne a chance to call Gil. He answered on the third ring.

"Great minds think alike. I was just going to call you. Is everything okay?"

"Yes, it's fine. Kids just got home." She told him about the other families being burglarized. "Is there a problem in the neighborhood?"

"Not that I know of, but I'll check."

"What happened with the waiter's car?"

"The kids, one sixteen, the other seventeen, claim they found it on a side street near a stop and rob on West Sixty-Fourth Street. Not the nicest of neighborhoods."

"Found it?"

"Said it was around one-thirty in the morning and they were on their way home from the convenience store when they came around the corner and saw this nice-looking car parked a few feet away. Nice-looking cars aren't the norm for that area. So, they tried the doors. They were unlocked and the keys were in the ignition. Had a wonderful time for a week."

"And nobody noticed they suddenly had wheels?" she asked.

"Claim they parked it in the alley behind the seventeen-year-old's house and their so-called friends never questioned its appearance."

"Do you believe them?"

"Yeah, they have no connection to Jeffrey Wainwright or to drugs, although we did find a small baggie of weed on the one kid when they were arrested."

"Would you like to come over for dinner tonight?"

"Can't tonight. How about tomorrow?"

"Deal."

"You sure you're all right? I could sleep on the sofa if you're scared."

Anne cast a quick glance down the hallway and lowered her voice. "I'm not scared. The kids are home now. And if you sleep over, I don't want it on the sofa."

Gil laughed before hanging up.

While making dinner, she thought about Wainwright's car.

The guy with Wainwright panics when the waiter dies, takes the car, drives it to a location he knows is unsafe, leaves it unlocked and the keys in the ignition in the hope someone steals it. And then what? He walks home? And what about his car? Did he come back later to retrieve it? He had to have come in some vehicle. Had he parked it at the house next door? Maybe he used public transportation.

She walked to the foot of the stairs and called out, "Dinner's ready."

As she served up the meal, another thought crossed her mind. *I wonder if he lives in that neighborhood.*

Chapter Fifteen

"Are you sure you feel well enough to go to school?" Anne asked her daughter the next morning.

"I don't feel real good, but not so bad that I have to stay at home," Lisa replied. "Besides, I have a history test on Thursday and don't want to miss a lecture."

Ken clomped down the stairs. "Come on, let's go, the bus will be here any second."

When the kids left, Anne poured a second cup of coffee, called a repairman for the sliding glass door, and then went upstairs to her office determined to get another scene written if it killed her. As she settled at her desk, her gaze fell on Gary the Gargoyle.

"The least you could have done was fall off the shelf or something and scare the intruder away," she told it before turning her attention back to the computer.

After two hours, she rose and paced the floor trying to untangle a plot problem. Ten minutes later, she still had no answers. Her phone ringing gave her a much needed diversion. It was Jen.

"Hey, Anne, how goes it?"

"I've been better."

"What's wrong now?"

Anne hesitated. She hadn't seen Jen in over two weeks. In fact, the group hadn't been together in longer than that. While she didn't have anything for critique, she could use their input on what was in those folders.

"Jen, are you available for lunch today at my house?"

"Sure. I missed talking to you guys and not being in on what the Snoop Group is doing. What time?"

"Eleven-thirty sound all right?"

"Great. See you then."

As soon as she hung up, Anne called Nancy and Rose. Nancy was available and Rose promised to find a sitter for the kids.

A quick inspection of her pantry told her lunch would have to be basic.

Surprisingly, Rose was the first to arrive with a big grin on her face.

"You are now looking at an emancipated mother—at least for two days of the week. Thanks to a new Mother's Day Out program at the church, I am free to pursue whatever I want on Monday's and Thursdays from ten until two."

Anne laughed. "I see lots of writing in your future."

"And grocery shopping. Do you know what it'll be like to go to the store and not have to deal with a toddler and a baby?"

Jen and Nancy arrived simultaneously. They all gravitated into the kitchen where the menu consisted of soup, chicken salad sandwiches, chips, and cookies for dessert.

"So, Jen, how's your mother?" Nancy asked.

"Much better. I didn't really have to be there, but Dad on his own is a disaster. My husband and kids on their own are disasters, too. I spent the entire weekend doing laundry and cleaning the place. Honestly, you'd think someone would have thought to dust or run the vacuum cleaner while I was gone. What's been going on here—other than Fran getting offed?"

"For starters, Nancy has a boyfriend," Rose said with a chuckle.

"What?"

"Yep, it's Gil's younger brother, Brad. He deals with volcanoes."

"Volcanoes?" Jen squeaked turning her gaze on Nancy. "Come on, out with it."

Nancy shot them all a look of exasperation while Anne grinned inwardly.

"Blame Anne. We met here, hit it off, and are seeing each other while he's in San Sebastian. I doubt anything will come of it beyond that."

"Volcanoes?" Jen repeated, sipping iced tea.

"He's a volcanologist. It's really kind of fascinating—not that I understand much of what he does."

"Why don't you think anything will come of it?" Rose asked spooning soup into her mouth.

"Because last night he got a call about rumblings on some south seas island. He may be leaving soon."

"Rumblings?" Anne said.

"As in earthquakes or whatever. I guess that's a precursor of things to come. And I'm tired of talking about this. What is going on, Anne? Anything new on Fran?"

Anne spent the rest of the lunch bring everyone up to date on events, including her excursion to Fran's shop, and the break-in.

Nancy frowned. "I can see someone rummaging through your bedroom looking for stuff, but why your office?"

"Cash, maybe?" Anne replied.

"If I'm going to keep cash on hand, I keep it in an old teapot on my kitchen windowsill," Rose said. "That way if I'm going out and need some money, it's handy."

"Wonder why they didn't toss the rest of the house," Jen added. "I mean, why just target those two rooms?"

"Maybe Bruno barked and scared them off," Nancy said.

"Bruno was hiding under an end table in the living room. He probably dived there as soon as the thief opened the door," Anne answered. "Anything new on the chapter's financial situation, Nancy?"

She shook her head. "I turned everything over to Mavis Holloway's son last Wednesday. While he suspects there's going to be a lot of money unaccounted for, he also thinks we're not in too bad a shape."

Anne breathed a sigh of relief. "Well, thank God for small favors."

"My advice is to hold that special election within the next week. You have several qualified candidates. No sense in letting Susan get a foothold," Nancy added.

"Good idea. I'll call Kathy and Ellie. Maybe we can set it up for later in the week. Rose, what about you?"

"I've been going over the correspondence. Some of it is really nasty on Fran's part and I don't see any reason to keep it," Rose told them.

"Fran was a real piece of work," Jen stated. "From your experience the other day, I'd have to say so is George. I mean, seriously? Letting go a perfectly nice woman who'd worked at the shop for several years, and then replacing her with some rude asshole must have Fran turning in her grave."

"I'm more interested in those folders you heisted," Nancy said. "Let's have a look and see if we can come up with anything new."

Anne rose. "They're under the driver's seat in my car."

"Why are they there?" Rose asked.

"I was going to toss them, but decided I'd just hand them over to Gil—minus the part about how I got them. And they're in the car because I didn't trust keeping them in the house after the break-in."

She retrieved the folders and set them on the kitchen table. Everybody reached for one and opened it as Anne cleaned up from lunch.

"Something about this inventory thing is weird," Jen said a few minutes later. "I've worked retail before and this reads like something you'd find stored in a closet."

"How so?" Rose asked.

"For starters, it's a short list. I've been in Fran's shop and, trust me, it's chocked full of merchandise. If you take inventory, you take inventory of the whole store."

Anne shrugged. "She had vendors, so she wouldn't bother with those things. She'd only list what was hers. But you're right, that strikes me as odd, too."

"Could be an inventory of items that came in recently," Nancy commented. "Maybe George entered them into a computer with existing merchandise."

"What are all these numbers next to the delivery dates?" Rose questioned.

"I have no idea," Anne replied.

"Let me see," Nancy said reading for a few seconds. "Beats me. I wonder why it's the same delivery company for all."

Anne leaned forward. "I asked myself the same question when I saw it. Why would you have someone from Miami deliver goods if you bought them in Jacksonville?"

"Perhaps Fran or her husband knew the owners and got a deal for using them or the company has branches throughout the state," Rose added.

Nancy riffled through some papers. "Did the special orders listed here coordinate with the inventory?" She picked up Jen's list. "Hmmm, some of them show up, but not all. I suppose a customer could come in and request say, a steamer trunk, then Fran would tell George to keep his eye out for one the next time he went on a buying trip."

"You know, for someone as meticulous as Fran, this all looks sloppy," Jen added.

"It's this last sheet that I find interesting," Nancy said. "It says here, 'received, six thousand dollars' and next to it is 'paid, six hundred.' Does that mean they paid six hundred for an item, then turned around and sold it for six grand?"

"Wow, that's one hell of a profit," Rose exclaimed.

"And what was the item?" Nancy continued. "You'd think if you just received six big ones for some merchandise, you'd list what it was."

"I have an idea," Jen chimed in with a grin. "Let's take a road trip to Fran's Fabulous Finds. We go in and ask for items on the inventory and see what happens."

Anne shook her head. "No thanks. I've been in there two too many times."

"And I have to pick up the kids from the care group," Rose said with a glance at her watch.

"How about it, Nancy, wanna go?"

"Sure, why not. When?"

"Now, of course." Jen jotted a short list on a notepad, and then handed it to Nancy. "You can ask for these items and I'll take the others."

"What can it hurt?" she replied rising.

They all trooped into the foyer.

"Be careful what you say in the store," Anne reminded them. "That new guy is a not real nice."

"Don't worry," Jen told her. "We'll be discreet."

Anne waved goodbye not sure if the word discreet was part of Jen's vocabulary.

****

"There, that should take care of things," the repairman said.

Anne inspected the sliding glass door. A pin lock had been installed at the top.

"See, it's on a chain so that when you're not using it, the pin doesn't get lost," the man explained.

She nodded then looked at the horizontal security bar attached midway along the frame. She decided it didn't look too distracting.

"Just release this catch here, Ms. Jamieson, raise the bar upright and snap it into the holder. When you want to lock up, bring it back down and lock it into place. No thief who relies on the quiet approach is going to mess around with both forms of security."

"And the ones who don't care about noise would just smash the glass, I guess."

He nodded. "Very true. Can't help you with that."

She thanked the man, paid him, stuffed the receipt

in a drawer until she could present it to her homeowner's insurance company, and then turned to look at Bruno. Bruno's tail wagged and she swore he smiled.

"I guess we're safe now, huh, boy? Unless the next thief breaks a window. If they really want to get in, they'll find a way."

Anne now turned her attention to the dinner menu. With little in the pantry, she decided to wait until the kids returned from school to go to the grocery. In spite of the new locks, she was hesitant to leave the house empty.

I suppose I'll get over it eventually, but I hate the feeling of having been violated.

The front door slamming told her the kids were home. She hurried into the foyer to greet them.

"How was school?" she asked, eyeing her daughter.

"Fine," Ken replied. "Is Gil coming for dinner tonight?"

"Yes, why?"

"I've got an assignment for English that requires me to do something I've never done before, and then write an essay. I thought maybe Gil could let me hang around the police station or maybe ride along in a patrol car."

"I'm sure there'll be no problem." She turned her attention to Lisa. "And how do you feel?"

"Blech! I can barely breathe." She coughed to add emphasis.

"Oh dear, do you feel like eating dinner?"

"Yeah, I guess so, but it's going to be an early night."

With the kids home, Anne ran to the grocery. Not really in the mood to cook, she took the easy way out and picked up pre-packaged fried chicken and mashed potatoes with gravy. A couple of cans of corn, dinner rolls, and salad makings finished the list. She also added some over-the-counter medicines for Lisa.

She was assembling the salad when her phone rang. It was Jen.

"Hi, Jen. How was Fran's?"

"Wow, interesting to say the least."

"What happened?"

"Well, Nancy and I got there around two, and I even remembered to enter separately so we didn't look together, you know, like we did that time we all went to Aristotle's when investigating Dorie's murder. I went in first. What did the guy you saw look like?"

"His name was Carlos and he was about five-ten, built like a fireplug with slicked back greasy dark hair and these really penetrating brown eyes. He was also rude as hell. Very uncouth."

"Well, he wasn't there today. We talked to a skinny dude with messy blond hair pulled back in a pony tail. He acted like we were intruders or something. At any rate, I went in and asked for urns. Said I was redoing my den in the Grecian style. I had to explain to him what an urn was. He said they didn't have any. I asked if I could put my name on a list to get one if they came in and he said he didn't think so."

Jen paused for breath. So did Anne. Listening to Jen talk was an adventure in breath control.

"Jen, slow down."

Her friend laughed. "I know, but I'm excited. While I was asking my questions, Nancy came in and said she wanted to see what was available in old trunks. She got the same spiel I did—none available. As she was talking, I kinda wandered around until I found the office. The door was open and there sat good old George at the desk. He gave me the fish eye, but I just plunged in and asked the same questions of him I did of the sales guy. Got the same answers."

"That's weird. It's like he doesn't care one way or the other about the store."

"My thoughts exactly! Maybe he's going to sell it or something."

"That's not the impression I got," Anne replied, recalling the conversation she'd overheard the first time she was there. "How about Nancy?"

"Are you kidding? After she asked her questions, the guy followed her all over the store like a puppy. Maybe she didn't look as trustworthy as me. When we met up later, she said the guy started asking her questions about why she wanted trunks and how did she know about the shop. Nancy also said he gave her the creeps, so she left after only ten minutes. I stuck it out for twenty, and then beat it. I don't know what's going on, but it sure isn't any way to run a business."

"I agree. There's something wrong about the whole set-up. Thanks for helping. I'll call Nancy."

She hung up from Jen and called Nancy. Her story was more or less the same.

"Anne, there was just something off about his questions asking why I wanted trunks. It was almost as if he expected me to know they had them even though he denied it. If I were you, I'd get rid of those folders."

"I'll give them to Gil tonight. He's coming over for dinner."

"Good idea. Brad and I are taking in a seminar on the age of volcanic rocks around the world or some such at the local community college."

"Have fun."

"I will, but it won't be at the seminar."

Anne laughed and disconnected, then headed upstairs to check on Lisa. She handed her the meds with instructions to take them, and then entered the office. She had talked to both Kathy and Ellie earlier and both agreed the time was right to hold the election. Kathy had made up a ballot and e-mailed it to Anne. She had put out the information on the chapter loop immediately. Susan could still receive messages on the loop, just not write a response. All she had to do was download the ballot, and vote. With any luck, they'd have a new treasurer by Friday—and it wouldn't be Susan.

The loop was fairly quiet. Just several promotional "vote for me" entreaties. She hated those requests. Getting all your friends to vote for your book or cover was no indication of the quality of the product. Blurbs for various conferences and workshops available online also showed up. Anne wasn't sure Susan's absence was a good thing. It just gave the tiresome woman more time to let the paranoia run amok. *Lord only knows what kind of skullduggery she's hatching.*

A long e-mail from Ellie told her the critique group roundup was going well. Another message from Jane thanked Anne for her discretion concerning the resignation. She was being released soon and would go into therapy.

The last e-mail was from Becky Lawrence.

Anne, would it be all right if I dropped by early

tomorrow afternoon? I need to talk to you about something and don't want anyone else to know.

She replied that one-thirty would be good and wondered what Becky had to say. Something about the affair her husband had with Fran? Or maybe the late president's rumored affairs with other members' husbands.

With that done, Anne returned downstairs to assemble dinner. Gil arrived on time, but looked tired.

"Heavens, I hope you're not coming down with a cold. Lisa has one and there seems to be something going around."

"I'm fine, just not a whole lot of sleep the last few nights." He followed her into the kitchen where he opened a bottle of wine. "What's for dinner?"

"Store bought fried chicken," Ken said with a grin as he entered the room.

"Ken! Okay, he's right. I just wasn't in a mood to cook. Hope you don't mind."

"Not at all."

"Hey, Gil, while I've got you, I have a favor to ask."

While Anne slid the chicken into the preheated oven and turned her attention to the rest of the meal, Ken made his request.

"I can arrange for you to take a tour of the station and have you do a ride in a patrol car," Gil told him.

"Wow, that's great. Thanks."

Dinner turned out to be excellent, although Anne hated to admit the store bought fried chicken was better than hers. Lisa, however, picked at her food.

"Are you feeling any better," Anne asked her.

"Not really. Screw homework. I don't have that

much anyway. I think I'll go to bed early." She pushed back her plate and rose. "In fact, now sounds like a good time. I'm so tired. Goodnight, all. Nice to see you again, Gil."

"Hope you feel better," he said as Lisa left the room.

Ken followed shortly leaving the two of them alone. After cleaning up the kitchen, they retired to the living room.

"How are you holding up?" he asked. "Nervous about being in the house?"

"Not really. Did you check out any other break-ins in the neighborhood?"

"Been three in the past two months—yours, one on Seabreeze, and another on Kingfish. Money was taken along with some random items, but that's about all. In your case, they just messed things up."

"Funny, I don't see how they missed the two hundred dollars I have stashed in the sideboard drawer in the dining room. In fact, it's odd that only my bedroom and office were violated."

"Kids. They look in those places first."

"I can see the bedroom, but the office is the strange thing. And speaking of kids, anything new with Wainwright's car?" she asked.

Gil shook his head. "No. Kids were sent to juvie, but I doubt they lied."

"Pretty stupid to drive around in a stolen car for a week. They had to assume the owner reported it as such."

"These two didn't strike me as having a wealth of brains or deductive powers. They got away with it as long as they did because Wainwright's car was a small-sized white one. A ton of those on the streets, and unless the kids did something dumb like speeding or driving recklessly, any patrol officer seeing them wouldn't think to check. Can't call in every white car they see."

"I suppose, plus the kids may have suspected the car was stolen when they found it."

"I don't think that even crossed their little minds. They saw an opportunity and took it. And don't forget, they parked it in an out of the way area in an alley behind one of the kids' houses."

"Anything else on the waiter's death? Or Fran's?"

Once again Gil shook his head, a look of frustration on his face.

"Tons of fingerprints in Wainwright's apartment. It's taking a while to sift through them all. And so far, no one can identify the so-called ghost or the bogus waiter from your meeting. The wait staff says they never noticed him."

"That would make sense if he grabbed the plates set aside, slipped into the room, served Fran and Jane, and then split. How about fingerprints on the plate served to Fran?"

He shook his head. "Partials or smudged."

"What about the bag of coke?"

"Just Wainwright's, which leads me to think the killer wore gloves."

"Wouldn't Wainwright have noticed his supplier wearing gloves of any sort?"

"I think his focus was on the drugs, not his visitor."

Anne sighed. "Anything unusual turn up in Fran's financials?"

"Not on a personal level. Haven't completely

checked the antique store yet."

"I've discovered some facts concerning Fran and the chapter finances, but that's all. I'm more interested in the antique store. After all, Fran was investigating offshore accounts. Did the lawyers ever get back to you?"

Gil made a face. "Only to say they couldn't talk about it—attorney/client privilege. When I told them this was a murder investigation, they hemmed and hawed before saying that Ms. Harrison came to them with a personal problem and they recommended the private investigators she eventually hired."

"I suppose it stands to reason that if she was embezzling from the chapter, she'd be doing the same from the shop." Anne heaved a sigh. "You know, money really is the root of all evil. You don't have much so you lie, cheat, and walk all over people to get more. Only more is never enough. You just keep right on lying, cheating, and stepping on trusting friends and acquaintances to get even more. I wonder if more is *ever* enough."

She didn't like to remember what she'd done for the sake of money.

"For some people, no. They're never satisfied and that makes them unhappy. I believe the happiest people are those who have loving families and strong values regardless of their social or financial status."

"Which reminds me, I need to give you those folders I accidentally took from Fran's. They deal with the shop, but don't make any sense. Maybe they can help you in the investigation." She told him what she, Nancy, Rose, and Jen had speculated.

"I thought you were going to return them to Mr.

Harrison," Gil said giving her a sharp look.

"I planned on it. Then I saw what a shambles the chapter finances were in and forgot." She had to tread lightly and didn't look him in the eye. "Just a second, I'll get them."

Anne retrieved the folders from the secretary in the corner of the living room where she'd stashed them earlier and handed them to him.

"They're lists, but don't sound very businesslike to me. And if nothing else, Fran was sharp about business."

"Thanks, I'll look at them tomorrow." He glanced at his watch. "It's been a long two days. I need to get home. Are you sure everything is all right here?"

"Yes, it's fine. I had new locks installed today on the sliding glass door, and since nothing was taken, I have to assume the thieves won't think it worthwhile to take a second crack at me."

Gil rose from the sofa and lightly kissed her forehead. "Never assume. Just be careful, okay."

"I will."

He pulled her into his arms and kissed more than her forehead. Delicious heat rose from the pit of her stomach. Her toes curled and her fingers clenched his polo shirt.

"I think I'll sleep happy tonight," he said with a smile.

"I won't."

Gil laughed and walked into the foyer. "What's on your agenda for tomorrow?"

"I have no idea, but if I don't get something logical written soon, I'll scream."

"In that case, I'll call you later in the day." He

leaned down to kiss her again lightly. "Have a good night."

She waved goodbye, then wandered into the kitchen, poured a glass of wine, and sat at the kitchen table.

There! The folders are with Gil. Maybe he can make some sense out of them.

Her thoughts turned to the next day. Becky was due to drop by around one-thirty. Her e-mail hadn't sounded all that urgent, but Anne wondered exactly how truthful the woman had been about her husband's affair with Fran, and if she had more information concerning possible other love interests the former president kept secret.

Chapter Sixteen

"I don't care what you say, you are not going to school today. You have a fever," Anne said forcefully as she removed her hand from her daughter's forehead.

"But Mom, today and tomorrow are review for the big test on Thursday!"

"If you go to school today, you might be too sick to take the test on Thursday. And besides, you could infect other people. Now, march! I'll bring up some orange juice later." She used her "mommy" voice and pointed up the stairs.

With a heavy sigh, Lisa obeyed.

"Take your temperature along with some aspirin and crawl right back into bed," Anne called up after her retreating daughter.

"So, the sickie is going to lounge around all day watching TV and eating good stuff," Ken said as he assembled his books in a backpack. "Think I'll get sick tomorrow."

"Don't you dare. I haven't had both of you home sick at the same time since you were in grade school and got chicken pox within days of each other. If you want to be helpful, you can go to her classes and get any assignments she might have, especially from history. She's got a test soon."

"Will do. I'm off. Don't forget to lock up behind me," her son said as he opened the door and left.

She sighed. Now her sixteen-year-old son was giving her safety instructions.

Not being one to slack off when it came to her kids' health or safety, Anne waited another thirty minutes until the doctor's office opened and secured an appointment for ten o'clock. It would totally kill her day as far as writing would go, but that's the way it worked. *Family comes first.*

She took a glass of orange juice up to Lisa who had curled up under the covers.

"Did you take your temperature? How about the aspirin?"

Lisa nodded. "Thanks, Mom. And yes, it's a hundred and one, but I'll be fine by dinner."

"Well, just to make sure, you have an appointment with Dr. Brunner at ten, so catch a nap."

She entered her office and pulled up her latest work in progress. She had a little over an hour and a half before the appointment. Maybe she could get a few pages written.

Fate conspired against that idea when her phone rang. It was Nancy. At eight-twenty? Now what?

"Hi, Nancy, you're up with the birds this morning."

"Yeah, well, I just thought I'd give you a little heads-up here."

"About what? And please don't say the chapter finances."

"No, nothing like that. Jack Holloway has that under control. I just thought I'd let you know I'm going out of town for a while."

"Really? Good idea. You haven't had a vacation in years."

"It's sort of a vacation."

Her hesitant tone sent Anne's antennae soaring. "Sort of?"

"Brad decided that those rumblings I told you about can't be ignored much longer, so he's taking off for the South Pacific this afternoon. I'm going with him."

"What!"

"Brad's boss called last night and suggested he might want to have a look. Brad said that as long as the volcano is in this stage, it's not dangerous, and since I know next to nothing about volcanoes, he thought I might like to tag along. If things escalate, he'll send me home pronto."

Anne couldn't decide if she was appalled or envious.

"But this is so unlike you. What on earth are you going to do except get in the way? No offense," she hastened to add.

"Brad had that all worked out. I can take notes. I'll be his secretary or assistant if anybody asks."

"This is nuts."

"Yeah, I know, but kind of thrilling all the same. We fly to Port Moresby in Papua New Guinea, spend the night or early morning, whatever the time change is, and then hop a small flight to Lae. I'm not sure what island that's on, but the rumblings are coming from near there at a place called Rabaul. I guess that city has been destroyed a couple of times by eruptions."

For the first time in a long time, Anne was speechless.

"New Britain."

"What?" Nancy said.

"I think Lae and Rabaul are on an island called

New Britain. I can't believe you're doing this."

"I can't either, but you know, if nothing else Brad has taught me that life is too short to let it go by without an adventure or two. So, I decided to have an adventure."

"But what about the chapter? We can't do without a treasurer. Susan Lynch will have a field day crying foul if you're not around."

"You've got the election scheduled for next week, right? And Jack said the results of the audit won't be available for at least another three. Slide, you're covered. Just don't tell anyone outside of the group and board that I'm gone. Or just tell them I'm out of town for a while."

Anne sighed. Nancy had it all worked out. "Do me a favor, get international calling for your cell and keep in touch."

"Already done."

"What about a passport?"

"Got one a few years ago when I went on that cruise to the Bahamas."

"When are you leaving?"

"In about an hour for Miami. We fly out of there for Los Angeles, then on to Honolulu, and I'm not sure how many other stops there are. Probably Australia."

Anne sighed. "Have a good trip, and for crying out loud, be careful. Oh, and by the way—have fun."

Nancy laughed. "No matter what happens, I will. Talk to you soon."

She hung up and stared at her computer screen. Who would have guessed this turn of events? Not even Jen would do something this impulsive. Thank goodness, the treasurer's position would soon be filled.

She called Gil.

"Do you know what your brother has done?"

"I know he's headed off to another volcano site in a while. He was called last night. Why?"

Anne told him about Nancy's phone call.

"Wow, he must be serious about her."

"That's all you can say? Gil, it's dangerous. Nancy doesn't know jack shit about volcanoes."

"She's an adult and Brad wouldn't do anything that could harm her. If things get rough, he'll send her home."

She hung up from that phone call with a growing sense of frustration.

I don't care if one of my best friends is an adult, she's nuts!

On the other hand, there was little she could do to stop her.

****

Anne stumbled into the kitchen a bit before noon with a slow-moving Lisa behind her. The doctor's diagnosis was thankfully not the flu, but just a cold. Her temp had dropped slightly and her cough had all but disappeared.

"Do you feel like eating lunch?"

"Actually, I am kinda hungry."

"I'll heat up some chicken noodle soup and make you a toasted cheese sandwich. How's that sound?"

Lisa grinned. "Ah, the old chicken soup trick. Sounds good. What's the old saying—feed a fever, starve a cold—or is it the other way around?"

"I can't remember, but since you have both one is bound to work. Scoot on upstairs and try to take a nap later. I do know rest is at the top of the recovery list."

"If I sleep too much this afternoon, I'll never sleep tonight. Do you mind if I use your computer to game? There's no bed to tempt me in your office."

Anne made lunch and took it up to Lisa, and then stayed to chat.

"So, Mrs. Carlyle is running off to the south seas with Gil's brother to look at some volcano?" she said as she spooned broth and noodles into her mouth.

"So she claims. I have no idea what to think."

"I don't know, it sounds exciting to me, although if I had to pick one of your friends to do something like that it would be Mrs. Swanson."

"Now that I could understand."

"Are Mrs. Carlyle and Gil's brother like, an item?"

"Apparently," Anne replied with a shake of her head.

"Wow, wouldn't it be weird if you and Gil got married, and she and his brother got married? That would make her your sister-in-law and my aunt—or maybe a step-aunt. Not sure of the genealogy on this."

"So far, no one has even mentioned or considered the 'M' word," she said. "Finish up."

Lisa did as asked, and a few minutes later Anne gathered up the bowl and plate.

"See, I ate all of the soup and most of the sandwich."

"Now, try to take a nap."

"I will in a while."

Anne glanced at the grandfather clock in the foyer where she paused. It was nearly one. Becky would be here shortly. Once again, she speculated as to what kind of information the woman had. Whatever it was, she hoped it would lead to finding the killer.

She took a step toward the kitchen, and then paused again as a shiver rolled over her. Something was in the air. She had that feeling that comes right before a lightning strike when the atmosphere crackled with unseen energy. The hair didn't rise on her arms or neck, but the sensation was there nonetheless.

Lord, I wish I'd let Lisa go to school today.

****

Anne cleaned up what little had gone into making lunch deciding that Becky probably knew more than she was telling. If the woman had information that could lead to Fran's killer then she'd tell her to take it to Gil.

I'm tired of always being in the middle of things. And while I enjoy helping Gil with some aspects of his cases, I'm also tired of going through all that comes with them. How does he handle the stress?

Her thoughts were interrupted when the doorbell rang. Good. Becky was here and with any luck at all, she'd tell her tale of woe and be gone in less than an hour.

Anne opened the door surprised to see George Harrison standing on her porch.

"Mr. Harrison, what are you doing here?" She regretted her aggressive tone, but her dislike for the man mandated it.

"I'd like to talk to you about Fran, if that's all right. May I come in?"

"Um, I'm sorry, but now is not a good time. I'm expecting a friend to drop by."

"This won't take long, I promise."

With no graceful way out of his request, she stepped back. He entered the foyer and smiled. His clothes hung on him like a scarecrow. The oversized jacket looked like a bad thrift store buy.

She gestured toward the back of the house. "Do you mind talking in the kitchen?"

"Not at all."

She led him through the foyer and down the hallway. "Please have a seat. Can I get you something to drink? Coffee? Iced tea? A soft drink?"

"No, no, thank you," he replied taking a seat in one of the chairs at the table.

"What is it you want to talk about?" Anne jerked a pitcher of iced tea from the fridge and filled a glass, then stood on the opposite side of the peninsula as far away from him as possible.

George took a deep breath. "I've been going through papers at the shop and found some things that suggest Fran was not exactly, shall we say, accurate about certain business matters."

"What kind of business matters?"

"Well, her deposits didn't always match her accounts receivable. Sometimes the deposits were several hundred dollars less. I then found bank statements from another bank—not the Fran's Fabulous Finds account—but a different one. It amounted to well over fifty thousand dollars."

Anne sat back. And Fran investigated offshore banks. Was she skimming and planning on taking off for some Caribbean island or Central America after all? With another man?

"It was her store, Mr. Harrison. I suppose if she wanted to set aside some extra money for whatever reason, then that was her privilege."

"Only it wasn't her store. I own it. I let her run the

place." His gazed sharpened on her.

That uneasy feeling of a disturbance in the air before a lightning strike returned. Why on earth would he tell her this?

"Oh, I see. I didn't know that. But if it was your store, didn't you view the financials from time to time? I mean, you used to be a CPA, right?"

"I'm still a CPA, but my wife asked to do the books. She wasn't a dummy when it came to money, Mrs. Jamieson. I still freelance accounting from home. I kept my eye on things by doing some of the buying for the store and checking the merchandise, but then you already know that. You know, that iced tea does look good. I think I'll have some after all."

Once again, with no clear way out of the situation, she poured him a glass and set it on the table.

Some of what he said matched what she'd heard from the sales clerk on her first visit to the shop.

"Yes, your sister-in-law told me how you helped with the shop. How can I help *you* with any of this, Mr. Harrison?"

"I was wondering if you found anything of a suspicious nature among her papers from the writers group. I know you took a lot of folders from her office."

She sipped from her glass, and then took a larger gulp. *He's fishing for information, but what I'm not sure. Am I missing something in those folders I stole from his office? Good Lord, does he know about them? No, I checked carefully for surveillance cameras. There were none in that part of the store.*

"I'm afraid not. All the papers dealt with the usual stuff a chapter president has to do. There was nothing of an accounting nature."

"I see. I'm pretty certain she kept some of the shop files at home. She liked to work on them at night, you see. Unfortunately, my late wife didn't always keep such a good filing system in place. I often had to call her on that and go searching for things."

Something's not right about this. I remember George telling me how organized Fran was. Maybe the objectionable store clerk noticed I slipped out rather fast. Did he suspect I had stolen something? If so, why didn't he stop me? She rubbed her suddenly cold arms. *I need to get him out of here.*

As she contemplated how to do that, the doorbell rang again.

"Excuse me, but that must be my friend. I'm sorry, but could we discuss this at a later date?"

He rose and picked up his glass. "I…I really would like to get this straightened out. I'm afraid the tax man is on my back about things. Do you mind if I stay out of the way, say on your patio, and finish my tea? Perhaps your friend's business won't take long."

She didn't buy the pleading look on his face, but the doorbell pealing again had her agreeing. Besides, whatever Becky had to say, might not take but a few minutes.

"Oh, very well."

She hurried to the front door and opened it. Becky Lawrence rushed in.

"Oh, Anne, I'm so glad you agreed to see me." Her face was ashen, and her hands trembled. "I don't know what to do or who to talk to. I'm scared."

"Good grief, Becky, what are you talking about?"

"It's Jim. He really is leaving me, but Fran had

nothing to do with it. It was all so wrong!"

Anne stood near the stairs in confusion. *Why is she telling me this? Her personal problems are none of my business.*

"Becky, I'm sorry to hear that, but I don't think…"

"No, no, it has everything to do with you," the woman said with a sob.

"Me? I don't even know your husband!" From the bridge above the foyer, she saw Lisa lean over the banister then retreat a couple of steps.

"Of course, you don't, but we thought it was Fran and now we can't undo it."

Becky's words had a familiar ring to them. "You aren't making any sense. Calm down and tell me about it."

"Oh, it makes perfect sense to me," a voice from the back of the hallway said.

Anne turned to find George standing there holding a gun.

Anne gasped. Becky emitted a strangled cry and clutched Anne's arm.

Somehow, Anne found her voice. "Are you crazy? Put that gun down!"

Movement from the bridge above sent a jolt of terror through her. She didn't dare look directly up. *Lisa, go hide! Now!*

"George! What are you doing here?" Becky asked in a thin, reedy tone.

"Trying to retrieve the folders Ms. Jamieson stole from my office the other day."

Anne's heart skipped a beat. "What…what folders?"

"Don't play games with me, lady. You took three

of them. They were sitting on the corner of the desk in the office along with a note instructing Carlos to shred them. When I got back to the store and saw they were gone, I assumed he'd done it. Only later I learned he'd never seen them. I'd had a hidden camera in the office and it showed you snooping around and shoving them into a big bag. One of them has information in it that I'd rather the police didn't know about, so I sent him around to find them."

So Carlos was the intruder. Not some neighborhood kids.

Anne's chest constricted. The air was supercharged as if the lightning was moments away. She could almost smell the ozone. At least Lisa had left the upper hallway. She prayed her daughter was calling the police, and then hiding.

George turned his attention to Becky. "I knew you were a weak link."

Becky gestured with her hand and sobbed. "You said the peanuts would just make her sick. I never thought she'd die!"

Suddenly, it was all so clear. "You were the ghost," Anne said in a tremulous voice.

Becky nodded. "My job was to hang around, see where Fran was seated, send a text message to George as to where, sprinkle the stuff on her food. The cards on the table told me who was eating what."

Of course, the cards placed by the seats that designated who got which entrée. All Becky had to do was text George what other entrée to pick up and serve.

"And you were the waiter," she said turning toward George. "Becky sprinkled the ground up peanuts and shellfish on the food, and you served her. How did you know she was eating salmon?"

"I found the menu selections on her computer. She loved salmon. It was a no-brainer."

"You took a hell of a chance. I can't believe Fran didn't recognize you."

"Fran couldn't be bothered with waiters or waitresses. Trust me, she'd never give them a second look. I was right. Besides, I layered several heavy sweaters under the jacket to make me look bigger. I caught a break when she wasn't in the room."

"But why? Because she had lovers?"

"She could ball every man in San Sebastian for all I cared. No, she was planning on taking off with a lot of my money. It's a ton more than fifty grand. It's close to a million. No way was I allowing that."

A million dollars? What the hell?

"But why involve Becky?"

"I needed someone dumb enough to do what I wanted. I knew Fran had slept with Jim Lawrence, so I called Becky one day saying I thought the affair had heated up again. She agreed to help."

"You said she'd get sick and we'd teach her a good lesson. You knew the peanuts would kill her," Becky wailed.

Anne stared at George. "You added the shellfish just to make sure she died, didn't you? And the waiter?"

"I bribed him to let me borrow his uniform for a day. Told him it was to surprise my wife on our anniversary."

"You killed him, too."

"Had to. I knew the cops would eventually get around to questioning him. He could identify me, so he had to go. I called him to say I had a bonus for him. Showed up with a baggie of almost pure coke. It was the perfect set up. I figured he'd have a small hit, love the instant high and do it again. To a casual user like him, the potency would kill within a few hours. I hung around until he passed out, then held the baggie under his nose so he'd inhale more. Problem solved."

Just like Gil suggested.

"And then you took his car and left it in a neighborhood where you'd know it would get stolen," Anne commented with a glance at a frozen Becky, her face white with terror. "And *you* drove him to the house next to the apartment complex, then met him again to pick him up."

Becky nodded. "He said if I didn't he'd tell the police what I'd done and that he was nowhere near the hotel."

"Fran wasn't embezzling from the shop. You were." Suddenly, the baggie of coke made sense. "You were using the shop to smuggle drugs. Where else would you get pure cocaine?"

"You both know way too much. Guess your intruder of the other day came back. Shame he found both of you here. Had to kill you."

He took several steps toward them, then cocked the hammer on the revolver.

"You won't get away with this," Anne stated in a shaky tone.

"Of course, I will. I'll say I came by to talk about Fran, walked in, and found you both dead on the floor."

Anne detected movement from the top of the bridge. *No Lisa! Run! Hide!*

George stepped forward and raised the gun. He was

positioned just a bit in front of the bridge. Off in the distance sirens screamed.

"No! Don't!" Becky shrieked.

An object came hurtling over the banister railing. It hit Harrison on the side of the head and his right shoulder. The gun went off with a deafening bang. Becky screamed. He dropped like a sack of cement onto the floor, bleeding profusely. The gun skittered across the tile. Anne rushed to kick it farther into the living room. Becky lay on the foyer rug moaning and blood oozing from a wound in her shoulder. Anne ignored her not caring about either of them. She looked up.

Lisa stood there, her hand to mouth, and with tears streaming down her cheeks.

"I...I saw what was happening, so I hid in your office closet and called 9-1-1. I told them to send Gil."

"You should have stayed there!" Anne said.

"I did for a minute, but no way would I let him hurt you. So I grabbed the first thing I could find."

Anne looked at the unconscious George Harrison, his head gushing blood. Gary the Gargoyle lay wedged between his body and the staircase.

The more she stared, the more she had the urge to laugh hysterically.

"Oh shit, I'm going to throw up!" Lisa dashed down the hallway toward the bathroom.

Outside, squealing tires told her the police had arrived. She hurried to open the front door. A moment later, Gil entered with his gun drawn. Five other officers followed.

Anne's knees turned to jelly. Her head spun. She grasped the newel post and sank onto the bottom step.

Chapter Seventeen

"Annie, are you all right?" Gil demanded.

She nodded, gulping for air before leaping to her feet and racing upstairs, taking the steps two at a time.

"Stay put," he told her as the other officers called for an ambulance.

Anne ignored him. "Lisa! I have to get to Lisa!"

She reached the top of the stairs as her daughter came out of the bathroom. Footsteps pounded on the steps behind her. She gathered Lisa into her arms.

"Oh, Mommy! Is he dead? Did I kill him?" she sobbed as they held each other tightly.

Gil joined them and called down from the balcony. "Is he alive?"

"Yes, but just barely. He's hardly breathing. I called for an ambulance," an officer replied.

He turned and folded both women into his arms kissing first Anne's forehead, and then Lisa's.

"He's hurt, but still alive."

"I…I didn't know what to do. I couldn't just let him kill you," Lisa wailed. "I thought he had when I heard the gun go off. Am…am I going to go to jail?"

Gil gave them one last hug before loosening his grip.

"No. Here, let's go into your mother's office. You can tell me the whole story."

He led them into the room, told the men downstairs

where he was and instructed them to let him know when the paramedics arrived. He reentered the room and closed the door.

Anne sat next to Lisa on the sofa while Gil pulled her desk chair over in front of them.

"Now, Annie, you go first. What happened?"

Taking a deep breath, she gave him the details as he wrote things down in his notebook. "I suspected that *Becky* may have been the ghost, and while I thought Fran and George may have had problems, I didn't realize he had engineered the plan."

"We'll get a warrant for the antique store immediately." He turned his attention to Lisa. "Now can you tell me what happened from your point of view?"

"Should I leave?" Anne asked, remembering previous interrogations she'd undergone.

Gil shook his head. "She's a minor. A parent should be present. Now, Lisa, tell me what happened."

Her daughter nodded in jerky movements. "I…I didn't feel good today so I stayed home from school. Mom and I had lunch up here and she told me she was expecting a friend to drop by. I decided to use her computer to game for a while. I heard the doorbell ring and thought it was her friend, so I didn't pay any attention."

Anne rose and grabbed a tissue box, then returned to drop it in Lisa's lap. The girl pulled a couple out, wiped her face, and blew her nose.

"Are you all right, Mom? I mean really all right?"

"Yes, honey, I'm fine thanks to you. Go on."

Gil smiled as if trying to reassure them all was well even though she had two seriously injured people in her foyer.

"Well, like I said, I didn't pay any attention. The doorbell rang again, then again about a minute later. I was curious, so I came out onto the balcony as Mom let this lady in. I started to come back in the office when I realized the woman was really upset. I kinda stopped, wondering if I should offer to help when I heard a man's voice. Then I heard Mom saying something about putting a gun down." She paused to take a shaky breath. "I tiptoed to the railing and saw this guy holding a gun on Mom and the lady. I crept back into the office, closed the door as quietly as I could, called 9-1-1, told them what was happening and to notify you. Then I hid in the closet. Only, I couldn't stay there, not knowing what was going on. Don't be mad at me, Mom, but I was so scared he'd hurt you."

"I'm not mad, sweetie."

Gil wrote furiously in his notebook. A knock on the door had him opening it.

"Paramedics are here, Detective Collins."

"Tell them I'll be down in a minute." He resumed his seat. "Go on, Lisa. What did you do next?"

"I...I opened the door again and heard him saying something about how he killed some waiter or someone. I knew I had to do *something*, so I looked around the room for a weapon. All I saw was the computer. Then I spotted Gary. I thought that maybe if I tossed him over the balcony, it would distract him and Mom could get away."

"Gary?" Gil asked.

"Gary the Gargoyle—remember? I told you about him the other day," Anne said.

"Oh, that's right. So you grabbed this statue?"

Lisa nodded. "He's kinda heavy, but I was so scared I didn't notice. I just came to the railing. The guy was standing almost directly beneath me. I didn't stop to think. I just dropped it. It hit him in the head. Then the gun went off, Mom and the other lady screamed, and I felt really sick to my stomach."

Gil smiled, put his notebook into his jacket pocket, and pinched her daughter's chin between his thumb and forefinger.

"Kid, you did a great job. Now, I want both of you to go pack. You can't stay here tonight. You can bunk in with me. Okay?"

Anne nodded and rose. Helping Lisa to her feet, they left the room. She pushed the girl down the hallway.

"Start packing, I'll be along in a minute." She then dared a peek over the balcony. "Oh, my God, what a mess."

Blood was pooled near the living room archway and along the staircase. George Harrison still lay unmoving on a gurney. As the paramedics wheeled him out, a second gurney was brought in. Becky was loaded on to it where the medicos bandaged her shoulder. She continuously sobbed and repeated, "I'm so sorry. I didn't know she'd die."

Gil pulled her away. "Don't worry. I know a company who specializes in this sort of clean-up. I can have them here as soon as forensics is finished."

"I kicked the gun into the living room."

"We'll get it."

She started to move down the hall, and then stopped.

"Ken! Ken will be home soon."

"I'll send an officer over to the school to bring him to my house."

Anne checked on Lisa. "Need any help?"

"No thanks."

"Remember to pack those meds." Lisa nodded and headed for her bathroom.

Anne continued on to her room and stared at the walls. The clock on her nightstand told her it was not quite three. All this has happened in less than two hours. It seemed like a lifetime.

Shaking her head, she pulled a small suitcase from the closet and proceeded to fill it with clothes and toiletries, even remembering to pack a few things for Ken. Finished, she met Lisa in the hallway. They paused at the top of stairs. Harrison was gone, but the blood wasn't. His head wound had bled all over the place.

Several people were in the foyer and the living room, including Gil. He looked up at them.

"Come on down and go straight out the front door to my car. I'll be out in a few minutes."

"I think I'm gonna barf again," Lisa murmured as they descended.

"No, you're not. Just take a deep breath and walk on past."

She was on the front porch when she suddenly remembered.

"Bruno! Gil, I can't leave Bruno here alone. I haven't seen him since we got home from the doctor's."

"I'll find him."

She popped the trunk on Gil's car, tossed their bags into it, and then settled in the front seat. Lisa got in the back.

"Are you okay, honey?" she asked.

"Better than an hour ago. God, look! All the neighbors are out and staring."

"Let 'em stare. I'll explain some other time."

Her head felt like it was clamped in a vice. She leaned it against the headrest and closed her eyes. *Will this day never end?*

Several minutes later, Gil appeared with a shaking Bruno.

"Found him hiding in the corner of the laundry room." He dumped the shih-tzu in her lap and a plastic grocery bag at her feet. "His bowls and some food, his leash, and a box of doggie treats. I'll be back in a minute, then we can go down to the station and you can make your official statements."

"You mean I have to tell this all over again?" Lisa said in a tortured tone.

"Sorry, hon, but I'm afraid so. It shouldn't take long. Anne, Ken is on his way to my place. You might want to call him."

She nodded and pulled her cell from her purse.

"Mom, are you all right? What's going on?" His tone was part demanding and all scared.

She spent the next ten minutes telling him the events of the past couple of hours. "I'll go into it further when we get to Gil's, but first we have to go to the police station."

Gil got in the car as she hung up. They looked at each other. He reached out and smoothed his hand down her cheek.

"Lady, you gotta quit doing this to me. My heart won't stand it."

He started the car and pulled away.

****

The trip to the police station didn't take as long as Anne had feared. Both she and Lisa repeated what they'd already told Gil, signed the statements, and left.

It was a little after five when they pulled into Gil's driveway. A police cruiser was parked at the curb. Ken immediately bailed out of it and raced toward them.

"Mom! Are you all right? Is anybody dead?" he exclaimed as he hugged her tightly.

"I'm fine and nobody's dead thanks to your sister." She explained Lisa's part in the affair.

"You brained him with Gary the Gargoyle? Way to go, sis!"

Lisa stared at him and burst into tears. Ken released his mother and hugged his sister.

Meanwhile, Gil thanked the patrol officer and got the suitcases out of the car.

"Come on, let's get you all inside. We'll order in pizza and I'll contact the cleaning company."

"Cleaning company?" Ken asked, his arm still around his sister's shoulders.

"There was, like, blood everywhere," Lisa said mopping her eyes with the hem of her T-shirt.

Anne retrieved Bruno and his things from the car and joined them, grateful Gil had played dog sitter in his office while she and Lisa gave their statements. If she remembered correctly, Gil's house had three bedrooms and two baths. She hoped they didn't need to impose upon him for long.

"Have a seat and make yourselves comfortable," he said as he took their suitcases down the hallway.

Lisa and Ken flopped into a pair of armchairs, while Anne chose the sofa. Gil joined her.

"I imagine you can use a drink," he said to her.

"Oh, yeah."

"I wouldn't mind one myself," Lisa mumbled.

"Not on my watch, young lady," Anne said.

Gil laughed and headed for the kitchen. He returned with a glass of red wine for Anne, and a couple of glasses of soda for the kids. He then ordered a pizza.

Anne took a healthy swig and let the Chianti slide down her dry throat as Gil's phone rang.

"Collins... Good. I want the place picked apart. Did you also get one for the house? I requested that at the same time... Excellent. I'll meet you at the antique store in ten minutes. In the meantime, if you come across something that needs more warrants, let me know."

He hung up and faced Anne. "That was Detective Sawyer. He's at Fran's Fabulous Finds with a search warrant. They also got one for the house. I've got to go. Will you be all right on your own?"

"Sure. How long will it take?" she asked.

"Not sure, but the pizza is paid for. Just give the driver a tip, and remember to save me a couple of pieces." He kissed her forehead. "Oh, and I've got you and Lisa in the front bedroom. Ken you're stuck with the pull out in my office."

As he left the house, Anne rummaged in her purse for a bottle of aspirin.

"This has been a helluva day." She swallowed one with a gulp of wine.

"Amen to that," Lisa replied. "I'm not sure how much I can eat. The tomato sauce will probably remind me of all that blood in the hallway."

"Oh, thanks, like I need to hear that," Ken drawled.

"Oh, and Mom, you don't need to bunk in with me. I may be contagious. Besides, I'm sure you'll be more comfortable with Gil."

Anne stared. "Wha…what? What makes you say that?"

"Well, duh! Paula moved in with Daddy a few months ago. I just kind of assumed you and Gil had moved beyond the hand-holding stage."

She was saved from making a reply by the arrival of the pizzas. Her hot face told her she was blushing again.

Damn, they grow up much too fast.

****

Anne ignored her daughter's sage advice and slept on the sofa in the living room. She awoke sometime around six o'clock to the smell of freshly brewed coffee and the sound of the coffeemaker burbling in the kitchen. Rubbing the sleep from her eyes, she padded out to greet Gil.

"Are you just now getting home?" she asked noting his tired expression.

"Yeah, Ms. Harrison's shop took forever to search. The house wasn't so bad, but took time all the same."

"Find anything?"

"I'll say. How did the kids sleep?"

"Okay, I guess. I should be getting Ken up for school."

"Oh, and I called the cleaning company for an emergency clean. They came around midnight, so the foyer should be fine."

"Thank you."

She poured a cup of coffee and knocked on Ken's door, then poked her head in to wake him. She then looked in on Lisa.

"I'm awake, Mom, and feeling much better. Can I go to school?"

Anne felt her daughter's forehead. Cool to the touch. The fever was gone.

"Yes. Get dressed and meet me in the kitchen."

She returned to Gil and the tantalizing smell of microwaving sausages. "Can I borrow your car? I have to take the kids to school."

"Yeah, sure. I'm going to grab something to eat and then try to catch some sleep. I'll bring you up to date later."

After dropping the kids off, Anne cruised by her house. Opening the front door, she stared in amazement. The foyer hadn't been this clean since she'd moved in fifteen years ago. Even the grout between the marble tiles was arctic white. At least she and the kids would sleep in their own beds tonight.

Back at Gil's she let herself in quietly, and then called Jen and Rose with yesterday's events.

"You know, I've heard it said that when someone is murdered, the first suspects are the family," Jen told her. "We should have gone with that assumption. And you said he seemed so heartbroken at the funeral. Scumbag. I guess the Snoop Group can chalk up another one in the win column."

"Oh, my God, I don't believe it," Rose said in a horror-filled tone. "And Lisa saved the day? That is one fine kid you've raised, that's all I can say." She paused. "I don't suppose you've read your e-mail lately, have you?"

"Yesterday morning was the last. Hasn't been at the top of my to-do list. Why?" She really didn't need any more problems.

Rose sighed. "Kathy Samuels e-mailed all of the board members with the news that Susan Lynch contacted her and was irate that other candidates stepped forward for the treasurer's position, and that holding the election so soon didn't allow for campaigning. Claimed it was a conspiracy to keep her off the board. The upshot is Susan withdrew from the chapter and, get this, is forming her own writer's group to rival Writers Association of America."

Anne didn't know how hard to laugh. "Like that's going to happen. The good news is she's no longer a pain in my backside, and we'll have a competent treasurer soon. I'll call Kathy later. Thanks, Rose."

Gil rose in time for lunch. As they feasted on leftover pizza, he filled her in.

"The warrants gave us a lot of ammunition for prosecution. George liked to keep records. Must be the CPA training. It's also his downfall."

"So what did you find in the shop?"

"Plenty of drug residue in the warehouse—marijuana, cocaine, heroin, PCP, you name it, we found it."

"So George Harrison *was* using his wife's antique shop as a drug depository?" Anne said.

Gil nodded. "One of his CPA clients was Jorge Ramirez. He's a hood living the high life in Miami. Shipments of antiques stuffed with contraband would arrive at the shop. Harrison would hold the items concealing the drugs in the back room until the bag man could get them. Harrison got a nice cut of the action."

"Only one day, Fran accidentally saw a man leave with an urn she knew wasn't on the inventory and questioned George about it. He does a song and dance about a special customer who was in one day requesting a specific item while she was out. And Fran, being Fran, got curious. I wonder why?" Anne asked.

Gil shrugged. "She may have been suspicious about the books. After all, in spite of what he told you, George was a CPA and in charge of that aspect of the business."

"Fran worked there most of the week, so she'd know how many sales there were in general."

"And may have realized the end-of-the-month reports didn't jibe with her numbers."

"And one day when George is out of town on one of his so-called buying trips, Fran gets on his private computer and discovers a lot of money going overseas. Hence, the private investigators and the lawyers. I'll bet Fran *did* have the account numbers and every intention of bolting with the ill-gotten gains."

"No doubt."

"How's Becky doing?"

"Bullet went clean through. Forensics dug it out of your wall. She's under arrest in the secure wing at the hospital and singing like the old proverbial bird."

"She was duped by Harrison. I know, I know," she said when he gave her a stern look. "That doesn't excuse what she did."

"I will refrain from saying anything."

"How did George know Jeffrey Wainwright?" Anne asked.

"Seems Mr. Wainwright was distantly related through marriage to—you'll love this—Becky Lawrence."

"What?"

Gil nodded. "Yep, his mother was Ms. Lawrence's aunt's stepson. And she knew he was a waiter at the hotel. In fact, he'd served her several times during your meetings. When the plan was hatched to what she believed was to sicken Ms. Harrison, she gave Wainwright's name to George."

"Oh my God, I never suspected that connection."

"Ms. Lawrence claims she never knew where her ersatz cousin lived, so she had no idea when she dropped Harrison off at the house next door to the apartment, that it was his complex. She also admits to getting a call around one in the morning from Harrison demanding she come pick him up on a corner near— guess where?"

The light bulb lit up in Anne's mind. "The convenience store. She made some kind of reference to that at the house when George had us under the gun. How did she explain her absence at that hour of the night to her husband?"

"She says she was still up watching TV when the call came in. Mr. Lawrence was in bed sound asleep. He never heard her leave or return. Said the whole trip took less than an hour."

"And she never questioned why George needed a ride either time?"

"She claims he threatened her and by then, she was too scared to say anything."

"So when her partner in crime called demanding a ride to Wainwright's place, she didn't ask. And, of course, George didn't want to take a chance on driving his own car and perhaps being seen on surveillance. What was her reaction when she heard about Wainwright's death?"

"Says she didn't know until just a couple of days ago that he was dead."

After I talked to her at the mall.

"Also claims she didn't think George was involved and she never suspected he had anything to do with the drug trade."

"I wonder why she took Fran's purse and hid it in the restroom?"

"We asked her that. She said George told her Fran always carried a lot of money. He didn't want it to get lost. He suggested leaving it in the stall and that he'd get it on his way out."

Anne shook her head. "Only, he either forgot or just ignored it. What's going to happen to Becky?"

"She'll be charged as an accessory to murder, probably murder one."

"Doesn't that carry the death penalty?" Anne asked in alarm. She didn't want Becky who was basically duped by George Harrison to buy a needle in the arm.

"It could, but most likely she'll be offered a plea deal in exchange for her testimony against Harrison. He's the one who's likely to be put to death, provided he comes out of his coma."

"I don't give a rat's ass about him."

"Didn't think you did. How's Lisa holding up?"

"Pretty well. She seemed fine this morning. I told both of them to keep quiet about what happened, and if anyone at school asked about Ken being picked up by a police car to just say we'd had a break-in, but everyone was all right."

Gil nodded. "Good, although I'm sure being a heroine and not able to talk about it is killing her."

"Probably. Maybe someday."

"I read through the folders you gave me. They make sense now. Inspection of the furniture on the one list showed false bottoms, hollowed out legs, and numerous other hiding places. The delivery list was to make sure the moving van picked up most of those items on the next trip so they could be used again. The numbers were the weight of the drugs. A digital scale was found in the warehouse at the shop. The last one was who picked up the goodies and the container used. The list of numbers is what was paid to Harrison by the "customer." Later, a bag man picked up the money and gave Harrison his cut—ten percent. He should never have made that list."

"I don't understand why they used Fran's Fabulous Finds as an outlet. Just more people in the know," Anne said.

"The cartels ship the drugs to various other countries that turn a blind eye to what's happening. Then it's smuggled into the US. Ramirez made the pick up in Miami, hid it in different antiques bought by Harrison and delivered to Ramirez, then redelivered them to Harrison. He, in turn, handed the drugs over to the dealers. As for the number of people involved, well," he said with a shrug, "there's also safety in numbers. The more people between Ramirez and the street dealers, the better. Blurs the lines."

"So that's it? The case is all wrapped up?"

"Not entirely. As a writer you're going to love this. Both the FBI and the DEA had Fran's Fabulous Finds under surveillance for the past few months."

"What?"

"Seems both agencies had been suspicious of Rodriguez Moving for some time now. Informants tipped them off that the moving company was really owned by Ramirez. The frequent trips to the port followed by trips to the store raised a huge red flag. They were weeks away from making arrests."

"What irony. You're right, I may have another story in the making here. The only thing not cleared up is the fake doctor at the meeting."

"My guess is she was paid by Harrison to make sure the medics didn't get to his wife too soon. You said that the 9-1-1 call was delayed a few minutes because she claimed to be a doctor," he replied.

"I know. She was so assertive in what she was doing, we all just stood around and watched," Anne said with a shake of her head as Gil's phone rang.

"Collins here... When?" He paused to listen for several seconds. "Are they sure... And they have the guy... Okay, I'll be right down." He disconnected. "George Harrison's dead. Apparently, murdered right in the ICU."

Her heart rate sped up. "My God, how?"

"One of the station nurses saw a man dressed like an orderly slip into his room. What he didn't know was that those rooms all have security cameras. The nurse hit the panic button when she viewed him taking a needle out of his pocket and sticking it in Harrison's arm."

"Weren't there policemen at the door?"

"One was on break, and the other was down the hall stretching his legs. The guy took a chance and walked right in. When the alarm sounded, the cop down the hall nabbed the guy in the doorway."

"Who'd want to kill him at this stage of the game?"

"I'd say someone on orders from Ramirez who

wasn't smart enough to look for cameras in the room did it. And Ramirez would do it on orders from the cartel. There was always a chance he'd come out of that coma and talk. Can't prove it, of course, unless the guy talks." He rose and kissed her on the forehead. "I've got to go, honey."

Anne sat back to think as he left. Harrison got what he deserved. She was just unhappy that he was already in a coma and didn't suffer like his wife had. Greed killed Fran and George. Jeffrey Wainwright was what amounted to collateral damage.

She shivered, thinking how close she and Becky had also come to being another notch in George Harrison's gun

Chapter Eighteen

Anne sat at her desk determined to finish the chapter she'd begun last week. She and the kids had returned home two days ago, and while Lisa still walked through the foyer with wariness, she was back to her normal self.

Gil called at least once a day, but was busy tying up loose ends with the Harrison case, so she hadn't seen him. That was due to change tonight. He was taking her out to dinner.

News had spread like wildfire through the chapter about Fran's murder and Becky Lawrence's part in it. Anne hoped to put it all behind them after the next meeting. She was certain the chapter would run smoothly now that both Fran and Susan Lynch were gone. Plus, they had a new treasurer, Laura Denbow. She had accounting experience and would do well in the position.

I should feel badly thinking about Fran that way, but she really was a nasty piece of work. She didn't feel in the least bit sorry to see Susan go.

Jack Holloway, the accountant, had contacted her with the good news that while the chapter had taken a heavy hit financially, they weren't broke. As close as he could tell, Fran, with Jane's compliance, had sucked close to five thousand dollars out of the chapter.

Rose and Jen were coming over tomorrow for a

critique group meeting. It would seem odd not having Nancy around, but an e-mail a couple of days ago confirmed she and Brad had arrived safely in Papua New Guinea. Next stop was Lae on New Britain, and then on to the volcano.

Anne sighed and pushed her thoughts out of her mind. She had a book to write.

Gil rang the doorbell at precisely seven o'clock. She opened the door and he entered, stopping to give her a hard kiss.

"Hi, honey, how was your day?" he asked.

"Fairly productive. Got a chapter and two more scenes written along with an outline for my next book."

"Let me guess, it's all about a woman with food allergies who's killed in a room full of people."

She had to laugh. "Straight from the headlines to my eager little mind. How was your day and where are we going for dinner?"

"Interesting, and I was thinking Giovanni's."

"Hmmm, Italian. Interesting how? Come on in and have a seat. Would you like a glass of wine?" she asked leading him into the living room.

He remained standing. "No thanks, I'll wait until we get to the restaurant. Becky Lawrence was officially charged with being an accessory in the murder of Fran Harrison. Her lawyer immediately plea bargained from murder two down to manslaughter two. She accepted and will do the max. Her husband's attorney served her with divorce papers right there in the courtroom."

"Ouch, that's cold. Yet according to Becky's ramblings the other day, I guessed the marriage was over. Any more on Ramirez?"

He shook his head. "No, that's in the Feds' hands,

but we did contact the former sales clerk at the shop, Miriam Jackson. She said she'd been suspicious of some of George's so-called customers for several months. And the financials from the store show that George really did own it and had been peddling drugs out of it for close to four years."

"So it was only a matter of time. Can't believe it took Fran that long to figure it out. But then, I guess it would be hard to suspect your own husband of dealing drugs and fixing the books. I'm glad those folders helped."

"Ah, yes, those folders."

He said it in such a way as to make Anne hold her breath. "Well, as long as they helped. Shouldn't we be heading out to the restaurant?"

"In a minute. Yes, they helped, but I'm more interested in where you got them in the first place."

She squirmed inwardly. "I told you. I accidentally picked them up when I was at Fran's. They were mixed in with the chapter business."

Gil stared. "Uh-huh."

Clearly, he didn't believe her. She tried again. "I put them aside when I saw they referred to her shop. When I actually got around to reading them, they didn't make sense. What with Fran investigating offshore accounts and me suspecting she'd been embezzling from the chapter, I thought maybe you could figure it out."

"Uh-huh."

His continued staring made her shift her gaze around the room.

"Will you stop saying that?"

He shook his head. "Not a chance in hell. Annie, I

can read, too. The printout dates are on the bottom of the pages. All are at least a week after her death and since we'd confiscated her home computer, they didn't come from there. So where did you get them?"

Damnation! She hadn't thought about that.

"Promise you won't get mad?"

"No, I won't. Come on, honey, spill it. You're not a very good liar."

"I don't think you're going to be happy with me."

"I think I'm going to be damned unhappy."

Anne sighed and told him about her trip to the antique store on Saturday. She'd lit the match and put it to the fuse. As predicted, he exploded.

"Are you crazy! What if you'd been caught? Jeez, baby, why on earth did you do it? No, don't answer that! You won't have a good excuse."

"I know. I got carried away. I realized it was a stupid idea as soon as I'd done it, but I couldn't very well take them back, could I?"

"Annie, you're killing me here."

If she was coming clean, she might as well admit everything. "George confessed that he'd seen me on a surveillance camera and sent Carlos to look for them while I was out. He was my intruder."

"I know. We, the FBI, and DEA rounded up quite a few of Ramirez's men along with Ramirez. Carlos admitted George told him to find the folders. The guy we caught at the hospital was some crack head working off a debt. He also confessed to killing Harrison on orders from someone in Ramirez's organization." He paused and ran his hand through his hair. "The way I see it, there's only one way to keep you from playing Jessica Fletcher."

While she deserved the tirade, his words irritated her all the same.

"And what would that be?"

"We get married! That way I can keep an eye on you."

The breath left her lungs in a huge gasp and her heart beat ramped up to ramming speed. Married? Part of her was elated. Another part was pissed off.

"Married? Keep an eye on me? Why?"

His expressions softened as he pulled her toward him and folded her into his arms.

"Because you have this horrible propensity for getting into trouble. Besides, I love you, you beautiful little idiot."

His lips found hers. For the next few seconds, she forgot her irritation and reveled in the moment before finally pulling away.

"Idiot? I am *not* an idiot—a little careless, perhaps, but not an idiot, and what the hell kind of proposal was that?"

"The one I'm making! I'm not good at this sort of thing. Ask my ex-wives."

"Bringing up your ex-wives at a time like this is not good salesmanship."

"Maybe not, but… but damn! If you want me down on one knee, then I'll do it." His expression clearly stated he'd comply, but wouldn't like it. "So, what's your answer?"

Anne had to laugh. "That's the craziest proposal I've ever heard, including the one from Jimmy Hartwell when I was six years old."

"It's not funny!"

"Yes, it is." She ceased laughing. "Of course, I'll

marry you. When?"

He smiled and ran a gentle finger down her cheek. "The sooner, the better. Who knows when the next body will pop up."

"Oh, you!" She playfully punched him in the shoulder. "But I do think we'll need a few months to get the arrangements made."

"All right, but remember, no more sleuthing."

"Whatever you say, dear."

He rolled his eyes as if knowing full well, she didn't mean it. Bruno trotted into the living room and barked as though giving it his seal of approval.

She clamped her arms around his neck. "I love you, Gil Collins."

Their lips met again. Marriage—the perfect ending.

A word about the author...

I was born in Indianapolis, Indiana, but have been fortunate enough to live in several diverse cities—St. Louis, Missouri; Rockford, Illinois; Memphis, Tennessee; and Fort Lauderdale, Florida. I have two adult children and seven grandchildren. My husband and I recently moved back to Memphis to be nearer to family.

Much of my spare time is used to indulge in my guilty pleasures like floating around in my pool on a hot summer day. And if I happen to think up a good plot line while doing so, all the better. I also have little containers of ice cream stashed in out of the way places in my freezer.

I love writing and hope readers enjoy the journey of my stories along with me.

Thank you for purchasing
this publication of The Wild Rose Press, Inc.

For questions or more information
contact us at
info@thewildrosepress.com.

The Wild Rose Press, Inc.
www.thewildrosepress.com

To visit with authors of
The Wild Rose Press, Inc.
join our yahoo loop at
http://groups.yahoo.com/group/thewildrosepress/

www.ingramcontent.com/pod-product-compliance
Lightning Source LLC
Chambersburg PA
CBHW051517260626
47170CB00003B/662